THE DEEP ABIDING

A TY JOHNSON NOVEL

SEAN BLACK

ABOUT THE BOOK

From International Thriller Writers award winner Sean Black comes *The Deep Abiding*, the first novel to feature Ty from his bestselling Ryan Lock series.

When retired US Marine Tyrone Johnson is hired to protect a young reporter investigating the brutal, decades-old murder of a young African American woman in the Florida Everglades, he soon finds himself plunged into a living nightmare that will test the very limits of his endurance.

PRAISE FOR SEAN BLACK

"This series is ace. It stars bodyguard Ryan Lock, here hired to protect a glamorous movie star with a headless corpse in her car. There are deservedly strong Lee Child comparisons as the author is a Brit (Scottish), his novels US-based, his character appealing, and his publisher the same. " – Sarah Broadhurst, *The Bookseller*, reviewing Gridlock

"An impressive debut thriller from Sean Black that introduces a new full-on action hero. Clearly influenced by Lee Child and Joseph Finder, Black drives his hero into the tightest spots with a force and energy that jump off the page. He still has a little to learn when it comes to depth of character and pacing, but that won't take long. Lock is clearly going to be around for a long time. With a spine-tingling finale that reminded me of Die Hard, this is a writer, and a hero, to watch." – Geoffrey Wansell. *The Daily Mail*, reviewing Lockdown

"Sean Black writes with the pace of Lee Child, and the heart of Harlan Coben. Lockdown is a sure-fire winner" – Joseph Finder, New York Times Bestselling Author of *Buried Secrets*

"In Lockdown, Sean Black's hero, Ryan Lock, causes New York to be sealed against a terrorist threat. The synergy between name and title matters because it highlights the artifice underlying an excellent first novel. Like Lee Child's Jack Reacher, Lock is an ex-military policeman. Unlike Reacher, he has a job (as an elite bodyguard), a home, friends and a sense of humour. Lock's likeability contrasts with Reacher's pomposity and Black's style is supremely slick." – Jeremy Jehu, *The Daily Telegraph*, reviewing Lockdown

Sean's books that were nominated for, or have won, the International Thriller Writers Award (previous winners include Stephen King, Jon Gilstrap Megan Abbott & Joseph Finder) presented annually in New York City.

Post (nominated in 2015)
The Edge of Alone (nominated in 2017)
Second Chance (winner in 2018)

For the coaches, fighters and players of Team KF Martial Arts in Dublin.

1

D arling, Florida
1974

THEY LEFT her in the tree. Swinging in the Florida breeze. A warning to others.

All through the night, a steady southern wind from the tip of the Gulf pushed through the leaves, making a sound like a rattlesnake. From time to time the hanging branch creaked a little with the strain of the extra weight that pulled it straight to the ground below.

On the streets, no cars drove by. No people walked. Everyone was inside, drapes or blinds drawn, children sent to bed early with promises of rewards if they went to sleep and stayed asleep.

It was as if a storm was on the way, and they were waiting for its arrival. Only the storm had already been and gone, leaving a woman in a tree as evidence.

Nothing like that had ever happened here. People had worked hard to make sure it couldn't. All they wanted was to be left alone.

Unchanged. At least, that was what they'd say if they were pushed on the subject.

Now this. A late summer chill that had run the whole length of the town's spine.

THE NEXT MORNING, about an hour before sunup, a truck came by. RJ was driving, two of his cousins from Broward along to help.

They had to use a ladder to get up to the branch. Two held the bottom of the ladder while RJ cut through the rope.

She fell to the ground with a thump, the rope still tight around her neck. One of his cousins pulled out his hunting knife, ready to cut it off. RJ told him to leave it.

They laid her on the bed of the truck, slung an old hunting blanket over the body, then climbed into the cab. It was a tight squeeze but no one wanted to ride in back with a dead girl.

On the drive out of town, RJ gripped the wheel so hard that the next morning his hands ached. He was ashamed. Ashamed of the people who had done this. And ashamed of himself because he knew that he would take what had happened to his grave without telling a living soul.

About halfway there one of his cousins made a comment about 'gator bait, trying to be funny, to lighten the heavy mood that lay between them. RJ gave him a look that suggested a second body would be laid out in back if he said another word. His cousin mumbled an apology. The other stared out of the window as they whipped past a stand of dwarf cypress trees.

Sticky midsummer heat was already building. The radio had said today was set to be the warmest of the year so far.

RJ gripped the wheel even tighter. He felt like screaming and hollering, not stopping until he blacked out.

Maybe, RJ figured, the heat was to blame for all this. It made people crazy. Men got strange ideas. Women too. That had been what started this whole thing. A crazy idea. A whole bunch of them, really, one tumbling into the next until here he was, driving out into the swamp to dump a woman's body for the alligators to get rid of.

'Gator bait.

People had made jokes about 'gator bait ever since he could remember. Old Harold Sharmer had told him once how he'd read an article in the *Washington Times* about how the zookeepers in New York had used two little black children – *pickaninnies* was the word the reporter had used – like a fishing lure to get the 'gators to move to their summer enclosure.

RJ had figured he was kidding. Then he went to the library in the middle of town to ask Miss Parsons, and she'd looked it up for him, and said it was true. She'd been laughing fit to cry when she'd read it to him.

He couldn't see what was so funny. He was only eight, not that much older than the kids in the newspaper.

When she'd seen that he wasn't laughing along, she'd gotten annoyed and told him to hurry home. She'd scolded him, told him he shouldn't take things so seriously. The story in the paper was most likely a joke. Someone just having a little fun because the idea was so comical.

Now here he was, all these years later, with a dead woman lying less than six feet away from him. A woman they were about to take out to Devil's Pond and feed to the swamp. And there wasn't nothing comical about it. Not to RJ's way of thinking. Nothing at all.

He thought about a song he'd heard once on the radio. It was sung by a black lady. It was kind of slow and sad about how in the South the trees grew strange fruit. He couldn't exactly remember the lyrics. He'd only heard it the once when he was rolling the dial on the radio.

Now, in the hazy twilight, he knew what she'd been singing about, and it made the very depths of his soul hurt.

A billboard announced they were entering the town of Darling (population: 1235). It was like something straight out of the 1950s, but freshly printed.

It was full-sized—fourteen foot high and forty-eight wide. A white background with a peppy slogan—"You'll have a Darling time"—splashed in yellow lettering with a red outline, and a picture of a fresh-faced young family that could have been lifted from the back of an old cereal box: mom, dad, and two kids, a boy and a girl.

The mom was standing next to a kitchen island wearing an apron, her daughter next to her, blond hair up in braids. The equally blond father, sweater-model handsome, stood behind his wife, one hand on her shoulder, their cute, gap-toothed toddler son scooped up in his other arm.

"Is that like super-creepy or is it me?"

Ty Johnson glanced at the young woman sitting in the passenger seat of the Honda Civic they'd rented back at the airport in Miami. Cressida King was in her late twenties with mocha skin, long brown-black frizzy hair pulled back into a tight ponytail, sharp cheekbones, and blazing green eyes. She was an investigative journalist for

Larceny, a popular online and cable news site that was popular with millennials.

Ty had been hired as security by her boss in New York for reasons that hadn't been made fully clear to him. The six-foot-four retired Marine eased off the gas pedal, and slowed the Honda to a crawl, as they came up on the billboard. "What's creepy about it?" he said. To his eyes it seemed cheesy more than anything.

"You don't see it?" said Cressida, studying him.

"Maybe if you'd tell me what I'm supposed to be looking for."

"Blond hair, blue eyes. All of them. Like something from Germany in the 1930s."

Not for the first time that morning, Ty bit back a smile. As far as he could tell, from his short time with her and what he knew of her employer's editorial slant, Cressida, or Cress, as she'd insisted he call her, was . . . What did they call them? Oh, yeah, she was one of those social-justice warrior types, perpetually on the lookout for something to get offended by.

Ty had gone through that phase as a young man. Then he'd decided there was plenty to get annoyed by in this world without going around actively seeking out things to upset you. He blamed the internet and bad parenting: the internet for giving idiots a platform, and parents for not explaining to their kids that sometimes life just wasn't fair.

"You do know that's usually how it goes, right?" Ty said to her. "You know, when Mommy looks like that and so does Daddy, chances are the kids turn out like that too—'less, of course, Mommy's been sneaking around when Daddy's out working."

"You know what I mean," she said, irritation creeping into her voice.

"Maybe that's what people around here look like," he said, poker-faced.

She gave him another disbelieving stare, with a nod to the swampy terrain that had begun to fold itself around the road. "What? Like they just stepped out of a J. Crew catalogue?"

Ty shrugged, his expression cracking, a smile playing across his lips. "Maybe."

"You kidding me? We're almost in the middle of the Everglades. This is Redneck Central."

"Now who's stereotyping?" said Ty, following a smaller sign that signaled the turn onto the narrow road that would take them the last few miles into Darling.

"Wait. You think the folks here are going to look like those people on that billboard?"

"No, but that's advertising. You think if you drove into Crenshaw and there was a billboard with the Obamas on it welcoming you to the area that you're going to see Barack and Michelle when you stop at the lights?" asked Ty, referencing one of LA's most ghetto neighborhoods. "This is a white town we're rolling up on. Stands to reason they're going to have a white family on that sign back there."

Cressida stared out of the passenger window. The landscape had changed almost as soon as they'd made the turn. Pop ash trees crowded in on the road surface, branches arching high overhead, almost blocking out the midday sun. To his left, about ten feet beyond where the blacktop ended, the ground fell away to a swamp of more pop ash sprouting from bright green algae-covered water.

Ty had read that the Everglades had been like this for thousands of years. A dank, humid wetland. Looking out, he believed it. There was something primeval about the landscape, unbending. It was terrain that would bend someone to its will.

"Tyrone!"

Cressida's sudden shout snapped his attention back to the road where a low green-black shape was lumbering across the blacktop. Ty stood on the brake pedal. The Honda shook, the brakes squealing as the car came to a stop a few feet short of an alligator that was plodding across the road, oblivious to their approach.

It was big, maybe ten feet long and six hundred pounds. Ty guessed from the size it was an adult male. Hitting it at speed would have done bad things to the Honda. They'd seen signs warning about alligators crossing on the way down here, but he hadn't expected to see one. Not on the road anyway, although he had seen a sign for a ''gator farm' tourist attraction nearby, whatever one of those was.

The alligator kept moving, its pace never varying.

Cressida popped the door open. She had a Canon DSLR camera in her hand.

"Where are you going?" said Ty.

"Relax. It's fine," she said, walking in front of the car, the camera lens trained on the retreating alligator.

Ty reached down for his SIG Sauer 226 and cleared it from his holster. He hit the button to lower his window. The air outside hit him, boiling hot and muggy.

The young journalist was still hunkered down, capturing the alligator's retreat. It cleared the road and, a few seconds later, slipped effortlessly into the swamp water. A final flick of its tail and it disappeared under the surface.

Cressida stood up, turned back to Ty, and smiled. "Video. It'll make a great cutaway."

"I thought you were *writing* this story up."

She gave him a look with which he was already familiar from the few short hours he'd known her. It was the same pitying look that precocious kids (these days, pretty much every kid) gave their parents when they had to explain the latest app or technology.

"I am, but you have to have some visuals if you want to get the page hits. Video preferably. Big blocks of words? People just tune out."

She climbed back into the car, and held up the camera's display screen, running the short clip back so Ty could see it.

Ty waved his hand out of the window toward the edge of the wetland where the 'gator had disappeared from view. "Thanks, but I just watched it live, in high-definition."

She pulled the camera back onto her lap. "This is going to be a long couple days, isn't it? I never asked for anyone to come with me. I told Gregg I don't need a babysitter."

Gregg was the young reporter's managing editor back in New York. He'd reached out to a private security firm in Manhattan. They didn't have anyone available for a close-protection escort gig, but had provided a list of alternative companies. Ty had spotted the job on a circular email, and made the call.

He had spent the last few months doing dry-as-dust residential and personal-security reviews for Chinese nationals in the greater Los Angeles area. The work paid an absurd amount of money. Escorting a journalist was a low-level gig, with the pay to match, but he'd desperately needed a change of scenery, and the story she was investigating had intrigued him. His business partner, Ryan Lock, was on vacation with his girlfriend in Barbados, and Ty figured this was as close as he'd get to an actual vacation for a while. Once Cressida had what she needed here, he planned on heading back to Miami for a few days, meeting Lock and Carmen, and maybe doing some serious partying. Who knew? He might even persuade the reporter to come with him. Stranger things had happened, and their professional relationship would be over by then.

Ty's window glided back up. He hit the button to crank the air-conditioning.

"So why did your boss hire me if you can handle this on your own?" he asked.

"I have no idea. Didn't you ask him? I mean, isn't that part of your job?"

Ty didn't take the bait. "To be honest with you, the threat assessment was kind of vague. Until I collected you back there at Miami I half thought this might be a put-up job."

Cressida looked genuinely confused. "What do you mean 'a put-up job'?"

Ty immediately regretted saying anything. "Forget it."

"No, what do you mean?"

"Well, I've had a lot of reporters and media folks contact me over the past few months."

"Oh, yeah?"

Ty detected a hint of amusement in her voice. "Yeah, I had a little run-in with law enforcement back home."

She shifted in her seat, pulling her legs up, and scooting round so that she was side on to him. She was smirking. "Huh. Now you mention it, I did see something about that when I background-checked *you*."

Now Ty was *really* wishing he hadn't opened this can of worms. This was why he was better rolling with Lock. His partner would have shut this down and stopped Ty digging himself into a hole. "You background-checked me?" He wasn't sure whether or not to feel offended.

"Of course. Come on, private security? There's a lot of strange individuals in your business. I wanted to make sure I'd be safe."

That much Ty agreed with. "And?"

She took her time answering. Finally, Ty glanced at her. She was still sitting side on, her back to the door, studying him.

"Former Marine."

"There's no such thing," Ty said pointedly. "Once a Marine, always a Marine."

"Point taken."

"Anything else?"

"You seem to have a thing for being naked in public."

Ty laughed. "Come on. A thing? It was one time, and I was trying not to get shot by some trigger-happy cop."

"You locked one of them in the trunk of a patrol car."

"Again, I did what I had to do. Dude was fine. Anyway, I can't be that bad."

"Oh, yeah?"

"You checked me out and you're here."

"Correction, I did a background review. There was no checking you out involved."

Ty shrugged his shoulders. *Whatever.* "Hey, do you have the address for the place we're supposed to be staying?"

She held up her cell phone. Google Maps was pulled up on the screen. "About a quarter-mile down this road. Take a right. There aren't any motels, so it was an Airbnb or nothing. Place looked nice, though."

"There were a couple motels about ten miles back there," said Ty, with a nod.

"A story like this, it's better to be embedded properly in the community. Get a feel for the place. Y'know, who's who. You'd be amazed at the things people let slip once they get used to seeing someone around."

"You really think you're going to find out what happened after all these years?" said Ty.

"We know what happened. A woman was lynched for the color of her skin."

"I mean who did it. Why would someone tell you now?"

He glanced at Cressida. She had settled back into her seat. "I can be pretty persuasive."

Ty thought it best not to say anything to that. Up ahead the trees thinned, the swamp receded to reveal lush countryside and, laid out below them, the picture-postcard little town seemed like the last place where anything bad would ever happen.

TY PULLED the Honda into a space at the front of the house, an old white colonial with a hipped roof and a deep porch that wrapped around three sides. He and Cressida got out, and walked up the steps onto the front porch. There was a bench and two rocking chairs. It looked like the kind of house where someone would shoot a lemonade commercial.

The front door opened and an elderly man with an impressive mane of white hair hobbled out with the aid of a walking stick. He stopped when he saw them and smiled, fumbling with his stick, then placing it next to a rocking chair and putting out his hand.

"Adelson Shaw, pleased to meet you."

"Ty Johnson, and this here is . . ."

Cressida stepped forward and introduced herself. "Cressida King."

"Nice to meet you both. I have your room all ready." He turned and started back toward to the front door as Ty and Cressida exchanged a look, both thinking the same thing. *Room?*

"Oh, no, Mr. Shaw, I think there's been some confusion. The booking I made on the website was for two rooms."

Adelson Shaw stopped, and looked back over his shoulder at them.

"What's the matter? Did you two have a fight in the car on the trip down here?"

"No," Cressida protested. "We're not a couple. Mr. Johnson here is helping me with something."

Adelson grinned. "I know. You booked two rooms. I was kidding. Just wanted to see your reaction."

Ty broke out laughing. He was warming to this guy. From Cressida's expression, he wasn't sure she felt the same, which kind of made it funnier.

"I have a room for each of you," the old man continued.

They followed him into the front hallway, and up the stairs. The old man took it slow, using his stick for balance. Ty stayed behind him, just in case he lost his balance on the stairs and took a tumble.

They stopped about halfway up so that Adelson could catch his breath. "I'm sorry about this, folks."

Cressida touched his elbow reassuringly. "Honestly, don't worry about it."

"Okay," he said, having caught his breath. "Let's do this."

They reached the top of the stairs and he had another breather. "Not sure how much longer I'm going to be able to keep this place on," he said to them. "You might just be the last guests I have here."

"I'm sure you have a lot of life left in you yet."

Adelson looked down at the dark wooden floorboards. "Maybe."

He started down the hallway, and pushed a door that led into a large, bright bedroom with the same dark-wood floor, eggshell-blue walls, and three beautiful old sash windows. In the middle of the room was a king-sized bed with a floral comforter. There was a chest of drawers and a dark mahogany lady's armoire with a padded floral seat.

"This will be your room, Ms. King."

"Oh, it's lovely. Thank you."

She put down her suitcase and the bag that held her camera gear, notebooks and laptop. "Have you lived here your whole life?" she asked Adelson.

He was staring, with a beatific smile on his face, out of the far window to the lawn below. He didn't respond. Something about his expression suggested to Ty that he'd heard the question but had decided to pretend he hadn't.

Suddenly he turned back to face them. The smile was still there, but something about it was off. It took a moment for Ty to realize it was the old man's eyes. They weren't smiling. They looked narrow and irritated.

"Mr. Johnson, you're just down the hall. I'll show you."

Ty caught Cressida looking at him. He shrugged in her direction. He guessed she was trying to establish the same thing he was. Had Adelson Shaw heard her question or not? "Thanks," said Ty, following him out.

At the other end of the corridor, Adelson showed him into a bedroom that was the mirror image of Cressida's. Ty put his bag on the floor.

"Oh, I almost forgot," said Adelson, digging into his pants pocket and pulling out two sets of keys. "Big one's for the room, the little one for the front door. I lock it when I go to bed. Not that there's really any need to lock your door around here."

This last part took Ty back a little. It was a small town, and isolated, but he assumed crime was a problem everywhere, these days. At least to some degree.

"Pretty safe place to live, then?"

The old man looked straight at him. "If you're from around here then, sure, I guess so."

There was nothing unpleasant in the way he said it. No hint of threat or disapproval. If anything, his tone was a little weary.

Ty was about to ask him to expand on what he'd said, but decided to take another tack. "And you're from around here?"

"May as well be. Moved here when I was a teenager."

"You must like it," said Ty.

"Guess I must. Or I've been too lazy to move. Place kind of takes a hold of you, I guess."

Ty drew a breath. "You know Ms. King's here to investigate the Carole Chabon murder?"

The old man leaned a little heavier on his stick. "Terrible business. I was away on a dental conference when it happened, but I don't think this place was ever quite the same after."

"You were a dentist?"

"Yes, started my practice here about a year before it happened. Strange way to spend a life, looking into people's mouths," he said wistfully.

"Not that strange," said Ty, and tried to steer the conversation back to the Carole Chabon murder. "Funny that it never got solved either. No one brought to justice."

Adelson glanced up at him. "Likely never will."

"Why do you say that?"

"Stands to reason, doesn't it? If no one's come forward all these years, why would they do it now?"

Ty gave it some thought. "Maybe someone would want to make their peace with it before they went to meet their maker. Assuming they knew something."

"Mr. Johnson, I'm far too old and I've made far too many mistakes in my own life to be handing out advice to strangers."

"But . . . ?"

Adelson's entire expression changed. The kindly old man who'd struggled to make it up the stairs slipped away, replaced by someone younger with a little steel.

"Let your friend through there ask her questions, and speak to whoever she wants to speak to. But don't spend too long here. That swamp back there, it has a habit of sucking people into it. And once you're in it, it's a devil of a job getting out again."

3

Adelson Shaw watched from behind the shades in the living room as Ty and Cressida got into the Civic. He fumbled for his phone. It had an extra large keypad, and was for older people who had difficulty with their eyesight.

He punched in the number and waited for his call to connect.

"Yes, Mimsy, it's me."

Mimsy asked him if his guests had arrived.

"Yes, they're here."

Another question. The same question he was always asked, although it had been some time since he'd had this conversation. Thankfully there had been no call for it. It had been a long time since Carole Chabon's name had been uttered by anyone he knew. He had hoped he'd go to his grave without hearing it again.

He hadn't been kidding when he'd spoken to his guest. The swamp and the devil were real to him. As real as the people who lived here. It had taken his father to make him understand that. He had drilled into Adelson that the only way to be here was to mind what you said, be polite and avoid discussing anyone else's business.

"They ask about her?" came Mimsy's question.

"Don't worry, I didn't say anything, and I'm not going to."

He hung up before Mimsy could say anything else. He had done what was required. He could only hope that silence would be sufficient, and that this was the last time he'd have to make a call of this nature.

He hobbled over to his old armchair and eased himself into it.

His mind drifted back to what the tall man had said about making peace with your maker. It wasn't a new idea to Adelson Shaw. He had thought about it a lot over the years. But thinking was one thing, and doing was another.

His eyelids grew heavy and before he knew it he was asleep in his armchair. A few minutes after that he was all the way back to the bad place where he could hear that young woman pleading for her life as she was dragged towards an end that no one should have to endure. The terror wasn't in death. Death was the release. The terror in her shrieks must have come from realizing what would happen before she died.

4

Ty had to give credit where it was due. To look at, Darling not only lived up to its name but also its advertising. The billboard they'd seen on the way into town was a fair approximation of the place. Neat, tidy, charming and, apart from the cars, clothes, and hairstyles, like a snapshot of post-war American life.

He was sure he'd read somewhere that Disney had a town in Florida. He half remembered it was called something like Victory or Celebration. Looking around he wondered if this was where he had gotten the idea from. It was hard to imagine anything too bad happening here. And yet it had. Not just bad. Horrific. This was where a young black woman, who had come into town to sell Bibles and spread the word of Jesus, had been lynched and dumped a few miles away in the swamp to be eaten by alligators.

If it hadn't been for the sheer coincidence of a visiting botany student from the University of Florida, who'd been out in an airboat, collecting samples of indigenous plant species, stumbling across the body, it was unlikely anyone would have known what had happened. As it was, when the FBI were sent in to investigate, they were met with a wall of silence.

On the night that twenty-two-year-old seminary student Carole Chabon went missing, a lot of people in Darling were either visiting relatives out of town, or had their drapes pulled shut and their television sets turned up to full volume. Finally, after months of obstinate silence, and despite intense press interest, the FBI agents were recalled to Miami. No one was ever arrested for the murder of Carole Chabon, never mind put on trial or convicted.

Then, slowly, as the months and years rolled by, what happened was quietly forgotten. The victim's mother died. So did her older brother, killed during a botched robbery at a convenience store in Detroit where he was jockeying the register.

Ty couldn't imagine that anyone was likely to talk now, not after all these years, but he guessed that Cressida King had the optimism of youth on her side. He admired her for being prepared to take a fresh swing at it. That was another reason why he'd agreed to take on this close-protection gig. Although now, looking around the small town, he wasn't sure her editor back in New York had anything to worry about when it came to her personal safety.

Then again, maybe Carole Chabon had figured the same, and look what had happened to her. But that was over forty years ago. The world had moved on. *Hadn't it?*

They turned onto what Ty guessed was the main street, a three-block run of small stores, a diner, an upmarket restaurant with a French name, a church, a public library, and a scattering of offices that included a couple of lawyers and an accountant.

Ty had spent enough time in what people in LA patronizingly referred to the fly-over states to be suitably impressed. The main streets of a lot of small towns had been decimated by the likes of Walmart and Amazon. It took a genuine civic spirit to keep local businesses up and running. Folks might like to say they wanted to buy locally until they succumbed to the lure of free shipping and lower prices. It was one thing to talk the talk about supporting local business, something else entirely to match it with your pocketbook.

"Drop me over here, would you?" said Cressida, pointing toward the library.

"Sure thing," said Ty, spinning the wheel, and pulling into a spot out front.

He put the car into Park, and started to get out. Cress reached into the back to get her bag. "You're coming in?"

"That's usually the deal with bodyguards. I go where you go."

"You know this was Gregg's idea, not mine."

"You already said. However, he's the client, and you're what we call the principal."

"The difference being?"

"Shouldn't you have your notepad out for this?"

"Funny."

"Difference is, the client is the person who pays my fee. The principal is the individual I'm tasked with protecting. Sometimes they're the same, and sometimes they're not. In this case, they're not."

"So the client calls the shots. That what you're saying?"

Ty smiled. "You're a quick study."

"Well, this particular principal doesn't need some huge-ass bodyguard cramping her style. It's a library. The worst that could happen is I get a paper cut."

"Okay, I'll wait here," said Ty.

"I'm going to be a couple hours. There's a diner over there. Why don't you go get a cup of coffee or something? I'll call you if a shelf of books falls on me. How about that?"

Ty figured she had a point. "Bodyguard" didn't necessarily translate to "shadow".

"In any case," she continued. "People are way less likely to talk to me if you're hovering about in the background like a bad smell."

Ty lifted his arm, and took a sniff. "Subtle."

"I didn't mean literally, smartass," she smiled, "but you look like a cop or something, and people tend not be quite so open."

It was true, Ty did look a little like a cop. Undercover, narcotics, but definitely law enforcement. His years in the Marine Corps had given him an official vibe that he hadn't managed to shake off.

"Okay, I'll be in the diner," said Ty, closing his door.

"Great," said Cressida, exiting the car, then running up the steps of the library and inside before Ty could remind her to call him if she needed anything.

He decided to leave the Honda where it was, and walk across the street to the diner. As he hit the sidewalk his cell phone rang.

It was Lock, no doubt checking in and making sure that Ty hadn't done anything crazy. Ever since Ty had gotten involved in the hostage situation in Long Beach, Lock had become a little like a helicopter parent who wanted to track his business partner and friend's movements.

Ty hit the green answer icon. "Hey, Ryan, what's up? How's the hotel?"

Lock had booked himself and Carmen into a place called Sandy Lane, a jaw-dropping luxury hotel right on the beach. No-expense-spared vacations were one of the upsides of their new ultra-wealthy Chinese clientele.

"Off the hook. So what's this about you taking a gig babysitting a journalist?"

Ty had emailed Lock before he'd left Los Angeles to let him know about the job. Rich Chinese immigrants had been great for their bottom line so he wasn't sure how Lock would take the sudden shift.

"It's a one-off. There's only so many *erdai*s you can fend off in a day while you're explaining why they shouldn't leave the keys of their Benz in the car while they go shopping on Rodeo."

Erdai was Chinese slang for the mistress of a wealthy Chinese businessman. Many of them were stashed in multi-million-dollar mansions in Arcadia. They made up a largish sector of their new security-review business. Most of them hit on Ty. At first he'd been flattered, but after a while it had gotten irritating.

"So what's the story that they need muscle along for the ride?"

Ty bristled. "You're calling me muscle?"

"Apologies. A high-level elite close-protection specialist."

"That's better."

"Okay, so what's the deal? I mean, I know Florida has more than its fair share of wack-jobs, but is there a specific threat you're supposed to be looking out for?"

"Honestly? Not that I'm aware of. There wasn't a lot of time to do a full risk assessment, but nothing popped. If anything, apart from the murder she's investigating, the place is about as low crime as it gets. I guess reporters aren't the most popular people, these days. That, and she's a black reporter covering a hate crime, but it was a long time ago."

"Well, someone must have been worried about something, so keep your head on a swivel. People don't usually drop cash for protection for no reason."

"Always," said Ty.

"I mean it," Lock reiterated. "The situations that catch you out are usually the ones you think are low risk."

"Okay, Dad."

"Funny," said Lock.

"Look, I'll be fine. Just go enjoy your vacation."

"I'll check in with you tomorrow."

"Ryan, I'll be fine. You concentrate your attention on that lady of yours. If I need you, I'll be in touch. Listen, I gotta go. I just caught a whiff of the pancakes at this diner I'm standing outside. I think they're calling me."

Lock laughed. Ty's lifetime obsession with food was a running joke between them. "Okay, brother. You stay safe."

"Always," said Ty, ending the call, and pushing through the door into his date of destiny with some pancakes, and possibly a side of bacon.

As he stepped inside the diner the low hum of conversation fell away sharply to a stony silence.

An elderly man, sitting at the counter, slopped coffee down his shirt. A couple sitting in a booth glanced at him, then awkwardly looked away. The short-order cook, a heavyset man with sweat pouring down his face as he stood over the grill, was set statue-like, the ladle he was holding suspended in mid-air.

A middle-aged waitress with curly red hair, and even redder lipstick, broke the spell, sashaying over to Ty with a menu and a broad smile. Her name badge read 'Sue Ann'. "Take a seat, sweetie. I'll be right with you."

"Are you sure?" said Ty, taking in the other customers' reaction to him with a raised eyebrow.

"Oh, don't mind us," she said. "We don't get many visitors from out of town, that's all. Anytime someone walks through that door we don't know it's kind of an event."

She sounded sincere and it had a ring of truth to it. It would have been the same in a barbershop in Long Beach, or any number of places. Someone unfamiliar walking in where the crowd was always the same would draw glances.

He took the menu from her with a polite 'Thank you,' and slid into the nearest empty booth as the conversations started up again, and people went back to whatever they'd been doing before he'd walked in.

5

Lock accepted the two cocktail glasses from the waiter, and headed back to where Carmen was laid out on a lounger by the pool. He wasn't really a hotel-holiday kind of guy, but he had to admit he was enjoying this vacation. They even had a man who came round and cleaned your sunglasses for you, should they need it.

He took a moment to admire the amazing woman he'd found himself with. Intelligent, compassionate, engaging, funny, and pretty damn attractive, inside and out. They'd already been through more together than most couples experienced in a lifetime, and seemed to be stronger for it.

"Here's your drink, Madame," he said, kneeling down and handing Carmen one of the cocktails.

She took a sip. "Damn, that's strong. You trying to get me drunk, Mr. Lock?" She laughed.

"Absolutely."

"Were you back there checking in with Ty?"

"Guilty."

"How's he doing?"

Lock told her a little about the job Ty had taken, and the background to it.

"It doesn't surprise me that they'd want someone with her," Carmen said, when she'd digested what Lock had told her. "All this talk of fake news, and how the media are biased. Plus people get upset a lot easier, these days."

Lock agreed with the last part. As for fake news, he didn't believe in it, but he did know from experience that you could take pretty much any event and spin it to make a good guy look bad, and vice versa.

"It can be dangerous, being a reporter," Carmen continued. "Maybe not here so much, but overseas, it's a scary gig. You start looking into things that people don't want you to look into and things can get very real, real fast."

"Well, if anything happens, I'm not too far."

Carmen shot him a look. "Don't you dare. We're on vacation."

"I said, if anything happens. And, like you said, that's hardly likely in Darling."

6

For a town with the population of Darling, Cressida had to give it to them, the library was pretty impressive. It was set over two floors with the second floor being a galleried mezzanine that wrapped around the entire inside of the building.

Cressida stopped in the entrance and closed her eyes for a moment. She took a deep breath in, savoring the distinct aroma of all the books. She had always thought of libraries as magical places.

Off to one side there was a pinboard display with photographs of the town that stretched from its earliest origins. She took a moment to study it. Unsurprisingly there was no mention of Carole Chabon or the events that had led up to her death. The display was probably for the benefit of visitors, and no one would want to lead with such a horrific event. It didn't exactly fit the narrative of a mom-and-apple-pie small town.

From the research she had already done in New York, she knew that the town had done everything it could to wash Carole Chabon's murder from its history. Which was why she was standing there now.

"Miss King," a woman's voice called.

Cressida turned to see an elderly woman in a smart pants suit walking toward her. "You are Miss King?" the woman repeated.

"Yes," said Cressida.

"I thought so. I'm Claire Parsons. You emailed me."

Cressida shook her hand. The woman's skin was like paper. She must have been seventy if she was a day. It was one of the things Cressida was noticing about Darling. Besides being entirely white, a lot of the people were getting up there in age. It wasn't too surprising. It was off the beaten track, and there didn't seem to be much economic activity, apart from occasional tourism, and a visitor would have to be intending to go there. It wasn't a place you stumbled into on the way to somewhere else.

"Pleased to meet you." She turned side on to the pinboard. "That's quite the local-history display."

The librarian's polite smile struck Cressida as a little forced.

"I'm amazed we gathered enough pictures to fill a single board." She rested her hand on the crook of Cressida's arm. "It's a pretty boring place, if truth be told."

Cressida flashed on the crime-scene photographs she'd viewed online of Carole Chabon's ravaged body. "Oh, I wouldn't say that."

The librarian's smile receded a little, and she led Cressida into the library. "I've gathered up as much material as I could find. I even contacted some of my fellow librarians elsewhere in the county to see if they had anything that might be relevant. I have it all laid out for you down in the basement."

She stopped. Her arm was still linked through Cressida's. "Some of the material is sensitive," she added. "We have children who use the library. I didn't want them getting curious, peeking over your shoulder and seeing something they shouldn't."

I bet you didn't, thought Cressida. She smiled. "That's probably for the best."

Miss Parsons led her by the arm toward the main library desk. She opened the gate, letting go of Cressida, who followed her into a neat back office, full of publishers' catalogs and book request forms, toward a door at the back.

Miss Parsons opened the door to reveal a steep set of wooden stairs. She reached for a light switch just next to the door and flicked the stairway lights on. A little hesitant, Cressida followed her down the dozen or so steps into the basement.

"Mimsy lent me a desk so you would have somewhere to go over everything," said the librarian.

"Mimsy?"

"Oh, sorry, habit of a lifetime. Mary Elizabeth Murray, our mayor. Everyone still calls her Mimsy. Guess that's what happens when you grow up in a place like this. The nicknames stick around."

The name rang a bell with Cressida. More than one. The mayor was someone she had on her interview list for her week here. But she had wanted to find her feet first and, if she could, gather some more ammunition. She had questions for "Mimsy' that no one would enjoy having to answer.

"Small towns, right?" said Cressida.

"Quite so," smiled Miss Parsons, flicking on a lamp to reveal an old wooden desk laden with papers and newspapers neatly laid out in bundles. Several stacks of box files were piled next to the desk. There was a lot to look at. Then again, she had pretty much requested everything she could possibly think of that might be held here.

Cressida had believed since journalism school that, even with Google and other search engines, libraries were an underused resource. Especially small ones like this, with local news sources that they couldn't afford to digitize, never mind make publicly searchable. "This is great. Thank you so much," she said, pulling out the metal folding chair that was pushed under the desk.

"Can I confess something to you?" said the librarian, leaning in conspiratorially.

It was a little early for confessions, but Cressida was happy to hear whatever it was. "Sure," she said casually.

"This is terrible, but . . ."

"Believe me, I'm pretty hard to shock."

"Well, when I got your email, I was kind of . . . excited."

"Excited?"

"It's like one of those crime shows on TV, isn't it? What do they call them? Cold cases."

Cressida hadn't been sure about Miss Parsons, and how she was behaving, but this seemed real enough. The woman was almost giddy with excitement. It wasn't a feeling she shared. Not having learned about Carole Chabon's horrific fate. Or what had come after it, the additional horror that had been piled on top. It wasn't entertainment. It wasn't a TV show. It had been all too real: a woman brutally tortured and murdered while, of all things, selling Bibles and spreading the word of the Lord. And for no other reason than the color of her skin.

She couldn't find it in herself to share the librarian's almost child-like glee, but she needed her help. She pasted on her best reporter's smile. "Well, maybe we can crack it together."

"Oh, I don't know about that," said the librarian, suddenly serious. "I mean, likely whoever did it is long gone."

She stared at Cressida, then brightened again. "It sure could be fun to try, though."

And with that she was gone, clattering back up the steps with a breezy "I was going to make some mint tea. I'll bring you some, if you'd like."

"That would be nice, thank you," said Cressida, and turned her attention to the paper-laden desk.

The librarian stopped at the top of the stairs. "Would you like me to leave this door open?" she called down.

"Please," said Cressida, not giving it any real thought.

"I may have to step out a little later, so if anyone comes and rings the bell on the desk, be a dear and let them know I won't be gone long."

Cressida glanced up the stairs to where Miss Parsons was standing at the top, silhouetted in the doorway. "Happy to."

"What I said earlier, about this being exciting. I didn't mean to be flippant. I'm sure you take your job very seriously."

"I do, but it's okay. Miss Parsons?"

"Yes?"

"There was one thing I wanted to ask you."

"Go right ahead. If you'll pardon the pun, I'm an open book."

"You said you grew up here?"

"Yes," said the librarian.

"So you would have been in your teens when Carole Chabon was murdered?" Cressida had estimated she might have been a little older than the victim, maybe by ten years, but part of being a reporter was getting on someone's good side: thinking they were younger than they were was a proven way of doing that. She'd used it lots of times in the past. Flattery almost always worked.

"I was twenty," Miss Parsons corrected her.

"So you were here?"

"Thankfully, no, Miss King. I was at college. Florida State. I'm afraid I only heard about it like everyone else did."

"And what about friends, Mimsy for instance?"

"I couldn't really say. But she'll be along later so I'm sure you'll have the opportunity to ask her."

Cressida had the feeling she wasn't going to get anything else from Claire Parsons, but it was a start. Better to let it go for now and circle back. "Thank you."

The librarian stood for a second longer. She didn't say anything. Finally, she turned, and disappeared just as Cressida thought she heard something scuttling about in the basement. She looked in the direction of the noise, but it was way too gloomy. The sound faded and she sat down, ready to dig in.

7

Ty sat in a booth, ate his surprisingly good pancakes with maple syrup and a side of bacon, watching small-town life unfold outside. People might have seemed a little startled when he'd walked in, but that was hardly a new experience. He was six feet four inches tall, 220 to 230 pounds, and less than ten per cent of that was body fat. Plus he carried himself like a proud US Marine, chest out, shoulders back, chin tilted up.

Black, white or yellow, a man of his size, who occupied a space in the world in the manner he did, often drew attention. He didn't doubt that his being African American dialed up people's curiosity switch a couple of notches, but he wasn't about to get paranoid just yet.

He finished his food, drained the last of his coffee, and signaled for the check. The waitress came over with it.

"Now that's what I like to see, a man who enjoys his food," she said, lifting the empty plates.

"It was delicious, thank you."

"Can I get you anything else, honey?"

"No, thank you, ma'am," said Ty.

Bearing in mind it was the South, Ty was careful to be polite. "Please" and "thank you" counted for something among people here in a way that they didn't back in Los Angeles. Also, he was thinking there was nothing to stop him seeing if he could assist Cressida's investigation into the Carole Chabon murder, even if it was only by preparing the ground for her.

"You lived here long?" he asked the waitress, giving her his usually winning smile.

"All my life."

"Must be a pretty special place."

"Oh, it is."

"Looks pretty quiet too."

Her easy-breezy manner was starting to fade. "Is there something you want to ask me, honey?"

"I don't want to put you on the spot, but I'm here with a reporter who's looking into the murder of that young black girl back in 'seventy-four. You were probably only a kid, but . . ."

Before he could finish, she'd slapped the check on the table in front of him. "You have a nice day, y'hear."

She walked back to the counter and settled into a whispered conversation with the cook, who shot Ty a couple of hostile glances. Ty shrugged it off. It was worth a shot. He studied the check, dug out enough cash to cover it, along with a hefty tip, placed it on the table and got up to leave.

The cook abandoned his grill to intercept him on the way out.

"Great pancakes," said Ty, hoping to wrongfoot him.

"Let me give you some friendly advice, boy," said the cook.

"Boy" was not a word you used lightly to a black man. Not here. Not anywhere. And certainly not to Ty. His fists clenched. "Boy?" he said.

"This is a quiet town. We'd like to stay that way. Don't come in here upsetting my staff. Keep your questions to yourself."

Ty took a half-step towards the cook. He wasn't a small man, but he was out of shape. Doughy and red-faced. "Call me that again and you and me are going to have a problem," he whispered.

The cook swallowed, loud enough for Ty to catch it. He'd made his point, but he wasn't going to back down, not in his own establishment. "You take care now," he said to Ty.

Ty stared at him until the man finally dropped his gaze to the floor, then pushed past him to the door as the silence that had accompanied his entrance made a return.

He stood on the sidewalk outside the diner, his body still tense, his anger still raw. Across the street a pickup truck was parked. A man sat behind the wheel and spat a wad of chewing tobacco into an empty Coke can. He had shoulder-length white hair, and a long white beard, but his eyes told Ty he was younger than the hair made him seem.

He was studying Ty. Not hostile. Not friendly. His expression passive but unyielding.

Ty had had enough small-town bullshit for one day. He stepped off the sidewalk, ready to confront the man, who hurriedly started the truck's engine, and pulled out. A Confederate-flag sticker rode on the bumper of the truck as it melted into a cloud of dust.

Maybe, thought Ty, he shouldn't have left Cressida alone after all. Perhaps there was more to this place than he'd thought. All it had taken was a couple of questions for that sunny image on the billboard to slip away. It was well off the beaten path. Maybe it hadn't moved on.

8

It had taken Cressida less than half an hour to realize she was unlikely to find anything in the papers that the librarian had gathered for her that would lead to any fresh revelation as to who had killed Carole Chabon. The local newspaper had gone out of business, like so many others, about five years ago. But back in 1974 the only thing noteworthy about its coverage of the murder was how sparse it was.

For most local newspapers in a quiet backwater, a murder like this would usually have been manna from Heaven. In the news business, crime sold. The old saying was "If it bleeds, it leads." But the *Darling Gazette* had barely covered either the original search for Carole, or the subsequent discovery of the body. They had played it off as little more than some kind of random mystery. They hadn't even gone after the killer on the loose angle.

The last mention of it that Cressida could see in the old back issues came two years after the murder when it had been announced that it was no longer an active investigation. She wondered about the motive for how the story had been covered. Was the editor, who'd passed away in the late nineties, afraid of local reaction? Had he come under pressure to downplay the seriousness of the story? Was it about maintaining the town's reputation as a safe community to live? Or was there a more sinister reason?

None of that meant the *Darling Gazette* was a bust, though. Far from it. Local papers offered one major advantage over larger media sources. They told you who was who in the area.

She opened a fresh page of her notebook, and began to jot down names, especially where their owner's age was included and suggested they had been young enough at the time to be around to speak to her now. The librarian had been away at college, but some of the people mentioned must have been here, with some memory of what had happened. The official town policy might have been one of studied silence, but Cressida had yet to work anywhere where there wasn't at least one person who was prepared, even eager, to talk.

It was simply a matter of finding them.

She got up from behind the desk, and did some stretches. She could already feel a nagging ache in her lower back from hunching over. It was good of Miss Parsons to have set up a desk but it wasn't exactly ergonomically balanced.

The bell sounded from somewhere above her. The librarian had stepped out and someone was looking for service. Cressida climbed the stairs, pushed through the door, and went to the front counter.

No one was there. She was sure she'd heard the bell. She reached down and picked it up. She rang it gently. Yup, that had been the sound.

"Hello?" she called out.

Silence.

She felt a little on edge and immediately chided herself. It was a small-town library not some cabin in the woods. The person had come in, seen that Miss Parsons wasn't at the desk, had rung the bell and left before Cressida had got up the stairs. In fact, she'd heard something that might have been the front door closing just as she'd hit the top step.

She walked around the counter and went over to the shelves where the fiction was arranged in alphabetical order. She ran her fingers along the spines, reading off the author names to herself.

Most were familiar, the obvious big names you'd expect to find in the fiction section of any respectable library: James Patterson, Danielle Steel, Nora Roberts, J. K. Rowling, mixed in with more literary fiction, and some regional authors. Cressida started to look for some of her favorite African-American authors, big names in their own right: Alice Walker, Maya Angelou, Toni Morrison.

She couldn't see any of them on the library shelves. She went back and started at the As. There were no African-American or even Asian-American novelists.

Then she turned a corner at the end of the Ys and Zs, and was met with a shelving unit of its own. A card at the top read: "Celebrating America's Diversity". Here she found pretty much every author she had been looking for, and dozens she hadn't.

Maybe she had been too quick to judge, hoping to be offended. If anything, when you looked at the shelf these authors were, someone might argue, over-represented. She reached for *The Color Purple* by Alice Walker and levered it out from between the other books. It opened with a distinct crack. It looked brand new. She checked the edition. It was a recent reissue, published this year. It looked like it hadn't been opened, never mind read: the pages were stiff and compressed so that you had to turn them with care.

So, she told herself, it was a new title that no one had had the chance to read. Plus it was popular. She imagined that most people who wanted to read it would have done so by now. Or had seen the movie rerun on television if they didn't want the effort of reading the book.

She took down another title, this one a more recent Toni Morrison. This copy, too, looked brand new and untouched. She put them back where they had been shelved, and selected something else. The same story. Every book was brand new. None of them showed borrow or return date stamps, which she had noticed in the other sections.

It looked like someone, Miss Parsons, was trying to make a point. No black people, but lots of books by black authors.

Cressida tried to shake away the thought. A staged display just for her? It seemed over the top and unnecessary. What did it prove anyway?

She picked up one of the other books. Then again, so what? Wasn't it better if people made the effort rather than not?

She wouldn't ask Miss Parsons about it. Unless she brought it up.

Either way, she wasn't here to decide if Darling, Florida, had a problem with racism. She was here to find out what had happened to Carole Chabon, and then, years later, to a man by the name of Timothy French.

9

The diner fell silent for the second time that morning as Mimsy made her entrance in a cloud of Chanel perfume, a long black skirt and a cashmere shawl that had to be way too warm, given that it was already in the high eighties outside and the diner's air-conditioning was patchy at best. She also had on what people in Darling referred to—behind her back, of course—as her war face: lips pressed tight together, eyes narrowed, chin jutting out. She was a stout woman, only five feet two inches tall, with short, mousy-brown hair.

"Lyle," she said to the cook. "We need to talk."

He looked up from the griddle and gave Mimsy a weak smile. Sweat was pouring from the top of his head, and trailing down a beetroot-red face. His shoulders rounded, everything about his body language suggested complete and total submission.

Lyle waddled across to the counter. "Sure, Mimsy. Can I get you something?"

She stared at him. He looked at the counter. Everyone else in the diner turned away. No one wanted to make eye contact with Mimsy when she was in this kind of a mood.

"Not here," she said. "Let's go out back."

He turned to the waitress who was standing, hands on her hips, giving him a told-you-so look, although what she might have told him wasn't entirely clear.

"Sue Ann, I'll be right back."

He lifted the counter flap that allowed access from one side of the counter to the other and, head down like a scolded schoolboy, followed Mimsy to a door at the back of the diner.

They walked down a corridor filled with cleaning and other supplies. He pushed open the fire-exit door and stepped out into the back alley.

Mimsy stood facing him, arms folded, her right foot tapping out an uneven beat. "You know why I'm here, don't you?"

He nodded. "Yes, ma'am."

"That man's a visitor to our community and you go behaving like, I dunno, some kind of crazy redneck."

"It slipped out."

"You know *they* don't like being called things like that, don't you, Lyle? It ain't the 1950s any more. People have to watch their tongues."

"Like I said, I reacted. He was being uppity."

"Uppity or not, we have to show our best side. That reporter and him won't be here for very long so let's not give her a story where there isn't one."

"Yes, ma'am."

"How long did it take this town to get over the last reporter who came here looking to make a name for themselves? I'm not going to let it happen again. We should count ourselves lucky we've been as fortunate as we have."

Lyle nodded. He knew everything she was saying made sense. He knew as soon as he'd faced up to the man that it was a bad idea. But he hadn't been able to control his temper. He would have thought Mimsy, of all people, would understand that.

"Now, Lyle, I want you to find him, and apologize to him for using that word."

"But, Mimsy——"

"But Mimsy nothing. You're going to say you're sorry, and you're going to make sure you sound like you mean it. And then you're going to offer him his next meal free. Dinner, in fact, with the young reporter."

This was too far. A fake apology he could just about stomach, but giving free food, bowing and scraping while he served it?

He looked up finally, squaring his shoulders. "I'll apologize, but I'm not doing any of the rest."

Mimsy's hand shot out without warning, fist clenched, her two rings catching the side of his eye and opening it up. "Don't you dare talk back to me," she said to him, her voice low. "Who the hell do you think you're talking to, you piece of trash?"

She raised her hand again. He flinched and stepped back. He was bigger than her, heavier, stronger, but he wouldn't dare fight back. No one would. Not to Mimsy Murray. Not unless you wanted to find yourself out in the swamp.

"Okay, okay," he pleaded, reaching for the rag tucked into his apron and using it to staunch the blood flowing freely from the cut next to his eye.

"That's more like it. Now, I'm sorry I struck you. But you and everyone else have to understand what's at stake here."

"I know."

"You'd better, Lyle. Because I don't want to see any more slips. Not from you. Not from anyone in this town. That reporter and her pal, or whatever he is, they're gonna leave in a few days. But you'll still be here."

She stared at him for a second, letting her gaze linger directly on him in a way that drove fear into his heart. "And so will I."

It was clear from Lyle's expression that he had got the message.

"I hear you."

"Good," said Mimsy, glancing around the alleyway with distaste. "You ought to keep this area out back a little cleaner before you get a citation."

She turned and headed back to the diner, stopping at the door. She smiled brightly, her entire demeanor changing in less than a second from one of menace to cheerleader pep. "Best foot forward,

Lyle. Let's make sure these people don't have any story to write, except that a nice little town has left the past behind and is trying to move on."

"Yes, Mimsy."

"Well, I'm glad that's settled."

She pulled the door open, and disappeared back into the diner. She caught Sue Ann's eye as she stepped inside. "Could you be a doll and take out a fresh towel and some ice for Lyle? He seems to have caught his eye on that danged doorframe. I keep telling him to get it repaired. It's going to really hurt someone one of these days."

"Coming right up."

Sue Ann snapped straight to it, ducking behind the counter for the items, as Mimsy walked past her and out of the door, leaving the smell of Chanel perfume and fear behind her. Slowly, for the second time that day, the conversation in the diner picked up again.

10

This time Cressida definitely wasn't imagining someone else in the library. She could hear footfalls on the floor above, heavy and definite, a large man or woman. More likely a man, as the sound of their steps was more like that made by boots than sharp heels. Definitely not Miss Parsons. Someone much larger.

She told herself it was likely someone who had wandered in to browse. She waited for the sound of the bell, but nothing came.

The footsteps stopped. The person sounded as if they were close to the desk.

She was starting to get creeped out. She reprimanded herself. She was in a dimly lit basement but it was the basement of a library, for Heaven's sake. Nothing bad happened in libraries. Alleyways, yes. Bars, sure. Lonely country roads, absolutely. But not libraries.

She looked down at her notepad. She had flicked to a section of notes she had written a few months back when she had first begun to research the Carole Chabon murder case. At the top of the page were four letters. They made her shudder every time she looked at them.

WKKK.

Beneath the letters was a list of names. She was attempting to see if any cropped up in the *Darling Gazette*. So far only one had: Murray.

The family had been in the area for generations. Originally Scots-Irish, they had settled down in the swamplands in this part of Florida, becoming not just slave owners but slave traders, who provided men, women and children to plantations across the South. Franklin Murray had founded the business and made a fortune by ruthless exploitation, with a laser-like focus on the bottom line.

After the civil war, the family had lost most of their fortune in a series of bad investments both in America and abroad. They had become a minor historical footnote, holding to the three-generation rule of wealth: the first generation made it, the second consolidated it, and the third lost it. But one thing had remained constant through the years: the power they held in this part of the Sunshine State.

The fresh press of boots on an uneven floorboard sounded again from above. It was no use. Cressida wouldn't be able to focus until she had satisfied her curiosity.

She got up from her desk, and started up the steep wooden steps. As her head cleared the basement hatch, she looked around. There was no one in sight.

She called, "Hello? Can I help you?"

A man appeared from behind a shelf of books about six feet in front of the main service desk. He was in his sixties with a scraggy white beard, trucker's cap and jacket, heavy boots and denim jeans. A thick mullet of white hair spilled out from the back of the cap. He shot her an unsettling gap-toothed smile.

"I was looking for Miss Parsons," he said, stepping towards the desk.

Cressida held her ground. Suddenly she wished she hadn't been so keen on not having Ty there. "She had to run an errand."

He smacked his lips. "You the reporter lady who's visiting?"

She didn't register the question at first, instead offering a hurried "She should be back any second," before her brain caught what he'd asked her.

"Yes, I'm the reporter. Did you want to . . ."

Before she could finish asking him if he wanted to speak with her, he was making for the exit with long, quick strides.

"Hope you're more careful than the last one who came down here," he offered, over his shoulder, as he pushed through the door and went out into the blinding sunshine.

Cressida ran after him as the door swung shut again, her heart racing. Was that a threat? Or was it something else? Whatever, she needed to catch up with the guy, and asked him what he meant.

As she reached it, someone pushed it open from the other side and she almost toppled over backwards. She ran straight into a man's chest and looked up to see Ty.

"Hey, thought I'd check on you."

She shoved past him.

"You okay?" he asked her.

"That guy who just left . . ."

Ty pivoted round, following her gaze into the street as the man climbed into a pickup truck. "Him?" he asked her.

"Yeah, that guy."

"Town eccentric," said Ty. "He was sitting in his truck earlier, staring at me. He took off. Hey, did something happen?"

Cressida had a decision to make. To share with Ty, or not? She didn't know why she hadn't already. Maybe because she was afraid that if Gregg, back in New York, knew everything about the story she was covering, he'd withdraw her, and send someone else to get it. A man, most likely.

It was part of the reason she hadn't protested more fervently when he'd assigned her Ty as a minder. Part of her wanted to be the fierce independent journalist who went where she wanted and asked the tough questions. The other part knew that someone had already done that, and it had not ended well.

She decided to keep that part of the story to herself.

"No, nothing happened. He was just kind of creepy, that's all."

Ty put a hand to her elbow. "You need to tell me if something happened, okay? It's the only way this will work."

"Nothing happened," she said, sounding shrill, even to her own ears. "He asked for the librarian. Then he asked if I was a reporter. Then he took off."

Ty didn't look like he believed her. "Okay."

They stepped back inside the library. Ty looked up at the beautiful mezzanine gallery. "Pretty nice."

"Here," she said, wanting to find a way to move the conversation on before he started asking her more questions about the redneck. "Come and look at this. I want a second opinion on whether this is weird or not."

Ty followed her through the shelves to the end of the fiction section where she had found the newly installed African-American section. She ran her finger along the spines. "They're all brand new."

Ty met her discovery with a shrug. "So?"

"Well, I bet you any money this section wasn't here until very recently. All these books were probably ordered and put out when they knew I was coming." She plucked a copy of *The Color Purple* from the shelf and opened it. "See? No stamps. Never been checked out or read."

"I don't get why you think this matters. You ever been at a military base when the brass are visiting or, worse, the President? The place is unrecognizable. Everything they want the VIP to see is out front and center, and everything they don't want them to see gets squirreled away until they've gone. It's just human nature."

The talk of squirreling away reminded Cressida of the basement and the boxes of books propped up against the door. "Okay, I accept that. Now, why don't we put all that brute strength of yours to some good use? I need some boxes moved."

She walked back behind the desk, Ty in tow, and towards the steps that led down into the basement. "Watch, they're pretty steep."

She started down, Ty following.

"This place was a sundown town," said Cressida, walking over to the pile of book storage boxes stacked against the far wall.

"That's not exactly a surprise," said Ty.

In sundown towns, which were usually in the American Midwest and South, it was made clear that African Americans weren't welcome after the sun went down. They were so widespread at one point that a guide was produced for African Americans, *The Green*

Book, which explained where it was not safe to spend the night while traveling across the country.

Often this unofficial form of racial segregation was aided and abetted by local law enforcement, who would find ways of dissuading black folks from sticking around in their area. More often places just got a reputation as best avoided because they were so unwelcoming. At the extreme were cases where African Americans, particularly men, were the subject of false arrest and violent assault, up to and including murder.

Over the years, the memory of sundown towns had slowly evaporated. But it was still the sad reality that there were parts of the country in which being the wrong color meant you were met with hostility and either the threat or reality of violence. Cressida had grasped long ago that the world still had a long way to go to realize the dream of everyone being judged on who they were and how they behaved rather than on how they were perceived.

"The theory at the time was that Carole Chabon had stayed too long here," said Cressida, leafing through a copy of *To Kill a Mockingbird* she had plucked from one of the book boxes.

"You think that's what happened?" Ty asked, as she peered a little more closely at the book's open pages, studying something inside the front cover that Ty couldn't see.

"I think it might have been part of it."

"But not the whole story."

She looked up at him. "Correct. I mean, I'm not saying the motive wasn't her race. The ligature marks they found around her neck, or what was left of it, proved she'd been hanged."

She held open the book to Ty. "I can see why they pulled this one from the shelf out there before I got here."

On the cover page someone had drawn a crude scaffold and rope, like a kid would to play a game of Hangman. Beneath it they'd scrawled "Niggers must die."

It took a lot more than some graffiti in a book to shock Ty. "Kids," he said, putting it back in the box.

"Yes, but where do they get it from?" Cressida asked.

They both knew the answer to that one.

"So what do you think's behind that door?"

"Only one way to find out," she said, straining to lift the box. He brushed past her, and picked up the box as if it was full of feathers and put it down to one side.

"So, you found anything interesting so far?" he said, moving to take the next box and nodding at the little desk laid out with papers.

"Not in any of that stuff, but yes."

He moved the second box, revealing a little more of the door. He put it down on top of the first, making a mental note that they would have to keep the same order when he put them back so that no one noticed they'd been moved.

"The librarian here told me she was at college when Carole Chabon was killed, but I emailed the University of Florida earlier to check her dates of attendance."

"And?"

"She may not have been here, but she wasn't a student there, not until the following year, 1975."

Ty seemed to chew it over. "Why make a point of lying about it?"

"I don't know. Distance herself from the whole thing, maybe."

"Or she knows a lot more than she's ever admitted," said Ty.

"Hello? Miss King, are you down there? Are you okay?"

The librarian's voice trickled down the steps. Her head appeared. "I thought I heard a man's voice."

Ty stepped in front of the boxes he'd been moving. He was hoping that the woman wouldn't spot they were trying to get to the door.

"Oh, this is Mr. Johnson. Tyrone. He's helping me out while I'm here."

"Helping?" said the librarian, cocking her head to one side. "Are you a reporter as well, Mr. Johnson?"

"More of an investigator," said Ty, unsure how the whole body-guard thing would go down.

"That sounds quite official. Guess I'd better watch what I say, then." She gave a little laugh that almost came off as sincere.

"Tyrone, I should be finished here for the day in about an hour. Would you mind coming back then?"

"Okay," said Ty, heading towards the stairs, his hulking frame blocking the librarian's view of the boxes. "See you in an hour."

The librarian stepped back as he cleared the hatch. She shot him the overly polite smile that hinted at more than a little discomfort at his presence.

"It's a beautiful library," he said, by way of conversation. "A real credit to you."

"Thank you, Mr. Johnson. I like to think so. We might not have everything that the folks in the big cities have, but what we have we like to preserve."

I bet you do, Ty thought. Like keeping the place free of black folks, or anyone else with a little extra pigment.

The library door pushed open. The cook from the diner poked his head around the side. He looked a little crestfallen as he made eye contact with Ty, who squared his shoulders, ready for another confrontation. Regardless of Cressida King's need to get on with the locals, any more mention of the word "boy" and things would get real ugly, real fast.

"I thought I saw you coming in here," said the cook. "Miss Parsons," he added, with a deferential nod. "May I speak with you?" he said to Ty.

"Sure."

Ty followed him outside. He could feel the librarian's eyes boring into the back of his head.

11

The two men stood on the steps of the library. Ty had about six inches and maybe sixty pounds on the cook. If there was going to be a fight, he didn't think it would last long. Although the man's demeanor suggested a fight wasn't what he was looking for. The shiner on his eye told Ty that he might have had one before he'd headed over here.

"Mr. Johnson, I just wanted to apologize for this morning. About what I said."

Ty stood tall. He wasn't about to make this easy for the man. Laugh it off and slap him on the back. Truth be told, he'd been called worse, much worse. And he'd dealt with a whole lot more than words. But the kind of behavior the cook had exhibited had no place. Not here, not anywhere, and the man needed to realize that.

"For calling me 'boy'. A grown man who's served his country in the Marine Corps."

"Yes. I'm sorry I used that word."

At least, thought Ty, he hadn't gone the 'I'm sorry if you were offended' non-apology route. That counted for something.

"It was wrong of me," the cook continued. "I'd really appreciate it if you'd accept my apology."

Ty didn't say anything, not yet anyway. He wanted to see what else this man might offer up. Not by way of a further apology, or groveling, but in terms of information. Someone who called another man "boy" and knew it was wrong wouldn't wait an hour to realize their error. Not to Ty's way of thinking. No. Something else had prompted this. Ty was sure of it.

"I don't want you to get the wrong idea about . . ." the man shrugged his shoulders ". . . y'know, this place. We're good people. It's just that. . ."

Another pregnant pause.

"It's just that what?" said Ty.

"We're not exactly used to folks who aren't like us around here. It's the way it's always been, I guess, and I'd like it to stay that way."

Despite himself, Ty smiled. He admired the man's candor. It was better than some mealy-mouthed explanation that danced around the elephant in the room. "Don't worry, I'm not planning on moving in," he said. "But I do expect a little respect while I'm here."

The cook's jaw bobbed up and down on his chest as he nodded in agreement. "Absolutely."

Ty figured there might even be what was sometimes called "a teachable moment" in here somewhere. He reached out his massive shovel of a right hand. "How about we start over?" Ty said. "Tyrone Johnson. Most people just call me Ty, but you can call me Mr. Johnson," he added, struggling to keep a straight face. He doubted the man had ever shaken a black man's hand before, or if he had, it was at some event where he'd had no alternative, like a graduation ceremony.

The man's hesitation confirmed Ty's suspicion. Finally he shook Ty's hand. "Good to meet you, Mr. Johnson. Lyle Ray."

Ty went easy on the grip, gave it enough time to be meaningful, then let go.

Lyle's hand fell to his side. Ty reached down and grasped the man's wrist. He pulled his hand towards him, and held it so that the open palm was facing the sun. "See?" he said. "None of my blackness rubbed off. I don't think you caught any cooties either."

The Marine Corps had been the first time that Ty had realized that, as an adult, there were plenty of people out there who had never mixed much socially, if at all, with those of another race. While he was growing up in Long Beach, his friends had been African American. His high school was broadly the same, and the church his momma had dragged him along to had consisted of an all-black congregation. It meant that he had grown up with his own set of prejudices about the white and brown brothers with whom he had forged deep bonds in the Corps. The only dumb thing was to pretend like none of this existed and that the country was some kind of join-hands-and-sing-together melting pot.

"You should wash your hands anyway, if you're preparing food," Ty added.

Lyle shot him a relieved smile. Ty could see that it had taken a fair amount of pride-swallowing to do what he had. It was worthy of respect, but it also made Ty more than a little curious as to what, or rather who, had prompted it.

Some kind of public-relations exercise was going on in Darling. This apology and the book display Cressida had shown him proved that beyond any reasonable doubt. But the question remained. Was it a genuine effort to show that the place had moved on from its past, or was it a smokescreen?

Ty hoped it was the former, but had a nagging feeling it wasn't. You didn't go to all this effort if you had nothing to hide. The question was what was it? And why was it so important to people here that it stayed hidden?

12

Curious George was sunning himself in the main pen as RJ pulled up in his truck. He'd set up the alligator ranch with money he'd inherited from an aunt in Tallahassee, but it had never taken off. He had burned through most of the cash setting the place up, and hadn't reckoned with the cost of the public liability insurance, and all the permits he'd need.

He'd hoped to create a visitor attraction where people could get to see 'gators up close and personal. What he'd ended up with was a three-bedroom ranch house on ten acres with a couple of ponds, three separate enclosures, and around forty or so alligators.

He'd had Curious George since he was a hatchling. He'd grown into a super-sized male, even by local standards. He'd given him the name because when he was young he had his nose in everything. If RJ had known the size he was going to grow to, he would have called him Big George, but Curious George still kind of fit.

Like any male adult 'gator, George was territorial, so RJ kept him in his own pen, apart from when he was called on to mate, which was quite a lot. Once George had begun to sow his wild oats with the female 'gators it had unsettled him. He couldn't go too long without love or he'd get even more ornery than he usually was.

With the idea of a tourist attraction shelved, RJ had begun breeding the 'gators to sell on, mostly for meat, and some for their skin, which rich ladies liked to use for handbags, and cowboys for boots. RJ killed them in a shed at the back of one of the ponds, then a guy came down from Gainesville to collect the carcasses and paid in cash. He had to use bait to get them into the shed. He'd make sure he didn't feed them for a few days before.

Hungry 'gators were dangerous so he'd let them eat whatever he'd used as a lure. Once they were fed he'd use a bolt gun to kill them. From time to time a slaughter would go wrong and he'd have to shoot them again. That was rare, though. He was pretty careful when he lined up the shot. The more holes the 'gator had in it, the less it was worth, not that the head was much use to anyone. Though he guessed that the teeth were used for necklaces and the like.

He watched old George lying at the edge of his pond. Only his eyes and the top of his head were visible. George would die of old age. RJ would see to that. He guessed he'd grown sentimental about the old guy.

Sue Ann's car was coming down the track. RJ started back to his truck, making a show of looking busy. What was it about women, and men not being busy? He glanced back toward Curious George. The 'gator had life figured out.

RJ grabbed some timber from the back of the truck and started moving it to the pile next to the house as Sue Ann pulled up and got out of her car. She looked tired. Waitressing, being on your feet all day, was a young woman's game, but they needed the money. Jobs were hard to come by around here, so people rarely gave them up.

Sue Ann walked over to him. He slipped his arm around her waist and gave her a kiss on the cheek. She made a show of pushing him away, smiling while she did it. "Get off me. You smell of 'gator."

"You like it." He grinned.

She put her hands on her hips. "What a day."

"Oh, yeah?"

"Mimsy tore a strip off Lyle."

"What for?"

"That reporter's in town. You know, about the thing."

RJ nodded. *The thing.* No one ever called it what it was—the murder or the lynching. No one ever mentioned the victim's name. In town it was always "the thing" or "the incident". RJ could barely remember Carole Chabon's name passing the lips of anyone he knew since it had happened. It was like a superstition or something. As if saying her name would raise her spirit from the swamp and it would come looking for revenge.

"Anyway, she has this guy with her. Big. Looks like a cop or something. Guess he's here after what happened to y'know."

"Y'know" was shorthand for Timothy French, the second Darling mystery.

RJ knew who she was talking about. The big guy he'd watched that morning from his truck. The black man with a chest big enough to block the sun and hands like shovels. He'd seen the reporter in the library and spoken to her before he'd lost his nerve, or had second thoughts, and bolted. He could only hope that Sue Ann hadn't seen him, but from the way she was talking she hadn't.

"So, Lyle got into it with him after he started asking me questions about that whole deal."

Oh, yeah, that was another phrase that got used. "The deal". "That crazy deal". RJ wondered if an entire town had pleaded temporary insanity as a defense.

"Mimsy must have got wind of it. Anyway, she comes tearing through the diner like a hurricane, takes him out the back, and he comes back in like a scolded puppy. With a black eye."

"She hit him?" he asked.

"Guess she must have."

She must really be riled up, he thought. Anxious. It had been a long time since they'd had someone poking around in town. He wondered if maybe this reporter knew something that had Mimsy worried.

"Mimsy doesn't want anyone upsetting this visitor. Guess she wants to play it like there's nothing to—" Sue Ann stopped herself.

"Nothing to hide?"

"Yeah. Anyway, she's having a dinner for them. Can you believe that?"

RJ could. It was Mimsy all over. What was that phrase? The iron fist and the velvet glove. That was Mimsy. Pour on the Southern charm, and if that didn't work then, well, watch out.

"She wants me to do the serving," Sue Ann continued.

"You're gonna do it?"

"It's a hundred bucks," she said, like that settled it, which it kind of did. "Who wouldn't want to be a fly on that wall?" She leaned in to kiss him on the cheek. "I'm going to take a shower."

He watched her walk into the house. His thoughts settled in around him again.

A dinner party? He could hear Mimsy already. It was a long time ago. No, likely no one will ever know the truth. There'd been talk of a drifter in town the week before the murder. Maybe he'd had something to do with it.

He blinked in the afternoon sun, and in that fraction of a second he saw the tree, and the rope. He heard the shouts this time, too. The catcalling. The frantic, fevered chatter, followed by the silence.

Reaching up a few seconds later, he felt his cheeks moist. He wiped away the salty tears with the back of his sleeve.

He thought of the black man he'd watched. He'd looked tough. Like he'd seen things. Maybe things even worse than RJ had. Maybe he was the person who could lift the weight of all this from them. Him and that young reporter.

But they'd need help. RJ knew that much.

The problem was, whoever helped them would still be stuck here. Living with Mimsy, and the others. Seeing them every day. There was Sue Ann to think about too.

RJ looked back to the pond. Curious George had sunk back down into the muddy water. RJ couldn't see him. But he was there all right. Lying low. Waiting for suppertime.

13

Ty held open the passenger door of the Honda for Cressida. She got in. He walked around and got into the driver's seat.

"You find anything?" Ty asked.

"No, and I'm not going to. Not in the stuff they've given me anyway."

"What about the locked door?"

"Too risky. The librarian kept coming down to see if I needed anything. I think she noticed that the boxes had been moved."

"She say anything?" said Ty.

"No, but it was kind of obvious, the way she kept looking at them."

"So why not just ask her? 'What's up with the locked store room and the boxes you had in front of the door?'"

Cressida chewed a little on her bottom lip. "I thought about it. I don't know." She paused. "It's like there's this really polite dance going on, but everyone's on edge. You know what I'm saying?"

Ty studied the main street. "Yeah. You ever see that movie *The Stepford Wives*?"

She shook her head. "Nope, but I kind of know the story. You think these people are robots?"

Ty smiled. "Not literally, no, but they seem pretty tightly wound. Like that cook at the diner is shaping up to throw me down, and the next second he's kissing my ass."

"They're hiding something. I know that much."

Ty switched on the engine, and placed the car in Drive. "So what's the plan now?" He nodded towards the library. "Assuming there's no answers to be had in there."

"Someone will talk."

"You sure about that?"

"Small towns. They're full of petty rivalries, people holding a grudge, just waiting for their chance. If Carole Chabon's murderer is here, and people know who it is, sooner or later someone will 'fess up."

"That's a lot of assumptions right there. What's to say it wasn't an outsider? Serial killer. Something like that."

Cressida shifted in her seat and looked at him. "You think it was a serial killer? Really?"

"No, but it's possible. Look, where do most investigations go wrong?"

She waited.

"The cops have a theory and they work to make everything fit, rather than keeping an open mind."

"I hear you," said Cressida.

They had reached the end of Darling's main street. There were two turns. One left and one right.

"So where we headed?"

"Back to the Airbnb to get ready."

"For?"

"The mayor has invited us to dinner at her place. Part of the charm offensive, no doubt."

"Man, if I'd known I would have brought my tux," said Ty.

"You own a tux?"

Ty side-eyed her. She had a habit, like Lock, of catching him out. "Okay, I'd have rented one."

"Let me guess. Burgundy crushed velvet," she said, smiling.

"You're funny."

"I was right," she said.

"So what's the plan for this dinner?" said Ty, shifting the subject.

"Plan?"

"Yeah."

She grimaced. "I don't know. Hope someone gets drunk and says something they shouldn't."

"How likely do you think that is?" Ty asked.

She shifted again in her seat. "It's not really a plan, is it?"

"Not really."

"Okay, I plan on playing nice. At first, anyway. And then when the time's right I have a couple of direct questions for the mayor."

"Which are?"

"You'll have to wait and see, but I guarantee you one thing, she's not going to like them."

"Is that so?" said Ty.

Cressida stared at him. "You didn't think I came all the way down here on a wing and a prayer, did you?"

14

Ty came down the stairs in a pair of neatly creased black trousers, a freshly pressed white shirt, and a grey sports coat.

Adelson Shaw's head appeared at the door. "Can I get you something to drink, Mr. Johnson?"

"No, thank you. I'm driving."

Adelson stepped into the hallway. "Are you sure? Mimsy's dinner parties can be pretty dull. Don't think I've ever managed to get through one without at least a few belts of something strong."

"Thanks, but I'm good. You haven't been invited to this one?"

"I was." Adelson smiled. "Sadly, I had a prior engagement."

He held up a tumbler with a couple of ice cubes and some bourbon. "Last offer," he said.

"Maybe when we get back." More like definitely when I get back, thought Ty. If the old man kept pounding bourbon, by the time they returned he might be oiled enough to let something slip about the Carole Chabon murder. Even if it was only unsubstantiated gossip, Ty was certain that in a small town like this one Adelson must have heard something about what had gone down and who was responsible.

"My, my," said Adelson, as Cressida walked down the stairs in a little black dress.

Ty had to agree. She looked stunning. She had put her hair up, and her makeup was expertly done. Her green eyes shimmered as she floated down the last few steps.

He did his best to pack away any thoughts he might be having about how she looked. She was his principal, and the rules about that were cast iron. Bodyguarding and close protection required a cool head at all times. Emotions were best kept out of it. They could make things very dangerous very quickly.

"Well, don't you make the perfect couple!" said Adelson, with a sly wink in Ty's direction.

"We're not a couple, but thank you," said Cressida, swiftly correcting him.

Ty walked with her to the door. "Save me some of that," he said to Adelson.

The old man raised his glass in a toast. "I got you."

Ty and Cressida went down the porch steps to the car. Ty held the passenger door open for her. She got in and he walked around to the driver's door.

Ty already had the route to the mayor's house scoped out. It was on the other side of town, about a seven-minute drive, assuming they didn't have to stop for any 'gators crossing the road.

"What do you think of our host?" Ty asked, as he pulled away from the house.

"I think he knows more than he's letting on," she said.

"I'd say that probably goes for most people around here."

She crossed her arms. "And not one of them is going to tell me a damn thing unless I drag it out of them."

"Why would they?" said Ty.

"If you knew something about an innocent young woman being murdered, what would you do?" she fired back, green eyes flashing in the light of the Honda's instrument panel.

"I don't live in a small town in the middle of nowhere with no one to watch my back when a reporter moves on to the next story."

"They're scared? Is that what you're telling me?"

"I'd imagine some of them are. And some are apathetic. And some probably figure talking now won't do any good anyway."

Cressida lapsed into silence. Ty studied the road ahead. Living in LA, it was easy to forget just how dark it got once you were outside the city. With no moon, the darkness was complete. All he could see was the forty feet or so of road carved out by the car's headlights.

They crested the top of a hill to see Darling's meager streetlights laid out below. Ty tried hard to imagine the kind of people who'd decide to settle in a place like this. Hot, humid, almost fully encircled by swampy wetlands full of things looking to eat you. People, he guessed, who weren't likely to give up their secrets easily, or cave to outside pressure.

Something else came to his mind. A question not for the locals but the young woman next to him. "What got you interested in this story in the first place?"

She made a face, like this was a question she'd anticipated but had hoped she wouldn't be asked. "I was researching a bigger story on sundown towns, and this was one of the most notorious cases."

Something about the way she rattled off her reply told Ty there was more.

"No, really," he said.

She sighed, confirming his suspicions. "It stays between us?"

Ty nodded. "Of course."

"It's personal."

"Personal how?"

"Carole Chabon was my great-aunt," said Cressida.

15

Mary Elizabeth Murray sat at her dressing-table, changed her earrings for the third time in the past ten minutes, and did her best to compose herself. The visitors would be here at any moment, and she wasn't sure she had done the right thing by offering this invitation.

Apart from maids and other domestic help, no African American had ever set foot in this house. Not as a guest. Apart, of course, from that one time. The time that had led to this horrible mess that was still plaguing them all these years later.

The whole affair was proof of what she had always believed. Of what her family had believed. That the races shouldn't mix. That no good could come of it.

And yet here she was, enabling just such a thing.

Had she done right? she asked herself. She could only hope she had, that this dinner would be sufficient to prove to this slip of a girl that the town had moved on. That there was no story here. That she should go back to New York and tell everyone there was no scandal to be found. That they were only simple people who wished to live their lives in peace. Others could move on if they wished, but Mimsy

Murray had no desire to follow them. No, she liked things as they had been. Every kind keeping to its own.

She took a final look at herself in the mirror, something she avoided most days. There was no cheating the passage of time and what it did to a woman. Men didn't know how easy they had it. No one minded that they lost their looks, assuming they'd had some in the first place.

Finally, Mimsy stood up. She adjusted her double strand of pearls and brushed at her dress. She took a deep breath, and closed her eyes. She had to keep her temper, she told herself, no matter what was said or what happened this evening. Her temper had been a problem for her over the years. It had lost her friends, and caused her no end of grief. Surprisingly, it hadn't receded with age as it did with most people. Didn't people mellow with age? Well, she hadn't. If anything, the shifting world had only consumed her even more.

But now, tonight, she had to keep herself in check. No matter what. She could rage all she wanted when her guests had departed, but while they were here, she was the public face of the town, and she had to play that part, and play it well.

She walked to the bedroom door. It opened directly onto the upstairs hallway. She stepped out. She was an actress, and this house was her stage. It was time to put her best foot forward.

From downstairs, she could smell something burning. She felt the anger well in her stomach. Sue Ann scuttled past the bottom of the stairs, heading with a tureen towards the dining room, which had been beautifully staged for this evening's dinner.

Mimsy cleared her throat loudly. Sue Ann froze in her tracks. Mimsy raised one finger, beckoning Sue Ann to stay where she was. Mimsy wasn't about to shout down the stairs, like some commoner.

She walked down the flight. Sue Ann was still waiting for her. "I smell burning. Might you go and see if Lyle requires any assistance?"

"It's okay. He left something on the stove a little too long, but it's under control."

Mimsy forced a smile. "Very well."

Headlights swept across the front of the house. She took another deep breath. "Well," she said, "don't just stand there. Put that down and get ready to greet our guests. Bring them to me in the drawing room."

TY KILLED the lights and switched off the engine. He'd backed into a space in front of the house and left the hood of the Honda pointing down the long driveway. He'd never had to flee a dinner party, not that he could remember, but old habits died hard.

Cressida glanced at him. "Do you have your gun with you?"

He lifted his jacket a little. "Of course. You want me to leave it in the car?"

She seemed to think it over. "No."

"You sure?"

"I don't think we're going to need it at dinner, but probably better not to leave it in the car."

"That was my thinking," said Ty. "Anything else?"

"Like what?"

Ty shrugged. "Anything you want me to ask? Or maybe not mention?"

"Just follow my lead, okay?"

Ty smiled. She might have been only in her twenties, but he had to hand it to his principal, she was pretty self-assured.

"The people around here . . ." said Cressida, doing a final check of her make-up in the vanity mirror ". . . they might seem all sweetness and light, but they can be anything but."

"That's why you're here."

"Correct," she said, opening the passenger door, and getting out.

Ty followed. He stood with her for a second, and took in the house that loomed above them. It was similar to the one where they were staying. It had the same porch that wrapped around it, like a skirt, and the same roof, but it was even larger. From what Cressida had told him on the way here, the family had originally been slave owners, and this was the main plantation house.

That knowledge sent a shiver down his spine. Even now, Ty found it hard to fathom his country's history. How could people own other people, like livestock, and not only see nothing wrong with it but go to war to retain the right to do so?

The wind, as if sensing his unease, picked up a little, as a breeze rattled through a stand of nearby gumbo-limbo trees. Ty put out his arm, and Cressida linked hers through it. They walked up the steps towards the front door and Ty rang the bell.

A few seconds later, the door was opened by the waitress from the town's diner. Ty remembered her name as Sue Ann.

"Really is a small town," he said to Cressida, as they walked into the hallway.

Sue Ann had traded her yellow and white diner uniform for something black and a little more formal. "Welcome, may I take your jackets?"

"Thank you," said Cressida, slipping hers off to reveal her strapless black dress.

"I'm good," said Ty, aware that taking off his blazer would reveal the SIG Sauer holstered beneath.

It didn't look the kind of house where you'd eat dinner with your side arm, although it was Florida, so who really knew?

Sue Ann took Cressida's jacket as the lady of the house appeared from another room. She walked over to them, smiling.

"Mayor Mary Elizabeth Murray but, please, call me Mimsy. Everyone does," she said, putting out a delicate, wrinkled hand.

Ty spotted Sue Ann tamping down what looked to him like an eye roll.

Cressida shook her hand. "Cressida King. Thank you so much for welcoming us to your home."

There was an undercurrent to how both women were looking at each other, but Ty couldn't get a handle on it. Somehow the vibe was like two gladiators circling each other in Rome's Colosseum.

Ty offered his hand. "Tyrone Johnson."

There was a fractional hesitation, which Ty also noted, before she shook it. "It's a pleasure to meet you. Now, can I have Sue Ann fetch you something to drink? A bourbon, perhaps? A glass of wine?"

Ty demurred. Notwithstanding that he never drank while he was working, he had a feeling he wanted his wits about him this evening. "Nothing alcoholic, but thank you."

"An Arnold Palmer? Dr Pepper? Something cool and refreshing. I would offer you water, but we've had a little problem with the town supply and I'm all out of bottled."

"An Arnold Palmer sounds great," said Ty.

"Miss King?"

"Please, call me Cress. A glass of white wine, please."

Mimsy turned and snapped her fingers. "Sue Ann. Some white wine for Cress, and an Arnold Palmer."

Inwardly, Ty grimaced. Finger snapping at staff was one of his pet hates. He reminded himself that they weren't there to make friends so much as get some answers.

"Actually, you know what?" said Mimsy. "I shall fetch them for you myself. I'll be right back. Please, go into the drawing room and make yourselves comfortable."

Ty traded a look with Cressida as both women left. She walked towards the room Mimsy had indicated. Ty followed.

The drawing room was all dark wood and heavy red drapes. There were two club chairs and two red couches, all antique. There was money in the family, but Ty could tell it was old, and no doubt dwindling. One of the couches was showing a badly repaired tear that had been partially hidden by a cushion.

Above the fireplace a faded rectangle of wallpaper indicated a missing picture. Ty wondered if it had been sold. "This is going to be a long night," he said.

"What are the odds we're the first black people to be in this house who weren't servants?"

"Not a bet I'd take. She's doing her best, though, right? Have to give her credit for that."

"Let's see, shall we?"

The door opened and Mimsy bustled back in with Sue Ann, who

was holding an ornate silver tray with their drinks. Mimsy plucked them off and handed Cressida her glass of wine and Ty his soft drink. They thanked her.

"You're not having anything?" said Cressida.

Mimsy seemed to flush a little. "I've never had alcohol pass my lips, my dear, but don't let that stop your enjoyment." She smiled. "Please take a seat."

They sat, Ty in one of the club chairs, Cressida in the other and Mimsy on the edge of a couch as Sue Ann left them to it. Ty wished he could go with her. The kitchen, or wherever she was headed, had to have a more chilled atmosphere than there was in here. The whole thing was taking him back to visiting elderly relatives after church on a Sunday when you were a kid and having to be on your best behavior when all you wanted to do was play ball outside with your buddies.

"So," said Mimsy, folding her hands into her lap, "what do you make of our small town so far?"

Before either of them could offer an opinion, she shifted to face Ty. "Mr. Johnson, I heard about the little difficulty you had with Lyle Ray."

"It's fine, he apologized," offered Ty. "Consider it forgotten."

She gave him that more than slightly forced smile. "All the same. It should not have happened."

"Just to let you know," said Ty, pausing to take a sip of his Arnold Palmer, which was so damn sweet he wished he'd gone for the Dr Pepper option, "that shiner he has, nothing to do with me."

"I never thought otherwise. Anyway, I'm glad it was settled. I'm afraid with Darling being such a small place, and so isolated, people around here aren't quite as progressive as people from bigger places."

To Ty's ears she'd said "progressive" like she was talking about Communism. He wasn't exactly sure why she was trying so hard. It wasn't as if racism wasn't an issue elsewhere. Darling, Florida, was hardly alone in that regard. In fact, in Ty's experience, any place in the world where the entire population looked one way, and had to deal with visitors who were different, the occupants reacted sometimes with hostility. It was human nature. You might not lynch someone or call them names, but you didn't pretend you didn't notice a difference when you did.

Cressida returned the mayor's forced smile. "So, would you still consider Darling a sundown town?"

Ty took another sip of his drink to cover a laugh. Talk about being direct.

Mimsy rocked back a little but recovered. "Well, hardly. I mean, you and Mr. Johnson are sitting in the mayor's home, and I believe the sun's already gone down some hours ago."

As counter-punches went, it was, Ty had to admit, pretty good. She'd slipped Cressida's jab and crossed with a right.

"But it was a sundown town?" Cressida wasn't about to drop it.

Mimsy stared down at the carpet. "I'm ashamed to say it was. Things happened here that shouldn't have. But I would ask that when you come to write your story, you make it clear that we're trying to move on from our past."

She looked at Ty, like he was some kind of neutral arbiter, and continued, "I mean, places change. Don't you agree?"

Ty wasn't about to start taking sides. "They can change. I agree on that."

"But do they?" said Cressida. "I guess that's the real question. It's one thing to say you've changed, but another thing to actually do it."

"My, we haven't even sat down to eat yet, and we're already weighing some of the great questions," said Mimsy, primly.

"Mayor Murray, how old were you when Carole Chabon was lynched right here in Darling, then dumped in the swamp out there?"

Mimsy had to have anticipated that this was going to come up, thought Ty. After all, Cressida had made no secret of why she was here.

"I was, let me see . . ."

"It was 1974, if that helps," said Cressida, eyes lasering on Mimsy.

A bell rang in the hallway, as if on cue.

"Well, shall we continue this discussion in the dining room?" their hostess asked them, getting up.

Cressida stayed where she was. "I'm sure dinner can wait a few more seconds," she said, as Ty tucked in his elbow, feeling the reassuring presence of the gun tucked down by his side.

"Ms. King," said Mimsy, her tone hardening. "Am I on trial here?"

Cressida stared at her. "I don't know. Should you be?"

16

Boot heels scraped the rough ground as he made his way toward the car. Light spilled from the front of the house. From inside he could hear the low murmur of conversation. Then a woman's voice, raised.

He held the paper in his hand. He unfolded it again and read what was on it. He had spelled a couple of words wrong, crossed them out, and written them again. He should write it over fresh, but there was no time for that.

He couldn't risk being seen.

He looked up again at the window. There was the sound of a door opening at the rear of the property and something being thrown into the trash.

He froze.

"Come on," he whispered to himself. "Do it, and leave."

Was he doing the right thing? He still wasn't sure. He was scared. What if they knew what he'd done? There would be hell to pay. More than hell.

But not to do anything, wouldn't that be worse? Hadn't that been as bad?

He thought of a passage he'd read over and over until he had committed it to memory. It came from the Good Book, from Hebrews 10:26–27, to be precise.

If we keep on sinning after we have received the knowledge of the truth, no sacrifice for sins is left, but only a fearful expectation of judgment and of raging fire that will consume the enemies of God.

He thought again of that passage as he folded the piece of paper and stepped in closer to the car. As gently as he could, he reached out, lifted the windshield wiper, tucked the paper under, and lowered it again.

He stepped back as he heard someone walking down the side of the house, whistling.

Startled, his heart pounding so loudly he could hear it in his ears, he turned and ran. He was making noise, he knew he was, but he couldn't risk slowing down.

If they cleared the side of the house before he got away he'd be seen. He couldn't be seen. Not now. Not ever.

He would give up his secrets, their secrets, but he wasn't brave enough to do it in the daylight.

17

Over the years, Ty had broken bread at some tense dinner tables, but that evening had to have set some kind of record. When he, Cressida and Mimsy had finally moved through into the dining room, things had appeared to settle down. But the peace hadn't lasted.

Cressida had continued to ask Mimsy what she knew about Carole Chabon's murder. Mimsy dodged and deflected, but rarely came close to giving a direct answer. Instead she would attempt to shift the conversation back to the town's new image, and Cressida would listen politely for a time before dragging it right back to the murder.

Through all of it, Ty noted the voice recorder that Cressida had placed in her handbag, picking up everything that was said. It was a classic reporter's trick. Unless someone specified that something was off the record, and the journalist agreed, you could assume it was on the record.

Ty didn't know if Mimsy was aware of the protocol or the recording device, and he figured that now was not the time to ask. He'd kept his head down, accepted another Arnold Palmer, and sat back to watch the fireworks between two women who couldn't have been more different.

At one point, he excused himself to use the bathroom. He walked toward the back of the house and, through a doorway framing the kitchen, saw Lyle, the cook from the diner, in a hushed but heated conversation with Sue Ann. They had their backs to him, Lyle hunched over the stove, Sue Ann standing at the sink, elbow deep in dirty dishes from the first course.

Ty stepped off the side, and dialed in to their hushed conversation for a moment.

"I knew this was a bad idea," Sue Ann was saying.

"Why didn't you say anything?"

"And get a black eye like you did?"

Ty hadn't figured Mimsy as the hands-on type, but maybe she'd gotten someone else to do it for her. Either way he guessed her intervention had been behind Lyle's supposedly heartfelt apology.

"You'd better get these plates in to them," said Lyle.

Ty took that as his cue to step toward the bathroom before Sue Ann came out and caught him eavesdropping. As he closed the door his cell phone chimed with a text. It was Lock, checking in.

Ty tapped out a quick reply.

Tense, but all good. Will let you know if anything happens.

He hit send, unzipped, relieved himself, then washed and dried his hands. As he stepped back out, Sue Ann was carrying the main course toward the dining room.

"Can I help you with those?" he offered.

She smiled. "Thank you, but I got it, and you're a guest."

He let her walk ahead. In the dining room, some kind of temporary *détente* seemed to have settled between Cressida and the mayor. Ty took his seat. Before Cressida started up with the questions, he figured he might try to build some rapport.

"You have a beautiful home," he said, settling into his seat.

"Thank you, Mr. Johnson," said Mimsy. "It's a lot of upkeep, but it's been in the family for a long time, and I didn't want to be the one to let it go, although when I pass . . ."

Ty sensed Cressida about to jump when Mimsy mentioned the

ancestral inheritance. No doubt it would be some question about how they'd made their money, with the answer being slaves. Ty managed to cut her off with a look, and for once she allowed him to continue.

"You don't have children?" said Ty.

"Never married to have any," she said, staring down at the fresh white tablecloth, which had been pressed to within an inch of its life.

It was the first time Ty had seen anything approaching a truthful human reaction from the woman since they had arrived. Despite himself, he felt a little sorry for her. Looking at Cressida, he noticed that her expression had also softened a little.

"Must have been difficult to meet someone. As you say, it's a very small town," Ty went on.

"Oh, there were suitors, of course," she said.

"I'm sure," said Ty, working in a little flattery. If he had learned anything over the past few years' working with Lock it was that people could reveal their deepest, darkest secrets at the unlikeliest of times. He might not approve of Cressida's confrontational approach, but only because it was never likely to work with someone who was clearly set in her beliefs.

What Ty had found, what Lock had taught him, was that many people had a deep-seated need to purge themselves of their sins. It was as if by sharing them with another human being it made them less burdensome. Ty guessed that, if they were religious, folks figured it was better to repent before they died and seek forgiveness on earth, rather than wait until it was too late and their eternal fate had been sealed.

All you needed to do was give the person the opportunity.

"There wasn't anyone who . . ." Ty let the last part remain unsaid. He was pushing his luck, he knew that. But he sensed that by taking this woman into one part of her past, she might just reveal the truth of what had happened to another young woman who never got the chance to marry or have children: Carole Chabon.

"Oh, there was someone all right," she said, her eyes smoky and wistful.

"He met someone else? Moved away?" said Ty, praying that no one would blunder in, especially not Cressida, and break the spell that seemed to have descended over Mimsy Murray.

"No, he's still in town. In fact, you've met him," said Mimsy.

Ty did a fast inventory. It didn't take long to guess whom she meant. It had to have been someone around her age and, judging by her manner, someone of the same social standing. There was no way a woman like this, who obviously set such store by appearances and status, would have dated someone with a blue-collar job.

They hadn't met that many people in town, so it had to be their host.

"Mr. Shaw?" said Ty.

At the mention of his name, her manner changed. The mists lifted from her eyes, replaced by the same fierce defensiveness they'd seen before. She straightened up, and seemed to notice for the first time that Sue Ann had been serving them.

Mimsy fixed her gaze on the waitress. "Haven't I told you about hovering around the table like a bad smell?"

Sue Ann didn't bother arguing, or apologizing. She flitted out of the dining room without a word.

"Don't let old Adelson fool you," said Mimsy, directing the comment to Ty. "He's not what he seems."

"How does he seem?" Cressida asked.

Mimsy ignored the question. "Have you asked *him* about what happened? That might be a good place to start."

She turned her attention to the plate of food in front of her. "Well, this looks delicious, doesn't it?" she said, lifting her knife and fork.

"Wait," said Cressida. "He knows what happened to Carole Chabon. That's what you just said, isn't it?"

Mimsy eyed her across the table. She was holding her knife like she might just use it to cut more than chicken. The switch was unsettling to Ty. It was rare to see such white-hot rage in someone of Mimsy's age. People usually mellowed as they grew older, let things go.

"Let's just say a lot of things died back then," said Mimsy, hacking away at her chicken breast. "Now, I've said all I'm going to say on the matter. You know who you should speak with."

"But you must know what happened too," Cressida said, not about to give up. "Otherwise you wouldn't have suggested I speak with Mr. Shaw."

Mimsy set her cutlery on her plate. "You won't hear it from me. No one will. I made my peace with what happened a long time ago."

"How can you make your peace with an innocent young woman being murdered?" asked Cressida.

"Innocent!" said Mimsy, before noisily clearing her throat.

"She was on a mission," said Cressida, her voice tightening.

"Oh, she was on a mission all right," said Mimsy, a little hint of a smile playing at the corners of her mouth.

Cressida slammed her hand onto the table. "Why don't you stop talking in riddles? What do you mean by that?"

The atmosphere in the dining room shifted once again.

"It wasn't the word of the Lord she was sharing. That's what I mean. She was sharing herself, like a common whore."

Even Ty, who was used to industrial language, sat a little more upright at that word.

"That's a lie," said Cressida. "You know it is. Her pastor, her family, they all gave the same testimony. Carole Chabon was going to take holy orders, become a nun. She'd never even held a boy's hand, never mind had a boyfriend, so she certainly wasn't doing what you're suggesting."

Mimsy rose up. Her face pale, her hand clamped around the knife handle. She glared at Cressida from across the table. "Women like her come in all kinds of forms," she spat. "And the Negro ones are the worst."

Cressida smiled. "Now, you're finally being honest, aren't you? So much for times changing, people changing. Tell me, are you the fourth or the fifth generation of your family to have joined the Klan? The Women's Ku Klux Klan was pretty big around here, wasn't it? Your mother was an Exalted Cyclops, wasn't she? You were one as well, right?"

Mimsy was standing. Her fists, one still clutching her knife, were planted on the table, her chest and jaw forward. It was the posture of a raging bull ready to make its charge. Ty was glad of the table that lay between the two women. He didn't doubt that he could handle the old lady if she lunged for Cressida, that wasn't remotely in doubt, but it was the last thing he wanted to do.

"Get out of my home," she said.

"Gladly," said Cressida, getting up and pushing her chair back.

Ty looked down at the chicken. It was a shame he wouldn't get to eat it. It looked pretty tasty. He guessed that now wasn't the time to ask for a doggy bag.

"But don't think this is going away," said Cressida, as she stood, matching Mimsy's posture, equally fierce.

"Oh, you'll go away," said Mimsy. "I'll see to that."

"Like you did with Timothy French?" said Cressida. "You know what happened to him too, don't you, Mayor?"

"I have no idea what you're talking about," said Mimsy, the self-satisfied smirk on her face contradicting her words.

Ty wanted to know who Timothy French was, but it could wait until they were in the car and heading out of this crazy town. Old or not, frail or not, he didn't doubt that Mimsy Murray would make their stay uncomfortable.

"He was murdered, too, wasn't he? He didn't disappear. He's out there somewhere, dumped in that swamp like Carole," said Cressida.

Sue Ann had appeared in the doorway. She was holding Cressida's jacket.

Ty pushed back his chair and got to his feet. "Come on. I think dinner's over."

Mimsy sank down into her seat. She looked emotionally spent. Ty knew how she felt. This had been like everyone's nightmare family Thanksgiving dinner, only on steroids.

Cressida collected her jacket from Sue Ann, who was busy studying the floor, no doubt hoping the boards would open up and swallow her.

With Ty's hulking frame next to her, Cressida delivered her parting shot.

"Thank you for an interesting evening," she said, pulling the voice recorder from her bag, and making sure Mimsy could see the red light flashing. "You've given me more than I need for my editor to approve me staying down here for as long as it takes. Heck, I might even buy a place. The town could use a little color, don't you think?"

Mimsy turned her head and stared at them. The look she gave Cressida was chilling. Ty placed a hand on the small of his principal's back, and shepherded her gently out of the room, into the hallway and toward the front door.

Cressida stopped halfway down the steps and exhaled.

"You okay?" Ty asked. She was shaking, not enough to be noticeable to others, but sufficient that he could feel it.

She nodded. "Fine."

"You're just getting the aftermath of the adrenalin dump. That's what the shaking is. Your body's readjusting."

She smiled. "Good to know. I really thought she'd go for me in there."

Ty didn't say anything. It had been a possibility.

"You know," said Cressida, "I think she not only knows what happened, I think she was involved. Really involved."

"I don't doubt it."

They continued down the steps. He kept an eye on the house behind them while also scoping out the open ground around it. Not that he'd be able to see someone if they were skulking in the shrubbery.

That was the thing with places like this. When darkness fell it was all-encompassing. Your only hope of seeing anything was the moon, and tonight it was obscured by grey clouds that had only recently moved in, leaving the air muggy and brooding with the threat of a storm to come.

He walked Cressida to the passenger side, and opened the door, shielding her body with his as she got in.

"So what's the deal with Timothy French?"

She stared up at him. "I should have told you about that."

"Sounds like it."

"Can we get out of here first?"

"Sure," said Ty.

As he went to close her door, the front door opened. He stopped. Cressida got out of the car as Sue Ann hurried down the porch steps toward them. Every few steps she snuck a look over her shoulder. She was holding two brown-paper bags in her hand. "You never got to eat," she said handing them over.

"You didn't put rat poison in them, did you?" said Cressida, sharply.

Sue Ann's face folded in on itself, her upset impossible to hide.

"I'm sorry," said Cressida.

"So am I," said Sue Ann. "I know you have a job to do, both of you, but don't go judging Darling by Mimsy Murray. There are good people here too."

Cressida regarded her for a second. "Will they talk to me?"

"I think they will."

"And what about you?" Cressida asked her.

"Not here, not now. It's too dangerous," said Sue Ann, with another furtive glance back to the house.

Mimsy might be watching them from a darkened window and they'd have no way of knowing.

"When you're gone, I'll have to live here."

"You can remain anonymous. I won't use your name unless you give me permission."

Sue Ann nodded, her eyes moist. "Let me think about it."

"You know where to find me," said Cressida.

"I'd better get back inside," said Sue Ann, turning toward the porch.

Ty noticed something on the windshield. He lifted the note from under the wiper blade.

It had Cressida's name on the front. He palmed it to her. "Read it in the car," he said, as she got back in. He closed the door and walked around to the driver's side, suddenly tired.

He turned on the Honda's engine and switched the lights on. He pulled away from the house, checking his rearview every few seconds until they reached the end of the driveway and turned back onto the public road.

No one followed them. Not that Ty could see.

That didn't mean much. He knew from bitter experience that small towns rarely gave up their darkest secrets without a struggle. The more dangerous the secret, the more it took to drag the truth out into the light.

"So," he said, when they were well clear of the old slave house, "tell me about Timothy French."

18

Mimsy Murray paced up and down the length of the front porch, her phone clamped to her ear. Adelson's line rang out again. She clicked the phone off.

He was likely drunk. Or getting there. Either passed out on the couch, or hunched over a bottle of bourbon.

That girl walking through his door—it must have been like seeing a ghost. Who knew what feelings it might have stirred up in him? Even at his age, did a man really change? Women usually softened as their bodies did, but men could be different.

She called him once more. Again there was no reply.

Mimsy wasn't afraid of the reporter, and what she might be able to prise from Adelson. But the man with her, Johnson? He might be a different proposition altogether. He looked more than capable of getting the truth from someone if he set his mind to it, whether they wanted to give it up or not.

And even if Adelson kept his mouth shut, what then?

Mimsy had believed what the reporter had said about not giving up. There was no questioning her sincerity. Mimsy recognized a cussed streak in a woman when she saw it. She had stared at one in her mirror every morning for the past sixty-plus years: the unwillingness to bend; the ability to stick with something to the bitter end.

Sooner or later someone would talk. She had no doubt of it. And once one person started talking, others would join in. There would be nothing to stop them.

For the most part, the old ways were gone. The idea that you had to stand by each other against the outside world. The belief that you couldn't yield an inch. The modern world and modern ideas had seen to that.

There was only one way for the town to hold firm against the tide, and that was to cauterize the infection. The question was, how to do it without making the mistakes they'd made before? The reporter French, they'd never found his body. No body, no proof of foul play, only suspicion. Dumping Carole Chabon in the swamp had been the error. A million to one shot that she would be found, but sometimes million to one shots came in.

The door opened behind her, interrupting her train of thought. Sue Ann's head appeared around the frame. She was about the last person Mimsy wanted to speak with.

"I'm going to be heading home," Sue Ann said.

Mimsy stood on the porch and grasped the railing. She stared out into the darkness. "Your money's in an envelope on top of the fireplace. I left you something a little extra in there . . . for the upset. Don't go saying anything about this evening to anyone. Same goes for Lyle."

"I wasn't planning on it," said Sue Ann.

"Good," said Mimsy. She heard the door start to close behind her. "Sue Ann?"

"Yes?"

Mimsy closed her eyes for a second. She could feel the swamp in the distance, seemingly still, but quietly seething with movement beneath the surface. The hunters and their prey moved at night, the 'gators on an endless quest for sustenance.

"When you get home, maybe tell RJ not to feed those 'gators of his. We're going to need them hungry."

Her order was met with silence. She turned around.

"You go to hell, Mary Elizabeth Murray."

"If I do," said Mimsy, "I'm taking you and RJ with me. He's every bit as much a part of this as I am."

"No, he ain't."

"You ever hear of conspiracy?" Mimsy asked her. "That's what they call it. You help, you're as guilty as the person who did it."

"You wouldn't admit to anything," said Sue Ann.

Mimsy pursed her lips. She was thinking. "You heard her. She isn't going to let this go."

"She'll get tired, go back to New York."

"I wouldn't bet on it."

"I don't want any part in any of this," said Sue Ann. She was thinking of RJ, and of how he still woke up some nights screaming, and in a sweat so bad she had to change the bed sheets.

"Too late for that," said Mimsy, turning her attention back to the dark horizon.

19

The swamp closed in from both sides as the Honda took a sweeping bend. Inside, Ty's attention was split between the narrow country road and the story that Cressida inexplicably, and possibly unforgivably, had chosen not to tell him until now.

"He must have been getting close to what happened when he was murdered."

Timothy French, an idealistic young reporter from Minnesota, had also grown fascinated with the Carole Chabon murder case and come down to Florida to ask some of the questions that Cressida had.

"But you don't know for sure he was murdered," said Ty, as the road took another turn, and he eased off the gas to get round it safely.

"Come on," said Cressida. "He was last seen down here investigating the story. He told his editor and family he'd been threatened, and then he went missing. What else could have happened?"

Ty conceded the point with a shrug. She was likely right. "What did the cops say?" he said.

"What do you think? No body, no witnesses, not even a speck of blood found in his rental car, and no one was talking. They had to give it up."

"But they suspected foul play?"

"They did, but what were they going to do?"

"And you didn't think to mention any of this to me?"

"I'm sorry. I really am. I was going to tell Gregg, but I thought he might get spooked and not allow me to come down here. I said there had been threats to reporters covering the case so he would assign me someone like you, but I didn't give him the details."

"Did you tell him you were related to Carole Chabon?"

"Not in so many words. I may have said it had a personal connection to me or something."

"That could mean anything," said Ty.

"You think I've messed up, right?" Cressida asked, studying him with those blazing green eyes.

She was hoping he'd absolve her, Ty thought. "Yeah, you did. You've let me walk into this situation with a huge chunk of information missing. Threat assessments aren't just a box-checking exercise. I need to know what I'm walking into when I take on a close-protection gig."

"But we're still here. There's no harm done."

"No thanks to you," said Ty.

"Listen, they're not going to do anything to me. They wouldn't risk it. Not after everything that's happened."

Ty took a moment to ponder the naivety of youth. At Cressida's age he might have thought the same. But, then, he'd already seen some of the less salubrious parts of the world, and witnessed human nature at its worst. No, he reflected, he hadn't been that naive. "You think that why?" he snapped. "Because they might get caught? Because they're scared of the law? Listen, places like this, these people are the law. They're not scared of jack, otherwise they wouldn't do what they've done. And that's assuming the person or people capable of lynching a young girl and then disappearing a reporter are working with a full deck, which is highly debatable."

"So what are you saying? You're going to ditch me?"

Ty hit the brakes, and the Honda skidded to a stop. "No, I'm not. I have a job to do, which is keeping you alive, and I plan on doing that job. However, in order to perform my duties I expect full disclosure. No secrets. You feel me?" He stared at her.

She nodded. "Agreed, and I'm sorry. Are we good?" She reached out her hand.

He took it. "We're good." He took his foot off the brake pedal and got the car moving again.

"What do you think she was getting at when she was saying all that stuff about Adelson Shaw?" Cressida asked.

"Well, let's see. They were an item, or that's what it sounded like. Then all of a sudden they weren't. She never married anyone else, which sounds like she got her heart broken by the guy."

"Then all that stuff about Carole being a whore," Cressida continued. "You think Adelson and Carole . . ."

"Hooked up?" said Ty.

"Yeah. I mean those were some pretty heavy hints."

"Guess you'll have to ask our host," said Ty.

Cressida stared out of the window. Briefly Ty studied her reflection in the passenger side window. "She sleeps with a white guy, and next thing she's killed," said Ty. "That might just do it. Even back then."

"Sleeping with the wrong person these days can get someone killed. Except this wasn't a crime of passion. A crime of passion doesn't involve lynching someone. That's not a one-man job."

"Or a one-woman job," said Ty.

They were clearly thinking the same thing. Had the rift between Mimsy and her suitor had something to do with Carole Chabon's appearance in town? And was that what had led to the murder?

Lynchings often had an unspoken sexual component. More than one black man had been strung up because he'd whistled at a white woman. Even in the 1970s mixed relationships were still somewhat taboo.

It was certainly a possibility that Carole might inadvertently have stirred passions without even being aware of it. Nothing more would have needed to happen than her being alone with a white man. Ty was sure that Mimsy had also made a reference to her house. Could that have been where it all started? With Carole Chabon ringing the doorbell and Adelson Shaw, alone in the house, inviting her in?

"So tell me about this Women's KKK," said Ty. "I didn't even know that was a thing."

"Oh, it was, although they were called Women of the Ku Klux Klan," said Cress. "Most people don't know about it. It was real big in the 1920s. They had about half a million members at their peak. Mostly in the South and the Midwest. They were kind of a mix of a women's social organization—you know, bake sales, sewing circles . . ."

"Cross burnings?"

"Exactly." Cressida smiled. "You had to be a white Protestant woman to join. But they were also kind of feminist too. They had links to the women's suffrage movement, which kind of brought them into conflict with the regular Klan."

"But that was way back then."

"Yes, but Mimsy's mother was a member. She led a klavern around here. I guess she passed down the ideals to her daughter, who kept the flame burning."

"You knew about this before you came down here?"

Cressida nodded. "Want to know who else was involved?"

"Go on."

"Our sweet little local librarian, Miss Parsons."

"Damn. Can't see her galloping around in the middle of the night wearing a hood. What about our host, Adelson?"

Cress shook her head. "That's where it gets interesting. As far as I could discover, he never had any involvement with the Klan. In fact, in Darling the membership through the seventies was almost all women. It was like this strange little enclave all on its own, fighting a rearguard action to keep segregation. They've done a pretty good job too."

"So when Carole Chabon popped up in their town, Mimsy killed her?" Ty asked.

"Or directed it," said Cressida. "You saw how she is. The temper she has. And how everyone seems to be scared of her."

"Apart from Adelson Shaw."

"Apart from him. I have a hunch that if anyone's going to let something slip about what really happened it just might be him."

Ty remembered something. "So what did the note say? Get out of town? Or, let me guess, it was a coupon for the local car wash?"

Cressida unfolded the piece of paper. "It's kind of hard to tell exactly. I don't think English was the person's strong point."

She handed it over to Ty. He reached up and popped on the cabin light of the Honda, allowed the car to slow and took the note while keeping one hand on the wheel.

The handwriting was a chicken scrawl of capital letters.

I can help you. Meet me next to this place tonight at midnight. I'll be waiting for you.

Then there was a hand-drawn map of the road through town, and a turn-off beyond it, marked, according to an annotation, with a sign for an alligator farm.

Ty handed back the note. "I don't think so," he said.

"I have to go."

"You do? You don't think that if someone wants to talk they couldn't find a way to meet you that doesn't involve the dead of night next to an alligator farm? I mean, come on, that's like a set-up for a slasher picture."

"But I thought I had a bodyguard with me."

"You have a close-protection operative with you," said Ty, using his partner Lock's description.

"What's the difference?"

"Bodyguards have thicker necks, wear sunglasses indoors, suits that are so tight they can't actually move, and they do whatever the hell their principal tells them to do."

"And close-protection operatives?"

"I may not be a good example. My neck's pretty yoked and I've been known to wear shades inside."

"Come on, you're the one brought it up."

Ty sighed. "Part of my job, a big part, is to make sure that the principal makes good choices."

"Make sure?"

"Okay, advise."

"But I don't have to take that advice," said Cressida.

"Correct."

"So I say I'm not going to pass this up."

"Tell you what, we'll drive down there and I'll scope it out. If I deem it safe we can do the meet."

"And what if they'll only meet with me?"

"Absolutely not. Under no circumstances."

"But you can't stop me."

It was Ty's turn to get annoyed. "Listen, how about I don't tell you how to do your job, and you don't tell me how to do mine? You think Timothy French maybe got a note like this just before he went missing? I'd say the odds are good."

She drummed her nails on the dash. She must have known that Ty had a point. Ty decided to drive it home. "You want to get this story, right?"

"You think I don't?"

"You have to be alive to write it up," he said, as in his rearview mirror he saw a rolling flash of red lights.

A siren blast wailed behind him as a patrol car bore down on them. Ty reached up, clicked off the dome light, and hit his turn signal, indicating that he was pulling over.

Next to him, Cressida looked freaked out. "This isn't good," she whispered almost to herself.

"Chill," said Ty. "Cop's probably bored, saw the car with our cabin light on, and decided to check us out. Let's not get carried away."

20

Sue Ann sat in the front seat of her car at the back of Mimsy's house and opened the brown envelope with her payment for the evening's work. Inside were five one-hundred-dollar bills, five times what she had agreed with Mimsy.

There were no prizes for guessing the reason. Mimsy was hardly noted for her generosity. She used money like a weapon when intimidation and fear of her wrath had failed. She always had done, ever since Sue Ann had known her, which was pretty much her entire life.

At this stage what Mimsy had asked Sue Ann to tell her husband was almost irrelevant. Now it was about Mimsy making sure that Sue Ann followed orders. What the order was didn't matter but it had to be carried out. That was the Murray family way. Do as you're told? If the stick doesn't work, here's a carrot.

Sue Ann held the crisp notes in her hand. She and RJ sure could use the money. But how much? How badly did they need it? Bad enough to be involved in someone else possibly losing their life? Looked at like that, five hundred dollars suddenly wasn't a fortune.

Two killings, or a killing and a disappearance, might just be written off as coincidence. A third event of a similar nature? There would be no coming back from that.

Everything would spill out into the light, like the insides of a shark lying on a sunny dock in the Keys.

21

Ty hit the button to lower the driver's window, then placed his hands in clear view on top of the steering wheel. "Keep your hands in plain sight, and don't make any sudden move," he told Cressida.

"This is bullshit."

"Chill. I had my interior light on while driving. Any cop is entitled to pull us over. Not everything's *Mississippi Burning*."

"Oh, come on, you weren't even breaking the speed limit."

"And let me do the talking."

"Oh, yeah, like you're so reasonable. The last interaction you had with a law-enforcement officer, you locked him in the trunk of his own car."

"That wasn't the last interaction I had, and there were extenuating circumstances. I don't make a habit of it."

Ty figured that people were never going to get past what he'd done back in Long Beach when he'd gone to the aid of an old Marine buddy who was in a full-on meltdown. In truth, as he did with anyone, he always tried to see things from the other person's perspective. A solitary patrol cop rolling up on two people in a car late at night was likely to be on edge. There was no point in making their life more difficult than it had to be.

Remain calm. Be polite. Keep your hands in plain sight. Don't make any unexpected or sudden physical movements. It was hardly rocket science.

Ty watched the cop approach the side of the car. He looked from the uniform to be state rather than local. Ty also noted two other things. He was African American and he had his hand on his service weapon, ready to clear leather if he had to.

"Sir, are you aware one of your tail-lights is out?" said the cop, leaning down next to the driver's window.

"I wasn't aware of that, no," said Ty, his eyes flicking to the dash and looking for a warning light that wasn't there.

"Also," continued the trooper, "do you usually drive with your interior light on?"

"I'm sorry about that, Officer," said Ty. "We're not familiar with the area and we were checking a map to find our way back to where we're staying."

"May I see your license and registration?"

"Yes, sir, they're just up here," he said, making eye contact. The cop gave the nod for Ty to extract them from the sun visor.

He reached slowly up, extracted them from where they were tucked into the visor flap, and handed them over.

"Also, Officer, I'm carrying a permitted firearm. It's in a shoulder holster. I assume you'll want to take possession of it until the stop's concluded. How do you want to do this?"

For good reason cops rarely allowed people to reach in, pull a weapon and hand it over. It was way too risky, and too likely to lead to problems. It was preferable to make sure it didn't come as a surprise and give them the option of how they wanted to proceed.

The best way of making sure that a stop like this went smoothly was to make a cop aware that their safety was a concern. Again, it was something simple and Ty wondered how so many folks could get it so horribly wrong. Cops had no idea whether someone was a good guy or a bad guy so it was safer for them to assume the worst.

"I appreciate you telling me that."

The cop moved back and opened the door. 'Sir, if you could step out of the vehicle and place your hands on the trunk."

Ty complied, moving slowly. He exchanged a final glance with Cressida. She looked a little worried. He gave her what he hoped was a reassuring smile.

He stood, hinged at the hips, his tree-trunk legs wide, and his hands placed palm down on the back of the Civic. The cop reached into his jacket, and took the SIG. It was a dumbass move. He should have cuffed Ty first. If Ty had been a bad guy, it would have been easy enough to trap the cop's hand as he reached in, pivot, and take him to the ground, or turn and trip him, coming up with the SIG.

Ty decided that it might be wise not to share those thoughts.

"Stay right there. I'm going to run your details," the trooper said. "By the way, you haven't been drinking this evening, have you?"

"Only soft drinks," said Ty.

"Okay. I'll be right back."

Ty stayed where he was. A few minutes later the trooper returned. "You can take your hands off the trunk, and turn around."

Ty did just that.

"Sir, I'm going to need you to complete a field sobriety test for me."

"Not a problem. I haven't been drinking. Just let me know what I need to do," he said, keeping his hands by his sides.

The truth was that he'd felt a little woozy ever since they'd left the dinner, but he had put it down to travel, and the hot, sticky weather. It wasn't that he felt drunk, or anything like it, but he didn't feel entirely sober either. He'd had to focus hard on the road, but he'd put that down to it being unfamiliar.

Now that the officer had mentioned a sobriety test, Ty felt a fresh bout of wooziness rise up in him. His mind was no doubt playing a trick on him. Mention being sober and all of a sudden you become much more aware of your physical state.

Ty shook the thought from his head. It was his mind playing

tricks. It had to be. He hadn't consumed any alcohol, and he hadn't smoked weed, which he did from time to time, in months. There was no reason to worry.

"Okay, Mr. Johnson," said the officer. "I'd like you to take nine steps forward heel to toe, counting the steps out as you go. Then I'd like you to turn around, and take the same number of steps. You understand what I'm asking you to do?"

"I do."

"Okay, then."

Ty started forward, placing one foot in front of the other, the heel of the front foot touching the toe of the back foot. He counted as he went. As he reached nine, and turned, he found himself wobbling slightly. He had no idea where his sudden loss of balance had come from.

"Keep walking," said the officer.

Ty stopped at nine. He looked back. "Don't know what happened on the turn. Ground must have been uneven or something."

As soon as the words were out of his mouth he regretted them. It was the kind of thing a drunk person said to explain themselves.

"Okay, Mr. Johnson, I'm going to need you to turn around, and I'm going to place cuffs on you."

"Come on, man. It was a wobble. You're not going to arrest me for that."

The officer eyed him, his expression set hard. "Sir, we also had an anonymous phone call that someone in that exact car had been drinking. Now, if you haven't consumed alcohol we'll be able to confirm that and you'll be released. Until then you are under arrest on suspicion of driving while intoxicated. You have the right to remain silent."

Ty turned and allowed himself to be cuffed as the officer rattled through his Miranda rights. There were no prizes for guessing who had made the call, and Ty suddenly wondered about the overly-sweet Arnold Palmers he'd drunk. It would have been easy enough to add some vodka, and he wouldn't have tasted it.

Now his concern was Cressida, and her safety.

He waited for the cop to finish reciting his rights. "May I speak with my passenger for a second? I'd really appreciate it."

"Sure," said the officer. "But I'm not taking the cuffs off."

"That's cool."

The officer shepherded him over to the car. "Ma'am, you can step out," the officer told her.

She got out. The cop handed her the keys to the Civic.

"I think my drink might have been spiked," Ty told her. "Either way, I'm certain our host for the evening called this in."

"Officer, this whole deal is a set-up. I'm a reporter from New York. I'm here . . ."

"Save it," Ty told her. "He's not going to change his mind. I'm already under arrest. Are you okay to drive back on your own?"

"Sure. I can find it," she said.

"Forget that note, okay? If this is a set-up . . . Well, I don't have to fill in the blanks, do I?"

"No, you don't," she said.

"I need you to promise me you won't change your mind," said Ty.

"Okay, okay. I'll go straight back to the Airbnb."

"You're sure you're okay to drive, ma'am?" said the cop. "Were you drinking this evening?"

"One glass of wine, and I didn't finish it. Officer, I'll be fine. I'm a big girl, and it's just down the ways."

Ty half turned to the cop. "Could we follow her to the turn-off? I'm fairly sure it's the way we'll be going."

The man hesitated.

"I'd really appreciate it, Officer."

He shrugged. "Okay. Can't see what harm it would do to make sure she gets back safe."

"Thank you," said Ty.

The cop led Ty back toward the patrol car where he got in back. Cressida got into the driver's seat of the Honda. He watched the Honda pull back out onto the road. The patrol car tucked in behind.

They followed Cressida for two miles down the road. She indicated to turn off. The patrol car slowed until she had made the turn, then sped up.

"So?" said the cop, eyeing Ty in the rearview mirror. "What brings you all the way down here?"

22

In the back of the patrol car, hands cuffed in front of him, Ty cycled through the evening's events, and beyond. The traffic stop had caught him off balance. So, for that matter, had the revelation about Timothy French and all the other stuff Mimsy had spilled.

The reporter going missing gave him the most immediate concern. He understood why Cressida hadn't wanted to tell her editor about it. He might have pulled her investigation. But by not telling him she had potentially placed both of them in danger.

The same went for the Klan involvement, and a couple of other things she had either failed to mention or played down, either directly or by omission. A female Klan order was news to him, but it was hardly surprising. Ty had never bought into the idea that girls were all sugar and spice. In his experience women could be just as deadly, if not more so, than men. He could conjure up a couple of vivid examples including a dedicated white supremacist by the name of Chance, and a Chechen terrorist called Mareta.

Would Mimsy Murray be added to that list? He guessed that only time would tell.

To murder one person and cover it up or hide the culprits was bad enough. But to do it to two people, many years apart, raised the stakes considerably.

The patrol car was wending its way through the section of Everglades they had driven through on the way in. Thousands upon thousands of miles of wetlands. Terrain so immediately similar that stumbling into it would mean you would almost instantly be lost and disoriented. You might be a hundred yards from a road, but without the sound of traffic, you would have no idea.

It would have been easy enough to disappear the body of Timothy French in there. If the 'gators didn't take care of most of it, a thousand other smaller creatures would.

The miracle wasn't that he was still missing but that Carole Chabon's remains had been found. They had been one hell of a grisly needle in a monumental haystack.

Now here he was sitting in the back of a patrol car with his principal on her own. He should have asked her to follow them. At least that way he would have known she was safe. He cursed himself for not thinking of it until now.

"You okay back there?" said the cop.

"Listen, would you mind calling the lady I was with, see if she got back okay?"

"I wouldn't mind at all, but cell-phone reception around here is kind of patchy, at best. It might have to wait until we get back to the barracks."

"How long's that likely to take?"

The cop shrugged. "Not long. Roads are quiet. Maybe another forty minutes."

Ty guessed that around here the phrase 'not long' was relative. Right now forty minutes seemed like an eternity.

Ty leaned forward again. "Is there any way you could have another trooper or a local officer check in on her?"

The cop gave Ty a longer glance in his mirror. "You guys in trouble?"

"We're down here investigating the murder of Carole Chabon. It was a ways back—1974."

"I've heard of it."

"They never got anyone," said Ty, trying to avoid sounding accusatory. Unsolved homicides could be a touchy subject for law enforcement, understandably so.

"No, we never did."

"Why do you think that was?" Ty was pushing his luck, but he wasn't sure what he had left to lose. It wasn't as if the trooper could arrest him for a second time.

"Oh, I could tell you exactly why. No one was willing to talk. Not that they'd even seen her, never mind anything else."

The cop's frank admission caught him a little off-guard.

"But people knew?"

"Someone did. They had to. There were rumors, but you can't arrest someone on rumors."

Ty thought about the anonymous call that had just gotten him pulled over. He decided not to mention it. "What kind of rumors?"

In the mirror, Ty caught the cop's smile. "You just ease back there, and enjoy the scenery, partner. We can check on your friend as soon as we get back."

Ty did as he was told. The darkness was so complete that, looking out of the window, all he could see was his own reflection thrown back at him.

23

Cressida pulled up outside Adelson Shaw's house. She flicked off the Honda's headlights, but left the engine running. The short ride back had been uneventful. She had seen one other vehicle, a big rig with a full trailer, but it had been traveling in the opposite direction, and had barely slowed down as it had barreled past her.

The porch lights were on. So were some of the other downstairs lights. She wasn't sure if Adelson was still up, or if the lights had been deliberately left on for their return.

She wondered what it must be like to live alone in such a large house. The thought of it made her anxious, although she wasn't sure why. Maybe it was the thought of passing through life without a family or children.

What had really happened between Adelson and Mimsy? Had they been involved at one time? Mimsy had seemed to suggest they had, without directly mentioning an engagement or that he was her boyfriend. She'd said something about Adelson having been the man she was closest to. That much Cressida was sure of.

Was there a link between the two of them and what had

happened to Carole? Mimsy had dropped some heavy hints about that too. Perhaps Adelson would be more forthcoming.

One thing Cressida was certain of now was that people here knew what had happened to Carole Chabon. They also knew why. When she had been researching the story, which seemed like it had been going on for a long time, she had become more fascinated by the why than the who. In a way who had killed Carole, then Timothy French was less important to her than why they had done it.

Was there a reason that went deeper than the color of Carole's skin, and the need to stop Timothy French exposing the guilty? Although Cressida knew it happened, killing someone for their skin color seemed pathetic. Beyond pathetic. A feeble motivation for such a devastating act.

She dug the note from her bag, flattened it out, and held it at the top of the steering wheel.

She had given Ty her word that she wouldn't act on it. Not tonight anyway. But a tiny voice was nagging at her now. It was the part of her that had made her want to come down here, even though her presence would be unwelcome, a part of her that was anchored way back in childhood when she had first heard this story, and others like it, but before she'd had a name to put to them.

The note in her hand was calling to her. Would the person who had written it, and left it on the windshield, really arrange another meeting? Surely there had to be a reason why they had contacted her like that, and why they wanted to meet in – she checked the time on the car's display – a little under thirty-five minutes.

The area was quiet. No one would see them. Or her.

Ty was right to have his suspicions. But sources, informants, whatever you wanted to call them, were nervy for a reason. They had something to fear.

But what if it was a trap? Without Ty as back-up she would stand little or no chance. And his arrest seemed more than coincidental.

She took the note, feeling the texture of the paper between her fingers. She placed it on the passenger seat. She reached down to the ignition.

No, she told herself. Ty was right. It was too risky to meet someone like this on her own.

She put the note back into her bag, took the Honda's key, opened the driver's door, got out and secured the car.

THE FRONT DOOR WAS UNLOCKED. Cressida pushed it open, stepped into the hallway, and slipped off the heels she'd been wearing. She picked them up and walked over to the living room where the lights were still on.

Adelson Shaw was half sitting, half sprawled in an armchair. On the table next to him was the same bottle of Blanton's bourbon. Now it was a half to three-quarters empty. While they'd been out at the mayor's house, he'd kept working his way through it.

It took him a second to register her presence. He looked at her with red-rimmed eyes that gave him the appearance of a tearful drunk. He reached over and grabbed the glass that was sitting next to the bottle. He raised it high above his head in a toast. "Ah, beautiful lady, care to join me for a nightcap?"

Cressida didn't respond. She was already feeling the awkwardness of the situation.

"Where's your male companion?" said Adelson, hauling himself into a more upright position in the chair.

For a couple of reasons she didn't want to share the story of being pulled over and Ty being arrested for DUI. First, she didn't want Adelson to think that she was going to be spending the night alone in his house. Not while he was in this condition, anyway. He already had the hint of a leer to go along with his goofy drunken expression. She was confident she could handle the situation if he tried anything, but she didn't want to have to sleep with a chair wedged against her bedroom door.

"He'll be along in a little while."

He patted the arm of the chair he was sitting in. "Come on, sit down, have a drink with me. You must need one after an evening with that old dragon."

"It's been a long night. I'm going to turn in."

"Oh, come on," he slurred. "Indulge an old man. I don't get that much company, these days."

She thought about it. If he was this drunk there was every chance she might get something out of him. He seemed in a talkative mood, and he clearly wasn't a fan of Mimsy, whom Cressida was sure knew more than she was letting on about the murder.

"Okay," she said. "I'll have a drink with you, but there's one condition."

"Just name it, lovely lady."

"We're truthful with each other."

"I've never been known not to be," said Adelson, his eyes darkening. "Why do you think I ended up alone?"

Cressida walked over to the drinks cabinet by the window. She picked up two fresh crystal glasses, and walked back to the table. She poured two decent measures, handed one to Adelson, then took the bottle back to the drinks cabinet and put it away.

"You're probably right," said Adelson, downcast. "I've had too much already."

She recognized the drunk's swift change in mood from her own upbringing with a father who self-medicated his emotional pain with booze and whatever else he could lay his hands on. Happy to sad to angry to self-pitying, he could work through them all in a matter of minutes, without anyone saying or doing anything to prompt them.

She made sure to sit on the couch, maintaining a good distance from her drunken host. This he seemed to pick up on.

"Oh, relax. I'm too old to try anything, especially after so much of this," he said, raising the glass of burnished amber liquid. "I couldn't raise a smile right now, never mind anything else."

She ignored the comment. "Mimsy mentioned you at dinner."

"Oh, yeah? What did the Queen of Darling have to say about me? Nothing complimentary, I know that much."

"You guys were an item."

"Is that a statement or a question?"

Cressida took a moment to answer. "It was an assumption, given how she spoke about you."

Adelson took a sip and raised his glass. "You may be the first honest journalist I've met."

"I'm correct, though."

Adelson straightened up further in his chair. "Thereby *hangs* a tail."

His expression grew serious, as he seemed to shake off the drunken haze, like a dog coming in from a downpour. "If you'll pardon the pun," he added.

Inwardly Cressida grimaced at his attempt at humor. *Hang. Lynching.* It wasn't funny. Not to her.

"You want to tell me?" she said eyeing her bag, which she'd tucked next to her on the couch.

24

Sue Ann could feel Curious George's eyes on her as she drove along the side of the main enclosure and up to the house. As she came to a stop she couldn't see RJ's truck. It wasn't in its usual spot.

On the drive back all she'd been able to think about was Mimsy telling her to tell RJ not to feed the 'gators. It was equal parts unsettling and infuriating. She'd about had her fill of Miss Mary Elizabeth Murray for one lifetime. Just because she had a little more money than most folks around here, which was hardly difficult, she thought she could order them around.

She fumbled for her house keys. There was splash of water from the enclosure. If she had her way RJ would get rid of the 'gators. They'd fill in the pools with concrete and build a fence around the property to make sure the beasts never came back.

Don't feed them.

The hell with Mimsy Murray.

Inside the house she called to RJ. He didn't answer.

She walked into the kitchen, got herself a glass of water and drank it. Then she went down the hall and into the bedroom.

"RJ, I need to talk to you about something," she said, putting her hand on the bed.

It was empty. She sat on the edge and smoothed her hand across the covers.

"RJ!" she called again. She switched on the light. The bed was made up, the same as it had been when she had left that morning. She pushed open the bathroom door. Empty.

Back in the kitchen, she grabbed the phone from the wall and called his cell phone, hoping he would answer, or be somewhere that had signal.

Mercifully, he picked up.

"RJ, where the heck are you?"

"Oh, hey, Sue Ann."

"Don't hey-Sue-Ann me. I came home thinking you'd be in bed and you're nowhere to be seen."

"Yeah, I had to go out. Guess I should have left you a note but it was kind of a last-minute thing."

"What was?" A knot was forming in the pit of her stomach. With the phone pressed to her ear, she heard RJ take a deep breath. "RJ?" she said.

"I'm meeting with that reporter."

"You're what? Are you crazy? Have you lost your mind?"

"No. I'd say I've gotten it back."

She took a breath, fighting to compose herself. "What are you going to tell her?"

"I'm going to tell her the truth. It's about time someone did."

Sue Ann felt the floor giving way underneath her. She sank down, her back to the wall, until she was sitting on the kitchen floor. Outside, she heard Curious George making that growling sound he did sometimes when he wanted to get to one of the female 'gators, but they were in a separate pen.

"The truth?" she said to her husband.

"Yes. Like I should have done a long time ago."

Sue Ann couldn't believe what she was hearing. She'd thought about coming clean, but she knew she'd never be able to do it. It was just a pleasant little fantasy, imagining the look on Mimsy's face when she realized that someone had stood up to her and she'd have to face everyone knowing the kind of hateful person she was.

"And why didn't you? I'll tell you why, shall I? Because you tell the truth and you're going to prison, and what would I do then?" she said, her voice cracking. She was close to tears.

"I've been thinking about that. Maybe I could be like a witness for the prosecution. Make some kind of a deal. Only go to prison for a few years instead of for ever. We could pick up again when I got out."

Sue Ann reached up with her free hand and massaged her temple. She could feel a migraine coming on. It blossomed in the middle of her skull. "Do a deal? You need a fancy lawyer for that kind of thing, and we don't have any money, RJ. Or are you forgetting that? We can barely pay our bills as it is. I can't lose you."

"And I can't live like this. I thought maybe I could. I want to. I know it would be easier. I know that. But I can't," he said, his voice shrill and raised.

"Listen to me, this reporter, she'll leave. Everything will go back to how it was. You talking to her can only make things worse. I don't like any of this any more than you do, but you can't do this."

Now, sitting on the bare floor, Sue Ann knew she couldn't stand up to Mimsy. If RJ did this and Mimsy found out, Mimsy would be hiring a fancy Miami attorney, and RJ would be taking the fall. Then what would she do? End her life alone, with Mimsy Murray still around to make her miserable.

She had to stop her husband. But how?

She would make one last plea. "RJ, I'm telling you not to do this. Come on home now. We can talk about it."

"I can't do that."

"Yes, you can . . ."

He hung up. Frantically, she called him back. This time he didn't answer.

Sue Ann sat in the darkness, thinking long and hard about what to do. RJ wasn't going to be stopped, and once he had opened his mouth to that reporter the consequences would cascade through their lives.

She continued to turn it over in her mind. She kept returning to the same conclusion. There was only one way to stop him.

Finally, and aware that the clock was ticking, she picked up the phone, and dialed another number. She couldn't call Mimsy. And it wasn't like she could call the cops because they'd ask too many questions. It had to be someone who knew about most of it already and would understand her dilemma. And someone who'd be able to stop him.

It took a while for Lyle to answer, but finally he picked up.

25

"How much do you know about Mary Elizabeth?" Adelson asked, his bloodshot eyes staring at Cressida over the tumbler of bourbon.

Cressida figured that if he really was to tell her what had happened to Carole Chabon she should match his truthfulness. In her short career she had found that people responded in kind if she spoke the truth.

"I know her family has lived here for generations. That originally they were slave owners. That they were involved with the Klan."

Adelson gave an approving nod. "Very good. You've done your homework."

"It's part of the gig, Mr. Shaw."

"Didn't I already ask you to call me Adelson?" He took a sip of bourbon. "Oh, yes, the Klan. Do you know that the original Klan started out as a joke?"

"No," she lied. She wanted him to believe she knew less than she did. And she wanted him to get into a flow. The more people spoke, and the more receptive the audience, the more likely it was that they would keep talking until they said something she didn't know.

In that respect, being a reporter was like being a lawyer taking a deposition, or a detective interviewing a suspect. Create the right atmosphere in a room and people would tell you all manner of things that they probably shouldn't.

"The idea was that the white robes would make them look like ghosts. They pretended to be dead Confederate soldiers come back to haunt freed slaves. They never thought anyone would take them seriously. But when they did, when they saw the fear their appearance created, and the power that fear gave them, well, it became something else entirely."

"Was that why Mimsy got involved? For the power?"

"That, and family tradition, although she caught the wave a little late. By the time she was a young woman, the Klan wasn't the force it had been. Do you know that in 1924 the Klan had more than two million members in this country?"

Cressida feigned surprise. Many historians estimated that there might have been as many as four million, which was a solid chunk of the white population in many states. Many representatives and more than a few senators in Congress relied upon the Klan vote to keep them in a job, Democrats as well as Republicans.

"Was that what drove her to kill Carole Chabon?" Cressida asked.

Adelson held up his empty glass. "You don't really think Mimsy would have gotten close enough to a black woman to put a noose around her neck, do you? Perish the thought."

Cressida got up, took his glass and began to refill it. "She had me to dinner at her house, and I'm a black woman."

The same lascivious expression she'd seen earlier filled Adelson's features. "And a very fine black woman you are," he said. "But extraordinary times call for extraordinary measures . . ."

She handed him the glass, making sure to back off as soon as he took it.

"Thank you, my dear. No, don't get me wrong, it was Mimsy's idea. She was the one who got people excited enough to hunt down that poor girl and do what they did, but she didn't do it herself."

Cressida wanted to ask who did. She wanted names. But something told her that wasn't the right question. Not now, anyway. "You weren't involved, were you?"

Adelson took a sip of bourbon. "Goes down easy," he said. "What do you think?"

"No, I don't believe you were involved in killing Carole. In fact, if I had to guess, I'd say you tried to stop it."

"You're a good judge of character, Ms. King, I'll give you that. Did you know that when it happened Mary Elizabeth and I had just gotten engaged?"

Cressida shook her head. "I thought the two of you might have been involved but, no, I didn't know you were engaged to be married."

"We had an affection for each other, but it was mostly our family's idea. You know, the most eligible young woman in town and the future town dentist. A nice, solid respectable white couple, with a decent income and a big house. There was even talk of me maybe running for office."

"But you weren't into it?" said Cressida, reading his tone. He was talking like a man who'd been sentenced to life incarceration rather than someone looking forward to marriage with the woman he loved.

"As I said, I liked Mary Elizabeth. She was pretty, and she could be fun when she was away from her family. But she was also very traditional. There wasn't any spark between us. No excitement."

"Do you mean sexually?"

"You really are from New York, aren't you?"

"That doesn't answer my question."

"I was what a lady like her would call 'a tough dog to keep on the porch'."

"You had affairs?"

Adelson's posture stiffened. "I wasn't married so they were hardly affairs."

"Okay then, while you were engaged?"

"A man has his needs. There was no way Mimsy and I were doing anything before we got married. She wouldn't even entertain the idea. And I suspected that when our wedding night came around it would be with the lights out, and she'd approach it as a duty."

"No spark?" said Cressida, checking that was what he'd meant.

"Quite so."

"And what does this have to do with Carole Chabon?"

Adelson smiled at her. His eyes held hers, and she knew exactly what it had to do with Carole. This was Adelson's confession she was hearing, and it went in a straight line from his fondness for black women to his fear of being trapped in a sexless marriage and all the way, she suspected, to Carole Chabon hanging from a tree.

"Mimsy discovered you with Carole, and that was why she was killed?" she said.

"The heart wants what the heart wants," said Adelson Shaw.

26

The small Florida Highway Patrol barracks house was a forty-minute ride from Darling, a squat single-story red-brick building.

The trooper who'd arrested him for DUI slid the phone across the desk to Ty. "Go ahead," he told him.

Ty had one hand cuffed to the metal desk they were sitting at, and one hand free. Not that he was complaining. The trooper had been as good as his word, making sure Ty was booked as soon as they arrived at the barracks, and that he could make his call as soon as it was done.

Now he got up from his desk, and wandered over to the coffee pot. "You want one?" he asked Ty.

"Thank you. Black, no cream, no sugar," said Ty.

He punched in Lock's number, silently praying he'd pick up, and that it wouldn't just default to voicemail. A second or so later his prayer was answered.

Lock obviously hadn't recognized the number because he answered with his full name and business voice.

"This is Ryan Lock."

"It's Ty. I have a problem."

"I guessed."

"How'd you know it was me?" said Ty, a little taken aback.

"Florida number, but not yours. I figured it had to have something to do with you. And no one calls anyone after midnight unless it's a booty call, or they're in trouble. Seeing as I'm here with Carmen, I could discount the first option. So what's up?"

Ty brought Lock up to speed as quickly and efficiently as he could. He wasn't sure if there was a mandatory time limit for his call, and he wasn't about to risk exceeding it.

When he'd finished explaining about having his drink spiked at the dinner and being pulled over and arrested for DUI, Lock said, "I'm on the next plane."

Those were the words Ty had feared. Lock rarely, if ever, took a vacation. Ty didn't want to ruin this one. "You don't have to do that. I'll be able to post bail and be out of here in a couple more hours."

Lock was abrupt. "I'm not doing it for you. Your principal is my principal, and this mission sounds like it needed more than a sole designated bodyguard."

"Listen, Ryan, I messed up. I should have gotten her to follow the patrol car. It was the wrong call to let her go back to the house."

"You don't know it was, but listen," said Lock. "She lied about the risk level. That's not on you. But what matters now is that she's safe. I'll call her, mop up the immediate threat, make sure she gets to a clean location, and you can take it from there when you're released."

"Thanks," said Ty.

"What about your side arm?" said Lock.

"Cops have it."

"That's a shame. She could have used it. Listen, hang tight. If there's any snag with bail, give the bond company my number."

"Appreciate it," said Ty.

"Don't," said Lock. "You've saved my ass. More than once. When we get close to even, you can start thanking me."

27

RJ powered down his cell phone. He didn't want Sue Ann, or anyone else for that matter, trying to talk him out of this. It wouldn't take much for him to lose his nerve, go home and forget all about speaking with the reporter.

Doing nothing had always been a heck of a lot easier than facing up to reality. He guessed most people were the same as him in that respect. He sure knew that Darling people were.

Keep your head down. Keep your mouth shut. Let it be someone else's problem.

Except that wasn't how life worked. You paid a price for the quiet life. In your head. In the dark, lonely hours before dawn. When it was just you and your conscience.

Church was worse. It had gotten so bad that he had stopped going. Not that he loved God any less. It was just sitting with all those hypocrites who lived the exact opposite way to how the Good Book told them to.

What he was going to do felt right. Frightening, but right. It would be his confession. He would offer up what he knew, and then he would go to church to beg God's forgiveness for his sins.

He turned the steering wheel, hanging a sharp left and easing down the dirt track towards the dock where he kept his airboat. He switched off his radio and lowered the front cab's windows so he could feel the gentle breeze that whispered through the cypress trees.

At the end of the track, he turned into the parking area. He reversed into a spot, killed his headlights, and checked his watch. He was early.

He had hoped she might be here by now, that she'd be so anxious to get his story she'd be early, but the parking area was empty. Maybe she wasn't coming.

What then? he asked himself. He wasn't sure he had it in him to do this again.

He had resolve, but it was brittle and weak. It would crumble with even a little bit of resistance.

He wasn't a strong man. Physically, yes, but mentally, he couldn't say he was. He had come to realize that as he had grown older. It didn't make him feel good about himself, but there it was. Some people didn't look much but they had inner steel. Mimsy had it. So had that other young reporter, with his horn-rimmed glasses and small, probing eyes, who had come down here ten years before asking what had happened to Carole Chabon.

Not that it had helped him much. His resolve had ended in death. A horrible death too.

RJ grabbed the steering wheel and squeezed until his hands went white. He had to get a grip of himself, stop with all this thinking.

He prodded the button to switch the radio back on. It started up so loudly that he startled. He hurriedly turned down the song.

He looked again at his watch. Why, he didn't know. It had only been a minute since he'd last checked it.

Relax, he told himself. All you have to do is sit here until she shows up, then tell her what you know.

Then you need to get her the hell out of town before they kill her too.

The sound of a vehicle. The sweet, merciful roar of someone driving down the track.

For the first time in quite a while he felt something approaching relief. She had decided to come early after all.

His wait was over.

He switched off the radio and opened the door. He would get out of the truck, show her that he was alone and offered no threat.

She would be nervous too, meeting a stranger in the middle of the night.

But she'd have that big black guy she was with. He was some kind of bodyguard, something like that. That was the talk around town.

If he was with her, RJ really could relax. Put the guy at ease and it would all be smooth sailing.

RJ began to fantasize a little about how good this would feel. A burden shared was a burden halved—wasn't that how it went?

Headlights appeared on the track. They were bright, on the maximum setting. So bright that he couldn't make out the vehicle.

He stepped away from his truck and off to one side as the vehicle made the turn. It stopped.

He held up his hand and waved. "Kill your lights," he shouted.

They stayed on.

"We don't want no one seeing us," he shouted again, as the vehicle rolled slowly to a stop. He saw it was more a pickup truck than the Honda but he was sure the reporter and her bodyguard had been driving.

Maybe it was someone who'd taken a wrong turn. Or maybe they'd switched vehicles. Yeah, RJ told himself. That could be it. They hadn't wanted to be seen coming here in the Honda so they'd borrowed a truck. It was smart.

"Hey," he said, stepping towards the pickup, and holding his hands over his eyes to shield them from the glare. "You made it."

The passenger door opened. Looking at the ground, he could just about make out the person's lower half. They had slippers on their feet, and were wearing a robe. It was pink and white, with soft, fluffy edges.

What the hell was this?

The headlights were switched off. His eyes adjusted from the dazzling brightness to the gloom.

RJ's stomach turned over.

How? How was this possible? He had watched the big black guy pluck the note from the windshield.

How could she have known?

He looked at the figure in front of him. He took in the person driving. He thought back to his conversation with Sue Ann. That was how, he told himself.

He held up his hands for a second time, this time in a gesture of supplication. "Please," he said, his voice high-pitched. "Don't do this."

28

A s the Honda bumped down the dirt track, Cressida could only hope that whoever had left the note asking to meet her hadn't gone. It was already a solid five minutes after the time they had given.

Anonymous sources could be jittery. They were anonymous for a reason, and that reason was usually fear. Fear of losing their job, fear of someone looking for payback. In extreme cases, fear for their own life or those of their loved ones.

Off to the left there was a parking area. She headed into it. If nothing else, she could use the area to turn around. The note hadn't said how the person was getting there. Were they walking? Driving? Without that information it was hard to know what to look out for.

And there was still the possibility that the whole thing was a set-up. A lure to get her alone. The second part of a plan that had begun with Ty's arrest.

Driving in she had noticed a dock that led out into the swamp. She wanted to get out and go take a look, but something told her that wasn't a good idea.

She should stay in the car with the engine running and the doors locked. When the person arrived she would be able to make a call on whether she should stay and speak with them or run for it.

She settled in to wait. Five minutes passed. Then five more.

There was no sign of anyone. The place was deathly still.

The hell with it.

She opened the door, and got out. She looked around at the thick undergrowth. Apart from the slow symphony of crickets, there was only silence.

Was the person here? Were they watching her?

If it was a set-up, wouldn't they have made their move by now?

She walked away from the car and down towards the dock. She stepped onto it. She could see an airboat tethered at the end.

Cressida kept walking down the dock towards the boat. She reached it and peered down into it. It looked empty, bar some fishing gear and a couple of fuel containers.

She walked back up the dock. Suddenly from the water next to her a black shape seemed to rear up. Despite herself, she screamed, and started running as fast as she could back up the dock.

At one point, she tripped, and landed heavily on her right knee. She felt the skin peel back, and the painful jar of bone on wood. She managed to get back to her feet and hobbled the last few yards up the dock.

She reached down to her knee, and her fingertips came up slick with blood. She hobbled over to the car, got in, and locked the door. She started the engine, threw it into Drive, and took off, the back tires spinning on the dirt.

Turning back onto the track, she hunched over the wheel, feeling suddenly ridiculous. Something had moved under the dock. That was all. No one was after her.

The Honda reached the end of the dirt track and, without looking, she whipped the wheel hard, turning back onto the road.

An air horn blared behind her, lights filling the inside of the little Civic. Brakes squealed.

The metal grille of a big rig filled her mirrors. She pressed down on the accelerator as hard as she could as the front of the truck touched her rear bumper, sending her car lurching forward.

She was clear, pulling away, putting distance between the back of the Honda and the front of the huge truck. Behind her, the trucker pulled down on his horn a couple more times, signaling his displeasure.

Cressida kept her foot on the gas until she was at a safe distance. Gulping hard for air, she tried to gather herself but found herself laughing hysterically. All these imagined horrors and she had almost killed herself by pulling out onto the road without even looking.

Her cell phone lit up with an incoming call. She looked down at the display, trying to figure out who it might be.

The number read as withheld. She tapped to answer and put it on speaker.

"Hello," she said, hesitant.

"Cressida King?" said a man's voice.

"Speaking."

"This is Ryan Lock, Ty's partner. Where are you?"

"I'm in the car."

"That's good. Are you under any immediate threat? Is anyone with you? Anyone following you?"

Cressida exhaled, blowing a stray strand of hair out of her eyes. "No."

"Okay, here's what I want you to do," said Lock.

"I'm listening."

"Do you have satellite navigation on your phone or in the car?"

"On my phone, but signal's patchy."

"Okay, there's only one main road in and out of Darling. Can you get to it?"

"Yes."

"Okay, get on it, and drive out."

"But I have a story to cover, and I'm finally getting somewhere. Tonight, the man we're staying with—"

Lock cut her off. "Stop talking and listen to me. Your life is at risk. I need you to drive out of town about twenty miles. There's a Motel 6 just past exit seven. I want you to check in there. Do not give your real name, and pay cash. Park your car at the back, or anywhere that's out of sight of the freeway, then go to your room, lock the door, and don't answer to anyone but Ty. Can you do that?"

The adrenalin from the near miss with the rig had started to dissipate, replaced with violent indignation at being spoken to like this. She had the biggest story of her career right in front of her. It was Pulitzer stuff. There was a book in it. Her career would be set.

As a kid growing up she had been obsessed with Muhammad Ali. An unlikely hero for a little mixed-race girl, but her mom had indulged her interest. She'd even had a poster of him above her bed. Ali was coated in sweat, fresh from a long sparring session. There had been a quote on it. She thought back to it now.

Don't quit. Suffer now and live the rest of your life as a champion.

"Can you do that for me, Ms. King?" Lock asked again.

"Yes, I could," she said.

"Good. Call me when you get there."

I could, she thought. I didn't say I would.

Up ahead was the main road. Turn right and she'd head out, towards the highway, and the motel Lock had directed her towards.

She turned left. Middle of the night or not, she was going to speak to Mimsy Murray, and this time she planned on getting the truth.

29

The drunk-tank door slid closed with a clang. Cells didn't particularly faze Ty. He'd seen his fair share. He considered himself law-abiding, but he was hardly what anyone would describe as a choir boy.

Both he and Lock had found themselves in conflict with law enforcement about as often as they had found themselves on the same side. It had never been by choice as much as circumstance.

The law was an institution that moved slowly. Apprehension, ascertaining the truth: these took time. And the law was reactive. First a crime had to be committed. In the military, and now in the private sector, you couldn't wait for something to happen. By then it was too late.

Ty didn't pay much attention to his cellmates as he settled himself on a hard wooden bench at the far end of the room. It was around twenty feet long and ten feet deep with benches on two walls and a metal toilet at the opposite end from where he was sitting.

Despite the lack of fixtures and fittings and the spartan decor, the walls, floor and benches had still managed to absorb the fetid, dank odor of its transitory occupants. He rubbed at the stubble on his face, and tried to figure out his immediate next move when he was released.

Cressida would want to stay in Darling and keep investigating. Of that much he was certain. She had grit, but grit could get you killed.

He doubted she would listen to him. But she'd listen to her editor. She'd have no choice. But then Ty would have to share the details that she hadn't. But what then? She might be fired for not telling Gregg back in New York about Timothy French.

Ty didn't want to see her get hurt. But equally he didn't want to get her fired.

He would use it as leverage. Either she backed off, at least temporarily, or he'd have no choice but to share with her boss what she'd withheld.

That would do it. He hoped.

"What the hell are you looking at?"

It took the question to be repeated for Ty to realize it was aimed at him. He wouldn't be the obvious candidate given that, right now, he was staring down at the concrete floor, stained with who knew what.

It was a standard jail-cell query. The precursor to what prison slang called a heart or gut check. Not so much a question as a challenge to assert one's masculinity. The only snag was that any disturbance could delay his release. And Ty needed to get out of there way more than he needed to prove his mettle to some thug or drug addict.

Ty looked up. Three scowling faces stared at him from the other bench. They each had long, lank brown hair, beards, tattoos, earrings, and cut-off denim jackets that Ty guessed had some kind of outlaw motorcycle-gang patches sewn onto the back.

Although a few '1%' biker gangs had black members, they weren't noted for their racial tolerance. Ty guessed that was one reason the smallest of the three had decided to call him out. That, and the fact that Ty was the largest man in the holding cell.

Ty stared back at the diminutive biker as he got to his feet. He was maybe five feet four inches tall, at a pinch. "Why don't you do yourself a favor and sit yourself back down?" he growled. "Assuming you're not still sitting down already."

Sometimes a strong enough verbal pushback could settle a matter like this. Ty had a feeling this wasn't going to be one of those times. You never got the breaks when you needed them. It wasn't how life tended to work.

One of the biker's brothers in arms, the largest of the three, snickered, all but guaranteeing that things were going to escalate. Ty saw an opportunity. Glancing up, he located the lone security camera above his head in the far corner. Where he was sitting was a blind spot. He knew what he had to do.

Ty switched his attention to the largest of the bikers. He locked eyes with him. "What are you laughing at, asshole?"

30

Cressida looked down at her cell phone. The signal had dropped to zero bars and with it the Google Maps navigation that was directing her back to Mimsy's house. A few seconds ago Google had told her to take a right down a narrow road that would get her there faster . . .

She pulled over for a second. She had a decision to make. She could double back to the main road through town and pick up the route from there. Or she could keep going and hope her phone picked up fresh signal.

She bit her lip as headlights bore down on the Honda. Without thinking she hunkered low in the driver's seat as a pickup truck swept by, squeezing past her with only a few inches to spare, the driver honking his horn.

Cressida froze. She was sure she'd seen Mimsy Murray sitting in the front cab next to the driver. Either it was her or she had a twin that Cressida didn't know about. Seeing Mimsy, or a woman she thought was Mimsy, chilled her blood. What the hell was she doing driving around in the middle of the night?

For a moment, Cressida started to have second thoughts. Was it a good idea to confront her without Ty? Or was it foolhardy? Maybe

Ty's partner had been right when he'd told her to head to the motel and sit it out.

She'd hedge her bets. She could follow the truck, and see what Mimsy was up to. Then she could decide whether to confront her, or leave it until she had back-up.

She threw the Honda into Drive, and hit the gas, speeding up so that she kept eyes on the rear of the truck before it turned off and she lost it.

A voice came from her cell phone: "Drive for eight hundred yards, then turn left."

She glanced down at the phone, and saw two solid bars of signal. She took it as an omen that she was doing the right thing.

Speeding up, she saw the tail-lights of the truck ahead. She reached down and switched off the Honda's headlights before the driver of the pickup could realize she was following.

31

Mimsy checked the truck's side mirror. She glanced at Lyle.

"You see that?" she asked him.

"See what?"

She smirked. Lyle was a terrible liar. Always had been. Ever since she'd known him.

"The car back there that just switched its headlights off so we wouldn't know it was following us," she said, indulging him.

He scoped out his mirror, narrowing his eyes, making a big show of looking for it. "Oh, yeah, there is someone back there, I guess."

"It's that reporter," said Mimsy, watching Lyle's reaction.

"You think? What do you want me to do?"

Mimsy straightened up in her seat. "She's following us. We don't have to do anything. Just keep driving."

"Yes, ma'am."

A thumping sound came from the bed of the truck as RJ stirred.

"You want me to stop?" Lyle asked.

"Not now. Just keep going."

"You got it."

That was the upside to Lyle, she thought. He might be dumb as a sack of rocks, a terrible liar, and not always capable of keeping his mouth shut when it should be, but he did what he was told. And, right now, that was all she needed.

32

The rule rarely varied. When confronted by a group, figure out who the leader is—usually, but not always, the largest man. You could discern the alpha male by how the others reacted to them.

When Ty called out the biggest of the three bikers, the other two sniggered, like they were in on a joke. That confirmed his suspicion. It was laughter that suggested Ty had messed up in a big way.

The big guy took his time getting to his feet. His slowness suggested that he didn't anticipate much of a fight. He didn't even get up at Ty's first jibe asking what he was laughing at. Ty had to push out a few more verbal jabs before he finally rose from the bench. Even then, he didn't rush over. He did some stretches, cracked his knuckles, exchanged a few words with his two cornermen.

Ty watched him, with a smile. He already knew exactly what the guy would do. He would mosey over. Then, when he was within the last few feet, he would either rush him or, more likely, throw a wild haymaker of a punch.

The big guy bumped fists with his two comrades. Ty noted he was right-handed. That meant he'd jab with his left, and his big shot would be his right. Assuming he moved into a boxing stance, which

Ty doubted he would. It was more likely he would stand square on, and just throw from there.

As he ambled the short distance, Ty got to his feet. He rubbed at his chin with one hand, a gesture of nonchalance that was anything but. It was a way of keeping his hands high, ready to block, without it being obvious.

"Man, you made a big mistake," the biker said to him.

"Yeah, I do that," Ty said, still smiling. "It's a character flaw."

At the last second, Ty shifted his demeanor. His smile dropped. He brought up his other hand to his face, palms open, in a gesture of supplication. "Listen, dude, can we start again?" he said. "I'm sorry if I upset you or your buddies."

"You believe him?" the big guy said, twisting his neck to look at his two fellow bikers.

Seizing his opportunity, Ty stepped off to one side, creating an angle. Rather than throw a punch, he leaped onto the biker's back. One hand slipped under the biker's throat, corkscrewing rapidly through until his elbow was in a line with the center of the throat. Ty's biceps jammed in against the windpipe, while his other arm worked a pincer movement, the hand coming to the back of the biker's head.

Ty grasped his biceps with his choking hand. In the same movement, he had sunk his heels against the front of the biker's pelvis. He squeezed hard, moving his elbows towards each other to finish the choke as the biker's two buddies scrambled from the bench and an alarm sounded. Outside the cell, boots scrambled towards the door.

Sneaking his face round from behind the biker's ear, Ty watched as the big guy's eyes began to roll back and his eyelids fluttered closed. Ty shifted his weight, sitting down, his heel hooks still in, taking his victim with him.

With his back to the cell wall, and holding the biker in front of him, the other two had no way of getting to him without risking delivering a kick or punch to their now unconscious comrade.

As the first trooper rounded the corner, Ty let go of the biker, shoving him down to the floor, and sitting back with his feet up on the bench, one arm out, ready to deflect any last-second punches.

The jail cell opened, and a trooper rushed in, pepper spray in hand. The two bikers put their hands up, and began to back off. Ty lowered himself down, making it look like he was tending the fallen man.

"I don't know what happened," said Ty. "I think he may have had a heart attack." Kneeling down next to him, Ty sank his knee into the biker's solar plexus.

"Okay," shouted a trooper, as others crowded into the cell. "Move away."

The biker groaned in pain as Ty gently cupped his face and ground his knee into his chest.

Ty held up a hand. "It's okay. He's coming round. It must have been low blood sugar or something."

A hand reached down, and grabbed Ty under the armpit. "We'll take care of it from here."

Ty stood up, and backed into the corner. "I just hope he's okay."

The biker started to sit up, completely disoriented.

Ty looked at him and gave a gee-shucks shrug. "You had me worried for a second there, big fella."

The biker growled and lunged towards him. An officer's baton sliced through the air, catching the biker on the back of the head, and sending him back to the cell floor as Ty shrank further into the corner, a picture of complete innocence.

33

Mimsy could just about glimpse the front of the Honda following them down the narrow road at a respectful distance, its headlights turned off. Mimsy knew every square foot of this place. This was home turf for her.

She reached over, and jostled Lyle's elbow. "When you get round this bend you can pull in. You know the place I'm talking about?"

Lyle did. Many of the roads around Darling were so narrow that passing places had been cut out so that if someone met a large vehicle coming in the opposite direction, they could squeeze in out of the way. There was one just around the bend.

"Turn off the lights when you pull in," Mimsy added.

Lyle pressed a bit harder on the gas, going from a steady thirty-five miles an hour to over forty. Not so much that it would cause the Honda to speed up to close the gap, just enough to give him a little more distance around the bend.

He made the turn. As soon as the back of the truck was clear, he switched off the headlights, gently applied the parking brake, and pulled the wheel down hard, easing into the passing place.

The front of the truck nudged against some branches as he spun the wheel back around, ready to exit. He already had an idea of what Mimsy had in mind without her having to spell it out.

There was another thump from the truck bed.

Mimsy craned her neck around.

"Don't worry, he ain't going anywhere," Lyle said.

"Best hope not."

CRESSIDA STRAINED to see the road ahead of her. She had been using the truck's headlights to map out the terrain. It must have turned, or gone around a corner, but she couldn't risk using her headlights.

This section of the road was thick with trees. They were tall, maybe thirty feet, with long, looping branches that formed a thick, arching canopy that quelled the moonlight, leaving the road close to pitch black.

Her phone display lit up. She slowed to a crawl. She would let them get ahead a little more, and then she'd be able to use her headlights to navigate. She could switch them off again as soon as she caught a glimpse of the truck.

"Yes," she said, picking up.

"It's Ryan. Did you get to the motel, okay?"

She damped down her irritation. Here she was, out in the middle of nowhere, quite literally tracking down the story of her life, and she was fending off calls from a babysitter she hadn't even met. She didn't need this. Not now. "Yeah. I found it fine. It's all good."

She turned the switch, putting on the side lights. It was enough to illuminate the road ahead without being too obvious. She smiled at her own ingenuity as the car inched forward a few more feet.

"Okay. Ty will be with you in a few hours. Bail's been arranged but there's an eight-hour wait time for release in cases of DUI in Florida. Just sit tight until he gets there and then you can decide what you want to do next. Whatever that is, we'll have your back."

Cressida suppressed an eye roll as she hunched over the steering wheel and the Honda rolled forward, coming up on a bend in the road.

"I appreciate that," she said. "Now, if you don't mind, I'd really like to get some sleep."

"Of course," said Lock. "Good night."

Cressida ended the call and tossed her cell phone onto the passenger seat. The display faded slowly back to black.

Men. The way they carried on. Like she was a helpless damsel in distress who couldn't handle some small-town rednecks.

Rounding the bend, she looked for the tail-lights of the truck. There was nothing. Only a dark country road.

She thought about turning her headlights on full and decided against it. Maybe they were just a little further ahead. The phone-call had slowed her down. For all she knew there was another bend or turn a few hundred yards further down the road and they were the other side of that.

Tapping down on the gas pedal, she picked up speed. Her hands tightened on the wheel as she tried to shake off the irritation of Lock's phone call.

The lie didn't even so much as flit across her mind. Or the thought that no one knew where she was right now.

From behind her came the roar of an engine and a dazzling blaze of light. It was so bright that when she looked up at her mirror to see what it was, she was blinded.

The truck's throaty roar came again as the driver gunned the engine, and it lurched forward, bearing down on the rear of the Honda.

Cressida stomped on the gas pedal. The Honda lurched forward, its wheels spinning for a second as it struggled for traction on the loose, rutted road surface.

It kept coming, closing the gap, threatening to roll right over the top of her. Somehow she managed to keep control of the Honda on the narrow road. She pulled away, glancing back to see a gap emerge between the two vehicles.

When she looked ahead, all she could see was a thick wall of trees as she came up on a fresh bend. She spun the wheel, struggling to keep the car on the road as branches whipped against the windshield, and the pickup truck's lights engulfed her.

34

Carmen was lying in the suite's king-size bed as Lock padded in from the bathroom, cell phone in hand. She patted the mattress next to her. Lock smiled, laying the phone on the bedside table.

"Sorry, I know I promised no work."

Carmen shot him a look that promised more than sleep. "Oh, I'm going to put you to work on this vacation, Mister. Don't you worry about that."

Lock rolled back the covers. He slid his hand under, feeling for the inside of her thigh, and letting his hand linger.

"Everything okay?" Carmen asked, with a nod to his phone.

"Nothing to worry about. She's at the motel. No one knows she's there. Ty'll be released in a few more hours. I just left a message letting him know he can relax until he's out. It's all good."

"So you can give me your full attention?" she said, her hand sliding down, taking his and moving it slowly up her body.

"One hundred percent."

35

The Honda bounced along the narrow country road. It hit a bump and Cressida lurched in her seat, her head touching the cabin roof. The seatbelt cinched tight around her, cutting across her chest, and into her shoulder.

She kept her foot to the floor. Her hands were growing sore from gripping the steering wheel so tightly. She took a breath and peered out through the windshield into the cone of light.

A quick check of her side mirror revealed the truck. It had dropped back a little.

If she could just get off this road, and back onto some kind of a freeway, she was sure the little Honda could outpace the lumbering truck that was riding her rear bumper. It wasn't suited to this kind of terrain. It was a vehicle designed for cities, not whatever this was.

The twists and turns in the road had made it hard to keep oriented. She wasn't sure if she was heading into town, or away from it. At one point, as she had slowed coming into a bend, she had actually glimpsed the swamp a few feet beyond the trees. The water had folded in on either side of the road.

She looked down at the passenger seat and her cell phone. She thought about calling Ty's partner, Lock. But what could he do apart from contact the authorities?

She'd call 911 herself. Even if she couldn't tell them exactly where she was, they would know and be able to send someone out. She knew Mimsy was in the truck. She had seen her. She could give them that information too.

Taking one hand off the wheel, she reached over and grabbed her cell phone. From behind her came a fresh roar from the truck's engine. It had closed the gap again. It reared up behind her.

She threw her phone back onto the passenger seat, the plan abandoned. It slid across and fell onto the floor.

Cressida cursed under her breath as the truck's metal cow-catcher slammed into her rear bumper. She fought the wheel as she hit a fresh rut in the road.

With rising desperation she struggled to keep control of the car. The tires spun wildly as she hit a rise, and the Honda left the ground. It came down again with a bone-crunching lurch that juddered all the way up her spine.

Her head hit the roof. For a split second she lost her grip on the wheel. The Honda turned, leaving the blacktop, and finding the soft, wet verge.

Everything around her twisted and turned as the car launched off the road, tires slipping. There was a sickening crunch as the passenger side slammed into a tree.

The back of the Honda slung out wide as it kept moving forward, heading miraculously through a gap between two pop ash trees, then beyond them into the murky water.

Cressida was tossed around in her seat, like a rag doll. There was a small detonation as the airbag deployed, shoving her back hard into the seat. The car belly-flopped, side on, into the swamp. The engine died. The instrument panel flickered and went dark.

It took a second for Cressida to come to. She wasn't sure if she had passed out, or just lost her bearings. The airbag filled her vision. She twisted her head. It was hard to see anything. There was only darkness, total and absolute, and the low gurgle of swamp water pushing into the cabin.

36

Lyle slammed the truck into reverse and backed up to where the Honda had spun off the road. Mimsy popped her door open and got out. Lyle followed. They stood there, taking in the twisted foliage and sheared-off branches where the car had carved its path off the road and into the swamp.

Seconds passed. Neither of them said anything. Mimsy listened. There were no screams of pain or calls for help. Not so much as a murmur.

In the back of the truck, RJ stirred, prompting Mimsy to speak. "I'll keep an eye on him," she said, with a nod towards the truck bed. "You go take a look."

Lyle opened his mouth to speak, but stopped himself. He opened the driver's door, reached in, and reappeared a few moments later with a shotgun. He crunched a round into the chamber.

"Leave that here," Mimsy told him.

"But—"

The look Mimsy gave him cut him off. "I said go look, not anything else," she said.

He put his head down, like a scolded first-grader, and handed the gun to her. She hefted it up, resting the barrel against her shoulder, the muzzle aimed at the heavens.

Mimsy watched as Lyle turned up his pants legs and started down the slope towards the water. She walked to the rear of the truck to check that RJ hadn't managed to free himself.

It was a miracle he hadn't been flung from the back of the truck during the chase. The only thing that had saved him was a length of rope that Lyle must have used to secure one of the sacks to a cargo hook.

RJ lay there, trussed up like a turkey, his knees pulled into his chest. Blood ran down his face from a cut above one of his eyes. He stared at Mimsy, a thick piece of tape covering his mouth.

Mimsy's free hand shot out, her index finger jabbing in the direction of the swamp. "You see? You see what you've done?" she said. "This, this here, it's your fault." She lowered the barrel of the shotgun, clasping it with both hands, tucking the stock into her shoulder and taking aim at him. He wiggled around like a fish, his eyes wild. "I wouldn't waste good buckshot on you," she said, lowering the shotgun. With a grunt, she hauled herself up onto the back of the truck.

RJ wriggled into the furthest corner, his eyes still on her.

"You know what you are," said Mimsy, jabbing the shotgun hard into a kneecap, prompting a groan. "You're an ingrate. Bet you don't even know what that means. Well, I'll tell you. It means someone who's got no appreciation for what others have done for them. In this case for what I've done for you. You and everyone else in this town."

She took a step towards him, the barrel of the shotgun dancing over various body parts until her aim settled on his backside. The muzzle jabbed hard into his hip, then shifted around until it settled between his butt cheeks. He grimaced.

Mimsy threw her head back and laughed. "Always knew you couldn't be trusted, RJ."

She turned away. "Lyle? You see her? She dead or what?"

37

As the adrenalin jolt of the crash faded it was replaced by pain. The worst was in her right leg. It was excruciating, unrelenting, like someone had pushed a red-hot poker against her shin.

The airbag had begun to deflate, allowing her a better view of the inside of the Honda, although "view" was a rather grand word for the eight to nine inches of visibility she had in the darkness.

Slowly, she began to take an inventory of her body. What she could and what she couldn't feel and move. Her chest was sore from the airbag, but no more than that. She had been winded, but her breathing had slowly stabilized. Her arms, her hands, they were all working. She flexed her fingers to make sure. Her hips seemed fine, and she appeared to have sensation everywhere, which told her she hadn't sustained any spinal or neck damage, or at least no paralysis.

Her head was clear, although the blinding pain from her right leg made consciousness a mixed blessing. She wiggled her toes, the action sending a fresh flash of pain all the way up her right side.

She was alive. Maybe with a broken leg, but that put her in the lucky category. If she had hit a tree head on she was in no doubt she'd have been dead, even with the car's modern safety equipment.

From what she could tell, the car was lying passenger side down. It was in water, but not submerged. The water that had been seeping in appeared to have stopped, its level found. Another stroke of good fortune for which she had the Lord to thank. Some of her friends and colleagues in New York teased her for her belief in God, but at times like this she was glad of it. He would see her through, she was sure of it.

She reached down and grabbed the seatbelt. She tried to sit forward and free it from over her chest but the pain in her leg made her sit back, close to tears.

There was a splash outside the car. Her heart jumped, her mind suddenly filled with what might be outside, lurking in the water but now on the move.

From the dread feeling of entrapment she found herself thankful for the car's metal frame and body around her.

Could it be some of the local wildlife come to check her out? Possibly as their next meal? She scolded herself for the thought. She needed to stay calm and present, not allow her imagination to run wild. Any alligator or snake within half a mile would have taken off in fright at the sound of the Honda smashing its way through the trees and landing in the water.

But they'll be back.

She shook her head from side to side, trying to dislodge the unwanted thought.

The sound came again. Someone moving through the water towards her.

"Hey, I'm here," she called.

A rippled wave of water swelled against the bottom of the windshield. She called out again, only to be met with silence.

Then, from nowhere, a face appeared at the driver's window. A man's. He was staring at her with a blank expression.

He lifted his hand and the beam of a flashlight blinded her.

She watched as he looked back over her shoulder and called, "She's alive."

The way he said those two words chilled her. His tone was of disappointment rather than relief. The way he said it hinted at work unfinished, a job that was some way from completion.

She waited, staring back at him, hoping to find some flicker of humanity in his eyes as he looked back at her.

What would her end be? Would he haul open the door, drag her out and hold her under the water? Would his hand come up with a gun?

"Please," she said, still straining to find some connection. "I'm hurt."

He looked at her for a second more. She heard someone call to him. It sounded like Mimsy but she couldn't say for sure. Then his face disappeared.

Cressida bit down on her lip, bracing herself for the inevitable stab of pain as she grabbed for the steering wheel and tried to push the door open. It was no good. It was too heavy, and she was too weak.

She waited for the face to reappear. She heard the sloshing of water as he waded back to the bank. Then there was silence.

ON THE ROAD, Mimsy climbed down from the bed of the truck as Lyle walked towards her, shaking the water from his legs. He glanced at the shotgun.

"What do you want me to do with her?" he asked Mimsy.

38

The sound of the splash in the water echoed for a moment. Slowly, from the water's edge, dark shapes began to move, huge tails flicking as they scurried from the land, and slipped almost silently into the water, ready to gather whatever had just landed.

They moved just beneath the surface towards the receding sound. The darkness was no barrier.

A few seconds later the water erupted again as they went after it, tails and bodies thrashing as they fought for their share. One shape, larger than the others, cruised towards the churning water. The others melted away as Curious George bore down on the frozen hunks of meat.

At the side of the pond, Sue Ann lifted another chunk from the pile and tossed it as far as she could into the water. A few smaller 'gators moved into the water, ready to go after the scraps.

Sue Ann lifted more and more from the pile, tossing it in until it was all gone, and it seemed like the entire pond churned black and silver in the moonlight.

She paced back and forth, watching the feeding frenzy. She had been trying to contact Lyle for the past hour, with no luck, and she had a bad feeling that she had done the wrong thing. That her phone-call had put her husband in more danger than he'd already been in.

All she could do now was make sure his animals were well fed. That and pray. For her husband. For Lyle. For herself.

39

"Are you sure about this?" Lyle asked, pulling the final branch over the gap in the roadside carved out by the Honda.

Both he and Mimsy were covered with dirt having spent the past forty minutes or so running the truck up and down to cover the tracks where the Honda had left the road, then pulling down branches to conceal the gap.

Now anyone driving down this road in the daylight, which wouldn't be many people, would have no idea of what had happened. Not unless they looked closely anyway.

He had to hand it to Mimsy: for a woman of her age, she could do a power of work when she had to. She'd always had that inside her, the ability to get down and dirty with the best of them. Not that he was sure RJ would have agreed.

Mimsy put her hands on her hips. "You go and shoot someone, that's murder," she said. "That same someone runs their car off the road into the swamp and doesn't come out? That's just careless. Nothing to do with us."

Lyle looked at the branches. Mimsy had a point but he wasn't sure that was how other people would see it. If you left someone to die, maybe it wasn't a crime like shooting them, but it wasn't good either.

In fact, some would say it was worse. The woman was suffering bad. He'd seen it in her eyes, heard it in her voice.

And what if she made it out? he wondered. What then?

Mimsy seemed to read his concern. "Don't worry. She ain't gonna be going anywhere. You said she was good and stuck, right?"

"Yeah, she's pretty busted up."

"Tell you what, if it makes you feel better, I'll come down here in the morning and make sure she's still there."

He was going to ask if she wasn't worried about anyone seeing her if she came back but decided against it. She might change her mind, ask him to do it, and he'd done enough dirty work for one lifetime, never mind one night.

"What about RJ?"

"You leave old RJ to me," said Mimsy.

40

Cressida sat in the wreck. She reached up, pulled the handle, trying to push the door open, but gravity was against her. She scoured the cabin, hoping to catch sight of her cell phone, but she couldn't see it.

Last she remembered, it had fallen under the seat. It was probably still there, submerged in the water.

The pain in her leg hadn't subsided. If anything it had gotten worse. It was pain like she had never felt before, so persistent and sharp she felt almost feverish.

The truck that had been out there had left now. She had heard it drive away.

They were counting on her not getting out. On her dying there.

She had to steel herself. From somewhere she had to discover the strength to get the door open, and clamber out.

No one was coming to help her. No one knew she was here. This was on her. And if she did manage to get out of this alive, she was going to make old Mimsy pay. But not in the way she had planned when she had come down here.

41

Lyle pulled the pickup truck in next to the dock. He and Mimsy got out, both still caked with dirt from hiding the gap in the roadway. Mimsy was holding the shotgun as they walked to the rear of the vehicle.

She motioned for him to drop the tailgate. He climbed up onto the back, and hauled RJ to the edge, moving his legs so that they dangled over it and sat him up.

"Take it off," said Mimsy.

Lyle peeled back the thick grey strip of tape covering RJ's mouth. He had a bloody nose and his face was all banged up from being thrown around the back of the pickup when they'd been chasing down the reporter.

RJ took in a couple of deep breaths. He stared at them both.

"I'm sorry, RJ," Lyle told him. "You didn't give us much choice."

RJ kept staring at him. "That so?"

"Don't blame Lyle here," said Mimsy.

RJ's chin dropped to his chest and he let out a hollow, sarcastic laugh. "Nothing's ever anyone's fault around here, is it, Mimsy?"

Mimsy took a step towards him, the shotgun pointed to the ground, but her hand settled near the trigger. "You think I wouldn't find out about you trying to talk to that reporter? You've been hanging around town ever since she got here."

"I'm not going to apologize for wanting to tell the truth."

Mimsy threw her head back. "Oh, you're so high and mighty, these days, aren't you? Like you're innocent in all this."

"No, I'm not innocent. I'm going to have live with what I've done, and I'm going to have to answer for it too, when I'm gone."

Mimsy let out a loud sigh. "Things happen, RJ. Things that people don't mean."

"Like lynching an innocent woman because of the color of her skin?" RJ shot back.

"There was nothing innocent about her. You know it as well as I do."

RJ started to cough. He kept coughing, almost doubling over. Lyle looked worried. "You want some water?"

RJ spat out a gob of bloody phlegm onto the ground. "Sure."

Lyle walked back to the cab, and reappeared with a bottle. RJ's hands were still bound together with a length of rope. Lyle raised the bottle to his lips and tilted it back so he could drink.

"Thanks." He looked back at Mimsy with a mixture of pity and anger. "You know she was innocent. Innocent in all of it. At every single turn. But you wasn't."

Mimsy raised the shotgun. "RJ, I'm warning you."

"Go to hell, Mimsy. You know and I know what happened was all Adelson's doing. She didn't show up at your house with a stack of Bibles and fall crazy in lust with him. He forced himself on her."

As he spoke she grew more and more angry. Her face flushed, and she began to tremble with rage.

RJ looked at her, defiant, not caring if she pulled the trigger. He'd already accepted he was dead from the time they'd caught up with him, trussed him and flung him into the back of the truck. He guessed that went double after what they'd done to the reporter.

They probably didn't know it because they were too busy covering their tracks, but he'd seen the whole thing. He'd wriggled as hard as he could to get free, but it had been no use.

"You just couldn't accept that he wanted her more than he wanted you. Wanted her so much that he did what he did. That was why you made sure she was murdered. You didn't hang her from that tree, but you might as well have. And all because the man you were gonna marry was an animal who couldn't control himself."

Her finger was on the trigger now. She had the shotgun aimed straight at his head. She was all ready to blow it clean off his shoulders.

"You want to make your peace with the Lord, you'd better do it now."

RJ shuffled his butt cheeks from the tailgate and stood up. He stood where he was, not moving, less than ten feet from the hot end of the gun.

"Already done. Guess I'll see you down there, Mimsy."

Her finger started to squeeze. It was a tough pull and her fingers weren't as strong as they had been.

As she grimaced with the effort, Lyle's hand reached from behind her, and pushed the shotgun barrel into the ground in front of RJ. The gun went off, peppering the ground with birdshot.

Mimsy turned on him. "What the hell you have in this gun?" she shouted.

"Give me the gun, Mimsy," he said. "You ain't killing RJ. He's one of us."

"One of us? You hear what he was going to do? You were there too. In fact, if I remember rightly, you supplied the rope. Ran in and got it from the back of the diner."

Lyle's hands closed around the gun and he succeeded in wrestling it from her. He shifted his weight so he was facing RJ, and that was who he addressed. "That's right. I did. I brought the rope, and you got rid of her, RJ. That means we're all in this. No easy way out. Not for you. Not for me. Not for any of us. You think you're being all brave, clearing your conscience, but that would ruin how many lives? How many families' lives? You think Sue Ann would be able to cope without you if you're dead or in jail for the rest of your life?"

RJ cast his eyes down, his defiance diminished for the time being.

He didn't think Lyle had ever before spoken that many words at one time in his life. Lyle seemed to have surprised himself because he scuffed at the ground with the toe of his boot, and added, "You know I'm right about Sue Ann. And I can't live like this." He jabbed a finger at Mimsy. "Not with her lording it over everyone, pretending like her shit don't stink when this would never have happened without her and her crazy ideas."

Mimsy rose back up. "The Fourteen Words are not a crazy idea. It's what kept this country together. For years." The Fourteen Words ran: "We must secure the existence of our people and a future for white children."

"Oh, bull crap," said RJ. "Take people as you find them. That's the only thing that makes a lick of sense and you know it."

Lyle snapped open the shotgun. "We have to know what you're going to do, RJ. It's as simple as that."

"You mean am I gonna talk?"

"Yeah," said Lyle. "We have to know."

"And if I say I am, and nothing will stop me?"

Lyle stared at the shotgun chamber. "Then I reckon the next one won't be birdshot."

"That how it is?"

"That's how it is."

RJ stared up into the inky black night sky.

"Sue Ann would struggle. That's true. She didn't want me coming here." He looked at Mimsy. "Just in case you're looking for someone to blame, she tried to talk me out of it."

"We know," said Mimsy. "She called Lyle."

RJ rounded again on Lyle. "And you called *her*?"

"She's the mayor," said Lyle.

RJ shook his head. "Ain't that the truth. Okay, I'll stay quiet. How about that?"

Mimsy's eyes narrowed. She obviously wasn't sure whether or not she could believe him. Or trust him.

"You give us your word?" said Lyle.

"Yes, I do."

Lyle looked to Mimsy for the okay.

She seemed to be mulling it over. Her brow was furrowed with deep lines, and her lips were set in a pout. "If you don't, it's not you we'll be coming for next time. It's that little wife of yours."

RJ didn't take the bait. He offered a solemn roll of the shoulders and a nod. "I understand."

42

As Ty was being released, he walked past one of the three bikers he'd shared the tank with. The man did a good job of being distracted by the tiled flooring in the reception area. Ty pushed through the front doors of the Florida Highway Patrol barracks and out into the early-morning Florida sunshine.

The day was warm, and muggy, the air heavy with the threat of an impending storm pushing in from the Keys. Ty would have a court date to deal with but right now that was future-Ty's problem. Present-Ty needed to get to the motel and check on Cressida King.

Eight hours and counting was an uncomfortably long time to be out of touch with your principal when you were a lone bodyguard. He knew that Lock had spoken with her, and that she'd confirmed she was at the motel Lock had directed her to, but he'd be a lot happier when he was back with her, and they could plan on what she wanted to do next.

The hours inside the cell, with sleep next to impossible, had given Ty time to think. At first he'd been a little leery of the young reporter's idealism, but a short dose of Darling hospitality had given him a different angle. If she wanted to keep pursuing the story, he'd have her back, no matter how long it took. The gig might have begun as a diversion from reassuring super-rich Chinese folks about their safety, but now he was all in. If Cressida was seeking justice for Carole Chabon, it was his job to help her deliver just that.

He used an app on his phone to order up a car to take him somewhere he could pick up a set of wheels. It arrived less than five minutes later.

They were just opening up at the car-rental place so it took him a while to complete the paperwork and for them to take his credit-card details. He picked out the only SUV on the lot, figuring that something a little larger wouldn't do any harm.

"Sir, would you like the additional insurance?" the lady asked him.

"Yeah, give me everything," he told her.

She looked up from her computer. "Better safe than sorry, right?"

Damn straight, thought Ty. Those were words to live by right now.

She clicked the boxes, swiped his card through the reader, got him to sign the rental document, and led him outside to a new Ford Escape. She began to walk him around the car, checking for damage, standard car-rental practice.

Halfway round, Ty plucked the key fob from her hand. "I'm kind of in a hurry. Plus I'm fully insured, right?"

"That's correct, sir. However . . ."

Ty climbed into the driver's seat, turned on the ignition, adjusted the mirrors, and gunned the engine as the woman stood there, a little nonplussed. He lowered the window. "Thanks for your help."

He didn't catch her reply, he was too busy making the turn out of the lot and following the signs for the freeway.

TY THOUGHT about calling Lock but decided against it. He didn't want to wake him and Carmen. Not when they were on vacation.

He settled in for the short drive, keeping an eagle eye on the road. The last thing he needed right now was any more problems with Highway Patrol.

He tried Cressida's cell phone. She still wasn't answering. A knot of anxiety formed in his stomach. Or maybe it was just hunger. He really wanted to stop and get something to eat. Food would have to wait. He would take her to breakfast. They could discuss what she wanted to do next.

A HALF-HOUR LATER, he got off the freeway at exit seven, turning right at the bottom of the ramp towards the motel. He parked in back, scanning the other vehicles for the Honda.

There was no sign of it.

Strange.

Ty knew that Lock would have told her to park there so that no one could see it while driving past. It was their standard operating procedure in situations like this. If someone was looking for you, you didn't make it easy for them.

It wasn't complicated.

If no one could see, then no one could find you.

43

I'm going to die here.

The thought had come to Cressida as the sun rose, and the energy-draining heavy heat of the day began to build, leaving her soaked in sweat. She had done her best to push it away – *no, you won't, don't be so melodramatic* – but it kept filtering back into her mind like an unwelcome visitor.

At some point she hadn't so much gone to sleep as passed out, drifting in and out of the present until finally the sunrise and the slowly creeping heat of the morning woke her fully.

Apart from the seething pain in her leg, she was thirsty in a way she couldn't remember having been before. She would have done almost anything for a bottle of cold, fresh water. She had resisted scooping up some of the algae-green swamp water. Another hour and she wouldn't be able to stop herself. She had never thought that such dank, scummy water, full of who knew what, could be so tantalizing.

From her twisted vantage point she could glimpse the road. Or, rather, where she supposed the road had to be because Mimsy and whoever was helping her had obviously dragged tree limbs across the area where the car had crashed.

Looking at it, Cressida couldn't believe that anyone would fail to notice the disturbance. Then she remembered that, for one, people wouldn't be looking. For another, they would be driving past at speed. The only way it would be obvious to someone was if they were walking, and that was hardly likely this far out of town.

She had to face up to the same reality that she had last night. The cavalry weren't coming. Or probably not in time. If she was going to survive, she had to make it happen.

She shifted position, ducking under the seatbelt, and pushing into the footwell with her good leg. Pain cascaded through her with every fraction of an inch that she moved.

Finally, she had maneuvered her body in such a way that if she pushed the door open, she'd be almost able to stand, using the center console as a floor.

She popped the door open, and shoved up with her shoulder. It moved, only just clearing the frame by an inch, but it was something. Last night she hadn't been able to get it open at all.

Cressida gritted her teeth, clenching her jaw and tried to work herself further in under the door. The movement brought a fresh jab of pain. She pushed through it somehow and gave the door another shove. It moved up another few inches.

Twisting around, she used her head to wedge it open. Gravity was against her but she held firm. She had never before thought about how heavy a car door was. She had never had to. They were things you opened, not objects you had to press with your head.

She brought up her hands, and gave the door a solid push.

Now what? The door was open, but if she took her arms away or shifted her body it would close again and she'd be back to square one. It was like being in a cellar, having to hold up a hatch and climb through at the same time. And not a regular hatch, but one that would only open as far as sixty degrees. And all with a broken leg.

Keep going.

Do not give up.

She braced herself for another push. She brought up her good leg, and jammed it against the steering column. Her weight shifted onto her broken leg. It almost buckled under the strain. Somehow she managed to get the foot of her working leg against the steering column just in time. She used it push herself up. Her head, shoulders and upper torso cleared the gap between the car's door and the frame.

Almost there, she told herself. That had been the hard part.

The edge of the door rested against her belly. The discomfort of the metal digging into her abdomen seemed to lessen the pain in her injured leg, the way stubbing your toe might take your mind off a persistent toothache. It wasn't better so much as different and, as strange as it sounded, in the difference came some small measure of relief.

She took a moment to catch her breath. All she needed now was to lever her lower body and drop into the water, then swim, or wade, to the roadside. If she could only make it the sixty or so yards to the road someone would be able to see her.

After a few more deep breaths, she reached down and lifted the edge of the door. She used her arms and core to begin to lift herself out. The car was at such an angle that she wasn't able to sit there once she got far enough. She would slide off. No, once she got far enough clear, she would have to drop down into the water.

Her injured leg would take some of the impact. It was inevitable. Even if she tried to land on the good one. The thought made her stomach turn over.

She held her position, suddenly grateful for those early-morning yoga classes in New York that had strengthened her body, although not nearly enough for a situation like this.

Okay, Cress, you got this, she told herself. She would count down from three and then she would go, ready or not. It was that or sit there all day, getting weaker and more dehydrated by the second.

Three. Two.

That was when she saw it. An alligator. A big one. Maybe ten feet long, and two feet wide at its broadest point.

It was lying in the water, semi-submerged, under the branches of a bald cypress tree. She didn't know if it was looking at her, or the car, or anything at all, but its snout was pointed straight at her.

Worse yet, it was between her and the road. To get there she'd have to crawl straight past it. Even if she took a long loop around, or chose a different route, she would be in the water with it. And who was to say it was the only 'gator in the immediate area? The water was murky, and deep enough to conceal another dozen.

She laughed at her bad fortune. It had taken a Herculean effort to haul herself up and out of the car. Now this.

She scanned the area between where she was, and the bank that led up to the road. There was no easy route. She could either go direct, reducing her time in the water, or skirt around it. Whatever she did, she would be exposed.

If it decided to go for her, she would have no chance. If it was determined.

A thought occurred to her. She raised one arm above her head and began screaming and hollering. Maybe the commotion would unnerve it somehow, and it would move off.

She kept screaming.

The alligator stayed stock still.

For all she knew she could be drawing in other predators. Did she sound like a crazy person that they would do their best to keep away from, or like an injured animal?

She stopped, suddenly self-conscious. It hadn't moved. It just sat there, staring at her.

Come on, Cress, you need a plan here. It's a dumb animal. You're not going to be outsmarted by a freaking handbag, are you?

What else could she do?

Maybe, she thought, if she had a weapon. There was a tire iron in the trunk, but getting that out would be ten times harder than getting past the alligator and onto the road. The car was on its side. She wouldn't be able to open the trunk. Not without help.

What else? Come on. Come on. Think.

A fresh jab of pain from her leg made her catch her breath. She looked over to her left. Just off to the right and about a quarter of the way toward the road was a pop ash tree.

It might do as a staging post, although she had no idea how she could climb it with her leg like this. Even without an injury it wasn't like it had big low branches she could grab onto and pull herself up.

But it was something. Maybe she could break off one of the branches, and use that as a weapon. Or get behind it if the 'gator watching her made a move.

It would be easier to reach than the road. That was for sure. And if she could make it to the ash, she'd be a quarter of the way there.

What choice did she have? Stay perched on top of the Honda, scream and hope someone heard her before her voice gave out and she passed out from dehydration, or drink swamp water, get sick and dehydrate even faster?

44

T y stood next to the Ford, cell phone to his ear, and waited
for Lock to pick up.

"You're out?" said Lock, picking up.

"She's not here," said Ty, still scanning the motel parking lot.

"You're sure? I told her to check in under another name."

"Ryan, I'm positive. I slipped Reception money and checked every
room myself. The rental car isn't here, and neither is she. I've tried
calling her but either her cell is switched off or she's not answering."

There was a momentary pause at the other end of the line, then:
"What about other motels in the area? Maybe she was so freaked out
she drove a little further on, checked in somewhere else."

"Not her style. She's gone back there. I'm sure of it."

"Hundred percent positive?" Lock asked him.

"No, but it's the only thing that makes sense to me. She's the kind
of person who's going to dig in, not back off."

Ty could hear Lock's girlfriend Carmen in the background, asking
Lock if everything was okay. "I'm sorry about this, Ryan. You're on
vacation, brother. You shouldn't be having to deal with this."

"No such thing as a vacation in our world, Tyrone. You know
that."

"I feel you. Listen, I'm going to head back to Darling. If you're right and she really did get out of Dodge, then no harm done. But if she's gone back . . ." He trailed off. "I dunno, it could be bad."

"You still have your gun?"

"Yeah," said Ty, giving his holster a reassuring pat. "I do."

"Okay. I'll be there on the next flight."

"No, Ryan. There's no need. I can handle this."

"Nothing wrong with having back-up."

Ty was starting to regret making the call. He didn't want Lock to cut short his vacation for him. And, if he was being completely honest, his ego wouldn't allow the thought of his partner coming in to help clean up his mess. He'd made the wrong call, and it was down to him to remedy that. "Ryan, I mean it. I appreciate the offer, but I'm good."

He could hear more hushed conversation between his partner and Carmen.

"You're sure?" said Lock.

"Completely. Listen, if I need you, I'll call."

"It's not like I can just drive down there in a couple hours. If something happens . . ."

"Nothing's gonna happen," said Ty. "I got this." Lock started to object. He cut him off. "I'll call you as soon as I find her."

He climbed into the Ford, and sped out of the motel parking lot, heading back towards Darling. As he drove, he kept calling the number he had for Cressida.

She didn't answer.

45

Ryan Lock closed the bathroom door as softly as he could. He didn't want to wake Carmen any more than the phone call already had. She had asked him who it was. He'd told her not to worry and go back to sleep.

He had promised her this vacation. In its entirety. Quality time together was precious.

But something told him, a sixth sense he'd always relied upon, that he needed to get to Florida, and fast. That Ty might not need his help right this second, but that he would. If he was wrong it wasn't the end of the world. He was sure Carmen would understand. She, as much as anyone, knew what she was getting into when they'd begun dating.

Over a long career in the military and then the private security industry, Lock had come to believe that sometimes the most banal close-protection jobs had the potential to be the most dangerous. Very few people hired a bodyguard for no good reason. Sure, they were a fashion accessory in places like Hollywood, where image was everything, but for the most part close-protection operators were hired because of a threat to the principal's life or general wellbeing.

Obviously high-risk gigs, such as escorting someone in a failed state or ultra-high risk environment, took care of themselves. Everyone was on high alert, planning was meticulous, and the resources were at hand.

The problem came with more casual jobs. Or tasks where you didn't have the resources or time to know exactly what you were getting into. Ty's Florida gig fell into that category. Even if it didn't, an AWOL principal was by definition a major red flag. You couldn't protect someone if you didn't know where they were.

Lock pulled up flight details on his phone. There was an American Airlines flight out of Grantley Adams at 06:40. He was about to book a seat, his finger hovering over the screen, when he stopped. Carmen wouldn't want to cut short her vacation. And he wasn't sure she'd want to finish it on her own. He put the phone down, and walked into the bedroom. She was sitting up, the bedside light on, reading a book.

"I'm sorry, I'm going to have to get back."

"I figured."

"It's Ty."

"I figured that too," she said, smiling.

He loved her smile. She smiled with her eyes, and, boy, did she have insanely gorgeous eyes to go with the insanely gorgeous rest of her.

"You know," she went on, "the one good thing is that when you're whispering on the phone at two in the morning I know it's not another woman you're speaking to."

Lock laughed. His closeness with Ty was a running joke between them. When they had moved into their new apartment together, Carmen had even suggested they set aside a bedroom for Ty to have sleepovers.

"His principal, the reporter he's looking after, has gone missing and he got set up on a DUI bust. Someone spiked his drink, then called the car in to Highway Patrol. That's what it looks like anyway."

"Then it sounds like you'd better go. What time's the flight?"

"Six forty."

"So, let's see. Ten minutes to pack. Twenty minutes to the airport. Two hour check-in."

She put down her book, and peeled back the sheet, revealing her sun-kissed naked body. "I think that just about gives us time for a proper goodbye."

Lock walked over to the bed. "I think you might be right, Ms. Lazaro."

46

Eyes fixed on the pop ash tree that was maybe thirty yards from the car, Cressida began a fresh countdown, steeling herself for the short drop that she knew would bring her even more pain. There was no way she'd be able to keep all her weight off her injured leg. The thought of the impact made her wince, but there was nothing else for it.

She started her countdown, muttering the numbers aloud to herself. "Three . . . two . . ."

Palms down, she levered herself up, swung her good leg up and out, over the edge. She began to scoot round so she would have her back to the car. She couldn't get her injured leg moving. She had to grab it with her hands to bring it with her. There was blood on her legs. It was soaked in. She didn't roll it up. She didn't want to see the damage. The agony of it was enough to deal with.

Cressida checked the alligator. It was still there, statue-like, under the tree. "Okay, here goes," she said, pushing off the top of the car and landing in the water.

Her good leg took the impact but she tripped, her foot slipping out from under her. Her arm shot out instinctively, and she found herself falling onto her side, her face going under the water.

As quickly as she could, she stood up. The water was shallower than she had thought. About two and a half feet. It came above her knees but below her waist.

She had to stop herself laughing. Something about this was almost absurd, like standing in a very deep puddle, only one that extended for thousands of miles behind her. She swished her hand through the water, clearing the green scum that lay on top.

The alligator was still there. Unmoving.

Maybe it was asleep. Its eyes didn't give anything away, and it still hadn't moved, not even an inch.

She thought about abandoning her plan, and starting straight across. Something in her hind brain stopped her. Something instinctive and deep-wired that went back generations told her to stick to her plan and get to the pop ash tree, rather than making a mad dash for the road in one go.

She started to take her next step. Her weight shifted from her good leg to her bad. The jolt brought her up short. It was all she could to stop herself sitting down.

Since she had been a toddler, cruising along, using her mom's couch and coffee-table for support, Cressida had never had to think about walking, any more than she thought about breathing. Now it was all she could think about as she squatted, her ass touching the surface of the water. She reached out and leaned against the under-side of the car for support.

She tried again. This time she made it a full two steps before collapsing, her butt not quite touching the muddy ground.

"Damn it," she shouted.

Tears of frustration welled in her eyes. How could she get out if she couldn't take more than two steps without falling?

The 'gator was still there. With every second that passed she was growing more accustomed to its presence. Slowly, second by second, her primal fear was receding.

She had started to resent it being there, watching her, not coming after her but not leaving either.

"Why don't you get out of here?" she shouted at it, slapping the water with an open palm.

The slap brought movement. The alligator's eyes seemed to roll over, and suddenly it moved, sliding its nose into the water, its powerful tail flicking out, propelling it forward.

It was headed straight for her. There was no doubt about that.

She could see the gnarly ridge of its back as it glided through the swamp water.

She freaked, stepping back towards the car, raw fear pushing out the agony every time she used her bad leg. Not daring to look back, she pushed off as hard as she could with her working leg, grabbing for the top of the car. Her fingers found the lower sill of the driver's door, her nails working into the tiny gap between the sill and the door. There was the sound of splashing to her right. From the corner of her eye she caught another greeny-black shape dropping into the water from wherever it had been hiding unobserved.

Cressida began to haul herself up. She found the door handle, her hands slick and greasy from the swamp. Finding a strength she hadn't known she possessed she managed to tighten her grip around it. She hauled herself up, her free hand finding what had been the roof of the car.

Legs flailing, using every ounce of energy she had left, she pulled herself onto the car.

The two 'gators cruised in toward the spot where she had been standing then suddenly changed course and began to swim away.

She lay there and tried to catch her breath. Tears came and soon she was sobbing, her chest lurching up and down, unable to stop herself.

A few minutes later, the same large 'gator was back on the bank, sunning itself as the heat cranked up and the sun broke through the trees. She could feel the metal of the car starting to heat. She was spread across it, like an egg thrown onto a hot skillet.

She couldn't climb back inside without having to haul the driver's door open. She could do that, if she wanted, but she would be cooked either way so she stayed where she was. She scanned the swamp for a sign of the other 'gator, but it, too, had disappeared.

You were right, she told herself. *You are going to die here. This is where they'll find you, if they find you at all. Out here in this God-forsaken swamp, half eaten by bugs, flies swarming over your dead body.*

Just like your great-aunt. The woman you came here to get justice for.

47

The Ford swept to a stop outside Adelson Shaw's house, gravel flying up from the tires. Brake lights flared. Ty got out and ran up the porch steps, taking them two at a time.

He went to pull the front door open. It was locked. He fumbled in his front pockets for a key, but came up blank.

He pounded on the door. As he waited he scanned the area outside the house. There was no sign of the rented Honda Civic here either. Or anywhere on the roads he'd driven to get there: he'd taken a high-speed loop through Darling on his way, half hoping to see it parked outside the diner where he'd eaten.

He could hear the old man's voice from inside. "Okay, okay, don't make me have to buy a new door."

Ty could see him coming down the stairs. First he saw his slippers, then hairless bare ankles, and then the hem of his dressing-gown.

Adelson reached the foot of the stairs and walked toward the door, still mumbling. He saw Ty standing there and froze, eyes wide.

Ty squared his shoulders, his head tilted down. "Come on, open up."

Adelson didn't move. "Listen, she's not here."

Ty was in no mood. Everything about Adelson's reaction to seeing him raised a red flag.

"Can you open up?" he asked, doing his best to keep the rising anger from his voice.

"I told you, she's not here."

"I don't want to have this conversation through the door. Just open up."

Adelson stared at him. He didn't move.

Ty's hand reached up to his holster. "Listen to me. If you don't open this door I can only assume it's because you have something to hide, and that means I'm coming in." His hand settled on his SIG for emphasis. "So, what's it to be?"

Adelson shuffled to the door and unlocked it. He shrank back as Ty walked in. "I told you the truth. She's not here. Look around if you don't believe me. I don't have anything to hide."

Ty closed in on him, towering above him, letting Adelson experience his physical presence. Part of him felt bad about intimidating an elderly man, but there was a time for niceties and this wasn't it.

"She may not be here, and you may not know where she is, but saying you don't have anything to hide is stretching the truth."

Adelson didn't say anything. He smelled of bourbon and vomit. The odor came off him in waves. His eyes were bloodshot and his skin had the florid, blotchy pallor of a drinker. "I have pills I need to take," he said to Ty. "You can make us some coffee and I'll tell you everything I know."

He started to walk toward the kitchen. Ty followed him.

"She was here," he continued, "but she ran out."

"Ran?" said Ty, the tone of menace he'd been unable to suppress a moment ago creeping back into his voice.

Adelson walked into the kitchen and headed to a counter, where he picked up a color-coded plastic pill organizer. "Okay, she left," he said, popping open one of the compartments and palming the contents.

"Where'd she go?" said Ty, arms folded in front of him.

"She didn't say."

Ty walked over to him. As Adelson lifted the pills to his mouth, Ty grabbed the old man's wrist, hard enough to get his attention but not so hard he would hurt him. "Where'd she go?" he repeated.

Adelson looked down at his hand with the pills in it. "My heart medication's in there."

Ty stared at him.

"She went to speak with Mimsy Murray."

Ty kept hold of the old man's wrist. "Why would she do that? We'd just been there for dinner."

"Maybe she had some new questions."

Ty asked again, "Why?"

Adelson let slip an audible sigh. "We talked about some stuff."

Ty's expression suggested Adelson should continue.

"Let me have my pills and I'll tell you."

Ty slowly released his grip. Adelson walked over to the sink, filled a glass with water, and swallowed his pills.

"I don't have all day," Ty told him.

"You think five minutes is going to make a difference?" said Adelson, reaching over and hitting the button to start a coffee-maker on the counter. "Of course you do. You're young." He motioned for Ty to sit down at the small circular kitchen table. "Why would five minutes make any difference after more than forty years?"

Ty wasn't going to sit down and talk in circles. Regardless of what Adelson had just said, he needed to find Cressida King, and fast. The forty-year stuff and beyond could be dealt with after that. And Ty intended on making sure it was dealt with, one way or another.

"I need to know where she is. So I can find her. So I can ensure she's safe," Ty said, leaning over the table. "This isn't a game, Mr. Shaw."

Adelson looked up at him, eyes moist. "Believe me, I know that better than anyone around here."

"So she went to see Mimsy and then what?"

"She didn't come back. Not that I heard, and I don't think her bed was slept in either."

"You tell her what happened to Carole Chabon?"

"Some of it."

"Which was?"

Adelson traced a circle across the table top with the end of his index finger. "You're right. You'd better go see if you can find her, Mr. Johnson."

"I thought you said five minutes wouldn't make a difference."

Adelson stared at him, blinking, but not saying anything.

Ty leaned in close to Adelson's ear. "You and everyone in this town better pray I find her, and that when I do, she's okay," he murmured.

Ty walked out of the kitchen, leaving Adelson sitting there. He bounded up the stairs, turned at the top, and threw open the door that led into Cressida's bedroom. Indeed the bed hadn't been slept in.

He opened her suitcase and checked through the clothes she hadn't unpacked. Then he checked the drawers and the closet for dirty laundry, trying to remember what she had been wearing.

As far as he could tell she hadn't changed, apart from ditching her heels.

He didn't see any signs of a struggle. No blood.

He rushed down the stairs. Adelson was waiting in the hallway.

"I told you she wasn't here."

"I have a hard time taking people around here at their word," Ty shot back.

He flung open the front door, walked out, slamming it behind him. He ran down to the Ford, got in, gunned the engine and took off.

ADELSON WATCHED HIM LEAVE. He had hoped he'd be dead and gone by the time this came tumbling out in all its wretched detail. But now, watching all this unfold, part of him was glad that he was around to see it. To see Mimsy get what was coming to her. If she did, of course. Others had tried, and it hadn't ended well.

Still, in all of this, old loyalties died hard.

He picked up the phone to call Mimsy and let her know what was headed her way. He punched in the first few numbers then stopped.

No, he thought. Maybe let the storm headed her way arrive without warning. Give the other side a sporting chance for once.

He put the phone on the side table and went back into the kitchen to pour himself a fresh cup of coffee and try to shake off his hangover.

48

Ty's display of anger had been for Adelson's benefit. Inside, he was as cool as a man could be, given the circumstances. He had to be in control of himself. But he couldn't let anyone here know that. Not yet.

He needed to use the presentation of anger to help him find Cressida. Or, rather, he suspected, help him push someone into telling him where she was.

For now he had to assume she was alive. He wasn't naive enough to believe she was. There was every chance she'd already met the same fate as Timothy French. But for now this was his working assumption.

Believing he was searching for a living, breathing Cressida King would take him to the same places as looking for a corpse. If, at the end of his search, she wasn't alive, he would deal with it. The same as he'd dealt with other tragedies. And if she was dead, he thought, as the Ford rolled down the narrow swampland road, there would be a price to pay for those responsible. He would see to it.

On the drive from the motel he had tried to drag up the details of the note that had been left on the windshield outside Mimsy's. He would get to her, and soon, but the obvious place to scope out first would be the RV where she'd been asked to meet this anonymous source. Ty couldn't recall the precise details, and in any case they had never made it there, or even checked it out, because they'd been stopped by the cops. But he remembered one key detail, and that would be enough. At the bottom of the sketchily drawn map there had been a sign for an alligator farm. He'd glanced only briefly at the note, but that detail had stuck with him.

He knew Darling was right on the very edge of the Everglades. But he couldn't imagine there would be many alligator farms in the area. He pulled out his phone and checked for a signal. The display showed a shaky two bars. It was enough to open Google, type in the town, then search for alligator farms. Within a couple of seconds he had his answer, and a pin on a Google map showing it was just two miles from where he was.

"God bless the internet," he murmured, pulling a U-turn and heading back down the road toward the farm. From what he could tell, the meeting point was about three hundred yards north-east of the farm's perimeter.

As he drove Ty kept his eyes peeled. For the Honda. For Cressida. For anything that his partner Lock referred to as "the absence of the normal, the presence of the abnormal". That single phrase had saved them, and their principals, on more than one occasion. Ty figured it would serve him equally well now.

The drive didn't take more than a couple of minutes, even after he passed the turn-off to the RV point and had to double back. The place where Cressida had been set to meet whoever had left the note was the dead end of an old dirt track surrounded by a wide circle of cypress trees.

Ty had to say that if he was going to arrange to meet someone to share information this would not have been a spot he would select. There was one way in and one way out. It was overlooked. There was plenty of cover for someone to observe any meeting without being seen.

He stopped the SUV, got out and took a look around. There was no sign of the Honda.

Five minutes later he had scouted out the immediate area, including the cypress trees. He hadn't seen anything. No cigarette butts, no trash, no clothing. It was pristine.

He got back into the Ford, made a tight five-point turn, and headed back down the track. At the end, he turned onto what passed as a main road. He was headed back toward Mimsy's, but he saw a faded old sign for the alligator farm—or 'ranch', as the notice, rather grandly, had it—and on a whim decided to ask the owner if they'd seen or heard anything out of the ordinary the previous night.

It was a long shot, but once in a while a long shot came in. It would take five minutes.

He made the turning, and the SUV trundled down the rutted track, and through an open set of metal gates.

Ty had never been to an alligator ranch before. For a whimsical second he had visions of cowboys on horses corralling herds of alligators, ready for branding. The reality was more mundane: a run-down single-story wooden house, a couple of barns, and a large chain-fenced area that held one large and a couple of smaller freshwater ponds.

He couldn't see any alligators. They must have been in the water, or lurking in the thick vegetation at the far side of the ponds.

One thing immediately caught his attention. A pickup with a Confederate-flag bumper sticker that he recognized as the truck driven by the weird-looking redneck guy, who'd seemed to be stalking him and Cressida when they'd first arrived in Darling. Maybe this was one of those long shots that would come in.

He pulled around the pickup, parked side on to one of the barns, got out, and walked toward the house. It didn't look like anyone was around. The blinds were drawn, and he didn't see any movement inside.

Using an old trick to give him plausible deniability, Ty walked up to the front door. He didn't knock. Instead he waited about twenty seconds, turned around, walked back, took a look at the front of the house, and then went to the barns.

If anyone came out in the meantime, he would claim he'd

knocked at the door, and when no one answered he'd figured they might be working in one of the barns.

In truth, a barn next to last night's RV point was as good a place as any to stash a reporter.

The door of the first was slightly open. He pushed his way through, and softly called, "Hey, anyone here?"

Inside there was a jumble of old car parts and some large chest freezers. He walked over, and opened them up, bracing himself in case they revealed something grisly. They were both close to empty, apart from a couple of bags of unspecified meat, and in the second, some frozen rabbits. There was a work bench at the far end with cabinets underneath for tools, a lawnmower, and some other gardening equipment.

Ty moved on to the second smaller barn. He used the same drill. Call first, then enter. Plausible deniability.

The sight that met him this time was a little different. Bars suspended from the ceiling with chains that ended in meat hooks. Three dead alligators were suspended from the hooks, their white bellies facing him. They ranged from five to eight feet in length. Ty walked over to them, drawn by the somewhat macabre sight. He reached up and touched the first, running his fingertips over the cold body. A glassy black eye stared back at him.

There was a dripping sound, and he looked down to see drops of blood splashing onto one of his boots.

The barn door squealed on its hinges and he turned around. Spooked – he hadn't heard anyone approach – his hand went to his SIG, ready to draw.

He immediately recognized the man in the trucker's hat standing just inside the barn. He had shoulder-length white hair, and a long white beard. It was the man he'd seen in Darling. The man who had been watching him from his truck, and then Cressida. The only difference was that now he was sporting some fresh bruises and the beginnings of a black eye.

The man spat a wad of tobacco onto the floor. "Can I help you?"

He didn't look surprised to have found someone poking around in his barn. Not even a six-foot-four black guy with the frame of a line-backer. Ty assumed there was a reason for that.

"Sorry, I did knock. Thought you might be out here working or something."

The guy wasn't buying it. "Uh-huh."

He peered at Ty's hand on the butt of his gun, which was still holstered. Ty removed it, and extended his hand. "Don't think we've had the pleasure," he said. "Tyrone Johnson."

The man shook, no reluctance or awkwardness in it, unlike the cook from the diner, but he didn't give a name. "So how can I help you, Mr. Johnson?"

If this was the man who had left the note on the windshield, with good intent or evil, Ty knew he needed to handle him with care. Either way, the last thing that would work right now was confrontation. Ty could take that route in a few minutes if he had to.

As Ty spoke, he studied the man, measuring every gesture and shift in expression. "I'm with the young lady who's in town investigating the Carole Chabon murder. She's missing. I'm trying to locate her."

He shrugged. "She ain't here. I can tell you that. You're more than welcome to look around if you'd like."

The last part was classic deflection, along the lines of, *I may or may not know where she is, but I know for a fact that she's not here.*

"It's a pretty large property. Are you sure? I mean, you seem pretty certain, for a man who looks like he just woke up." As Ty spoke he didn't move his eyes from the guy, not even for a split second. He wanted him to know that he was observing his reaction, that he had him under a microscope.

He didn't say anything. Not a bad strategy.

Silence descended. The atmosphere between them was charged, although Ty couldn't pinpoint with what. It wasn't impending violence, not exactly. It felt more like the start of a fight when two men are trying to feel each other out, moving without throwing for fear of being caught with a counter, except the next move could be words as easily as a punch.

Usually Ty would have let the quiet keep running, but it was doing him no favors. And, he reminded himself, he was on the clock. Time was not necessarily on his side. The quicker he found Cressida King, the better. At the same time he sensed that rushing things here wasn't likely to get him anywhere.

The more he looked at the man with the long beard and the bruised eye, the more he got a sense of someone who wanted to talk but didn't know quite how to get started. In other words, he seemed like a man with a lot on his mind.

"How long you had 'gators?" Ty asked, with a nod to the three carcasses hanging from the chains.

"Those ones are wild," the man said. "I go out hunting them."

"Didn't realize that was legal," said Ty, keeping his tone conversational. "Thought they were a protected species."

"No one's going to make a fuss about a couple dead 'gators," the man said.

"That's probably true," said Ty, looking down at the floor. "So you haven't seen anyone?"

The man stared at him for a long moment, again like he had a big decision to make. He shook his head. "Nope. Sorry."

"What about last night? We were supposed to meet someone right around here. Someone who wanted to talk about who might have killed Carole Chabon."

No response.

"I was thinking maybe you saw someone. Heard something. It was that little dead-end road just past those ponds of yours. Maybe you saw someone drive down there."

Another shake of the head. "I was sleeping."

"That how you got the black eye?" said Ty. "Sleeping?"

The guy shifted his weight from one foot to the other. Ty tried to establish eye contact with him, but the guy kept looking away, a sure sign of avoidance and discomfort. He was edging into confrontation and he wasn't sure if it was doing him any good, or just closing the man down.

"Something like that," he answered.

Ty decided to give empathy, and an appeal to common decency, one last throw. "Look, she's a reporter, but she's only twenty-seven. A kid, really. You know what I'm saying? She might have come down here all guns blazing, and upset people who just want the past to be left there, but that's it. It's not something anyone deserves to get hurt over."

The guy looked beyond Ty to the three dead 'gators. "They're pretty good parents, alligators. You wouldn't think it, right? But they are. Especially the mamas. They don't let those eggs out of their sight. Same when they hatch. They put them in their mouth, real gentle like, take them down to the water. You go near them and, man, watch out. They'll die for their young."

"RJ!" A woman's voice. It seemed familiar to Ty. "RJ! You out there? Someone's here."

RJ turned away from Ty and walked to the barn door. "I know. I got it."

The waitress from the diner, the same woman who'd served them dinner last night, walked in. She stopped when she saw Ty, her surprise matching his. "Oh," she said.

"I'm sorry to bother you so early, ma'am," said Ty. "I was just asking your husband if he'd seen the young lady I was with."

If her husband was deadpan, Sue Ann was far from it. Her gaze kept shuttling back and forth to her husband, like she was trying to guess what he might already have said. Ty decided to barrel on, and not give them the time to get their collective bearings.

"She's missing," Ty continued. "I'm concerned that something may have happened to her. I need to find her, and I thought that, seeing as she was due to meet someone here last night, you might be able to help me."

"She was meeting someone here?" Sue Ann asked, pointing to the ground.

"A little ways down the road, but, yes."

"Over on the road behind the ponds," the guy corrected, looking at his wife rather than Ty.

"Okay," said Sue Ann. She sounded relieved. "Well, I'm sorry, but we haven't seen her."

Ty bit down on his lower lip. He wanted to give the impression of being resigned to not having found her, and taking them at their word. "That's too bad. It would have saved a world of trouble if you'd known where I might find her."

"I'm sorry we couldn't be more helpful," said the guy.

"If we do see her, or hear anything, we'll be sure and let you know."

"I appreciate that," said Ty. He pulled a business card from his wallet. He handed it to RJ. "Here. My cell phone is on there. If you do see her, call me."

The man took it, making a point of examining it. "Private security?"

"Yeah," said Ty, with a shrug. "But I think I'm going to have to hand this one over to the Feds."

"The FBI?" said Sue Ann.

In truth, Ty doubted that the FBI would get involved in a missing-person's case, even one like this. Not without more concrete evidence of wrongdoing. They would likely refer him to local law enforcement first. But these people weren't to know that.

He needed a bluff. And he needed to make it convincing.

He was as sure as he could be that the couple in front of him knew more than they were letting on. He also sensed that at least one of them wanted to talk. All they needed was a nudge.

"Yeah," said Ty. "One reporter goes missing while looking into a race murder, well, might be bad luck. Who knows, right? But two? I don't believe in coincidences like that, especially after everything I've found out since I've been here."

He walked to the barn door. "I'd say there are going to be a lot of nervous people around here over the next few weeks."

Now the pair were trading glances. Ty had them, and they knew it as well as he did.

He turned back, and pointed to his business card, still pinched between the man's fingers. "Don't lose that number. Oh, and maybe get some ice on that eye. Kind of makes you look suspicious."

THEY DIDN'T COME CHASING after Ty to ask him what he meant about looking suspicious. They weren't going to either. Their reaction told him that. They were hiding something. He'd have bet his life on it. The question wasn't even what. The question now was how much. How much were they not saying?

He got into the Ford and started the engine. They still hadn't come out of the barn by the time he rolled back out onto the road.

He pulled out his cell phone. The FBI might not give him the time of day, but he could still rattle some cages.

He dialed 911 and asked to be transferred to the local sheriff's department or nearest local law enforcement. After a few moments his call was picked up by a second dispatcher.

He explained the absolute bare bones of the situation, sparing them the full story of why Cressida King was there. He said he had been accompanying her. He'd had to leave. When he'd got back her car was missing and she was nowhere to be found. He was concerned for her safety.

He continued. There had been a note left on their windshield. He lied and said it had contained a threat.

"Sir, do you have any idea who left the note?" the female dispatcher asked.

He gave them the address of the alligator ranch and told them he didn't have an exact name, but explained about recognizing the truck and how the driver seemed to have been stalking them.

"And what about where you saw her last?" the dispatcher asked.

He was sure she wasn't at Adelson's, so there was no point giving that address. He needed to throw a rock into the hornet's nest so he lied for a second time.

49

M imsy hurried down the stairs still in her robe. Exhausted from the previous night, she had gotten home, taken a shower and lain down on her bed to take a nap. She must have fallen into a deep sleep because next thing she knew someone was banging at her front door loud enough to wake the dead.

Her shotgun, the one that been a gift from her daddy, was propped in a corner of the hallway right next to the door. Just in case. It was better to be safe than sorry.

The black guy who'd been with that smartass young girl was still around, so she'd heard. Well, she said to herself, if it was him, he'd get both barrels.

At the bottom of the stairs, she took a moment to compose herself. The banging on the door continued. The lack of manners, these days, was breathtaking. She couldn't have imagined someone thumping their fist against their front door when her daddy was still alive. They wouldn't have dared.

"Hold your horses," she called. She wasn't going to open the door without checking who it was first, and having her shotgun ready, if need be. "Who is it?" she said.

"Miss Murray, it's Deputy Carnes. I'm here with Deputy McGraw. We'd like to speak with you, if we can."

Her stomach did a back flip. She only vaguely recognized the names. They were from the County Sheriff's Department rather than the town's Police Department. Although "Department" was a rather grand description for the two officers they had in Darling who rarely did much more than issue parking tickets. Those two wouldn't have dared to appear at her door like this. But the county had just elected a new sheriff, an outsider from Chicago, or somewhere equally horrendous. She'd met him briefly at the town hall and taken an instant dislike to him.

She left the shotgun where it was and opened the door. "There's really no need to break the door down. I was asleep upstairs."

The two deputies stood on the porch. One was tall and gangly and looked like he'd barely graduated high school. The other, Carnes, was a heavyset man in his forties with a mustache and badly dyed hair.

"We're sorry to disturb you, Miss Murray, but we've had a report of a missing person, and this was the last place she was seen."

Instantly, she knew who they were talking about, and her stomach did another flip. She tried to compose herself.

They couldn't *know*. They couldn't know she had helped run Cressida King off the road and into the swamp, then left her there to die. If they knew, they wouldn't be here asking. If they knew, she wouldn't be missing.

She quickly decided on a strategy. She wouldn't lie. She wouldn't deny the reporter had been here last night. Or, if they probed, that things had gotten heated. But she wouldn't offer them anything more than that.

The reporter and her pal, or whatever he was, had come to dinner. It had been tense. They had left. That was as much as she knew. The only people who could say otherwise were Lyle and RJ. There was no way Lyle would say anything, and she was confident they had put the fear of something into RJ.

Her only concern was Lyle. He got nervous with things like this.

He could slip up without even knowing. She'd call him once she'd dealt with them. Make sure he had his story straight about where he'd been.

RJ knew where this would end if he gave up their secrets. In jail, with Sue Ann left to fend for herself. Mimsy had put down what had happened in the last day or so to a temporary bout of insanity on his part. Once he'd faced a loaded shotgun, and, more troubling, the reality of Sue Ann growing old on her own in worse poverty than she was now, with only a bunch of 'gators for company, he'd sobered up real fast. She expected that now he'd stay that way.

This was routine. That was all it was. What kind of a County Sheriff's Department would it be if the deputies didn't ask some questions of one of the last people to see someone who had gone missing?

"You wouldn't know where she is, Miss Murray, would you?"

"No, I have no idea. I thought they were going back to Adelson Shaw's. That's where they told me they were staying."

She watched their reaction, but they gave nothing away.

"But she and Mr. Johnson were here last night?"

"Yes, they were here for dinner, but then they left together, and that's all I know, really."

"So you didn't see her after that?" the deputy asked, his expression a little more loaded with skepticism, like somehow he knew the answer.

Stay calm, Mimsy, she told herself. Don't let your imagination run away with you. If they knew, they wouldn't be here. Not like this anyway, standing politely on the porch.

"No, I didn't. I'm sorry I can't be of more assistance."

Blank cop faces stared back at her. They were looking for her to keep talking so she shut up, and smiled instead.

Carnes, the older one with the mustache, peered beyond her. Her blood chilled as she remembered the muddy boots she had pulled off when she had gotten back and thrown into the corner of the hallway. Without turning, she could sense that was what he was looking at.

"You've been asleep this whole time?"

"This whole time?" she repeated after him.

"I mean since they left."

Yes, he'd seen the boots. That was what lay behind the question. She couldn't get defensive. That would only serve to make him more suspicious.

"Yes, although there was something after they left."

She had told herself to keep to the bare bones, not to embellish. But she needed to give him some explanation as to why she might have a muddy pair of boots in her otherwise pristine hallway.

Maybe she could turn this little hiccup to her advantage.

"Oh, yes?" said McGraw, the tall gangly deputy, like he didn't believe her.

"Yes," she said firmly. "Maybe a half-hour after, I heard a noise. I put some boots on and went out to investigate."

"By yourself?" McGraw asked.

"I was the only one here. Lyle and Sue Ann had both left at that point."

"Lyle?" asked Carnes.

Mimsy felt her face flush. Now she'd done it. She'd gone and given them details she hadn't needed to.

"Lyle Kincaid. He works at the diner—he was cooking for me. And Sue Ann, she was waiting on us."

"Must be nice to have staff," said Carnes, with a smile that managed to be warm. "If you run into her, just don't tell my wife you can do that."

Mimsy forced a smile in return.

"Okay, well, that's great," Carnes added. He turned to his partner. "Guess we can stop for breakfast after all. That diner's pretty good."

She thought now of Sue Ann. They'd let RJ go home, but his wife would have had questions. The idea of the two deputies speaking to her about the previous evening filled Mimsy with foreboding. She could feel everything spinning out of control.

"Thanks for your time, Miss Murray," said Carnes.

Both men tipped their hats, turned and walked to their patrol car.

Mimsy closed the door. She stared at the muddy boots sitting a few feet away. It would have taken her less than a minute to put them away. But she had been so exhausted by everything.

She guessed there was no point cleaning them now. Not when they were going to get dirty again.

50

"So you don't know anything about any note that was left on her car?"

Over the deputy's shoulders, RJ could see Curious George lying by the pond, staring at the patrol car parked next to the fence. He had crawled out of the water when it had arrived and stayed there, watching it, seemingly fascinated, living up to his nickname.

"RJ?" the deputy prompted.

RJ snapped out of his reverie about the big 'gator. "I already said, didn't I? I don't know about any note. I already had the guy who came over here earlier asking me."

"Well, now we're asking you," said the taller of the two.

"And now I'm telling you what I told him. I didn't see any note, I don't know about any note, and I sure as heck didn't leave any note."

"Okay," said the heavier one. "You see the car? It's a Honda."

"Nope. Ain't seen it," RJ lied.

Of course he had seen it. He'd watched as it sank halfway into the swamp, her with it. It was another picture he would take to his grave with him, along with all the others he had of cutting down Carole Chabon, taking her body out to Devil's Pond and dumping it in the deep water.

"Okay. Well, if you do—"

"I'll be sure and call you," RJ said, cutting him off.

He didn't know how long he could keep being asked these questions. Not because he was scared about lying to the cops, but because the longer it went on, the more he felt like he might start telling the truth.

As he was talking to them, it was as if he could see another RJ telling them everything from all the way back to now.

He'd once seen a TV show about people who had this problem with their brain that meant they just blurted things out, cuss words, things like that. Things they knew they couldn't or shouldn't say. But the more they felt they shouldn't say it, the more they did. It was called Tourette's Syndrome.

That was how he felt right now, like he was on the edge of something like that. Except instead of cussing, he would start shouting the truth, including the evil things he had done, or helped get done.

"I got work to do," he said finally, hoping this would get them moving before he lost his mind entirely.

"Okay. Well, if you see anything," the older deputy said, handing him a card, "give us a call."

Years without anyone giving him a business card, and now he'd had two in one morning. He took it, and tucked it into his pocket with the other.

He and George watched the deputies walk back to their patrol car and get in. George seemed a lot sadder to see them go than he was. He scuttled up to the fence, and pressed the tip of his snout against it, his teeth on show the way he did sometimes, like the world was one big joke he couldn't help smiling at.

RJ was just happy that Sue Ann hadn't been there. She'd had to go to work.

He walked over to Curious George, and hunkered down next to the fence. It was strange: he knew this animal could kill him with ease but he had never, not for a moment, been afraid of him. Careful, sure, but not scared.

Truth be told, Mimsy scared him more than any alligator. She was more cunning for a start.

After a minute, he straightened up. His mind flashed back on the car, and the woman who'd been trapped inside.

He had a thought. *Save her.* He pushed it away.

It stayed there. Nagging at him. He tried again to dismiss it. He couldn't. Now it was there, he couldn't rid his mind of it.

He cursed himself. A conscience was a burden.

He pulled his pack of smokes from his shirt pocket and lit one. He took a deep draw. He only ever smoked when Sue Ann was at work. They didn't have the money for cigarettes, yet when he was really stressed it was about the only thing that calmed his nerves.

What if he stumbled across the car? By accident.

She was probably already dead from the crash anyway. He thought he'd heard Lyle say she was alive, but she couldn't last long out there.

He could drive down. Take a look.

He didn't have to decide anything now. There was no harm in looking, was there?

51

T y parked the Ford across from the library and got out. There was a commotion outside the diner. He went down the sidewalk and joined the back of a small knot of people who were gathered outside. He braced himself for bad news. Murmurs of a body being found.

"My belly thinks my throat's been cut."

"What's the matter with him, anyway?"

"I was looking forward to some of those pancakes all morning."

He quickly established that Lyle, the short-order cook, hadn't shown up for work, leaving a sidewalk full of disgruntled, and hungry, customers.

Across the street, a County Sheriff's Department patrol car was parked. A few hundred yards further down there was another.

Ty had worried about the response to his call, but from what he'd seen driving around, conducting his own search, they had taken his report that Cressida was missing with the seriousness it deserved. Of course, their response could also have been down to his making a phone call to Gregg, her editor, in New York. He had presumably made his own calls after he had finished what had been a fraught conversation with Ty.

"What do you mean she's missing? You're supposed to be there to make sure nothing happens."

That had been the editor's first response to the news. Ty didn't blame him. He told him about the traffic stop and how he suspected his drink had been spiked. But he wasn't making excuses. If anything had happened to her, as far as he was concerned it was on him.

One lesson Ty had taken from his military service was that responsibility meant accepting the blame as well as the glory. So far in all of this there had been little glory, and plenty of blame.

He left the hungry diner patrons, and dodged through traffic into the library. It was a huge long shot, but he was running out of places to check. Maybe Cressida had snuck back in. She had been curious about the room down in the basement that had been barricaded behind boxes.

It still didn't explain why there was no sign of the car, but he figured it had to be a possibility.

Miss Parsons was behind the desk. She seemed surprised to see him.

"I'm looking for Miss King. She hasn't been here this morning, has she?"

The librarian got up. "No. Why? Is something wrong?"

Ty wasn't sure if she was serious. Most of the County Sheriff's Department was crawling over Darling, and the librarian seemed not to have noticed.

"Yes, she's missing. You haven't heard?"

She took off her reading glasses and put them down, getting up from behind the desk. "Oh, is that what all the commotion outside is about?"

She sounded concerned, but her smirk told a different story. She seemed to be enjoying this.

Ty had neither the time nor the patience for games right now. Or passive-aggressive bullshit, for that matter.

"Do you mind if I take a look in the basement?"

She smiled. "Be my guest."

He walked past her. Her face wore the same self-satisfied smirk as he opened the door, flicked on the light at the top and started down the stairs.

Ty was wasting his time and he knew it. But he didn't know what else to do, apart from keep driving around, or sit in the Ford and wait for a call to say she'd been found, dead or alive. His first real solo gig, and he'd messed up in a way that was off the scale. Outwitted by a racist grandma and a bunch of rednecks.

The desk where Cressida had been working was strewn with papers and notes. He gathered up her notes, leaving the old newspapers and press cuttings.

He walked across to the door that had been blocked by the stack of boxes. He lifted one of the last boxes and moved it to the side.

Above him he heard the door at the top of the steps slam shut. Then he heard it being locked.

Ty put down the box and headed up the stairs, more irritated than anything. The librarian had locked him down here. It was a childish gesture.

He tried the handle. It turned but didn't open. He rattled it a few times.

52

Lock looked up at the departures board in Grantley Adams International Airport. It was showing column after column of cancelled flights. He had been there for pushing three hours now, and his flight had already been delayed twice.

The word was that a storm was working its way toward the Windward Isles, disrupting both in- and outbound flights. He had tried making some calls to see if any private jets were operating, but they were subject to the same restrictions.

A tropical storm provided equal-opportunity delays. It didn't matter whether you had a billion dollars and a Learjet or were going to be tucked up in economy with your knees to your chest, air-traffic control was taking no chances.

He walked back to the check-in desk where two polite Bajans were busy dealing with a scrum of irate passengers, who had failed to grasp that there was little they could do.

A few people from his flight had already given up, and walked outside to take a cab back to their hotel, grab some rum punch and hunker down for the high winds and lashing rain that were forecast to hit at any time.

Under normal circumstances he would have done the same and

been grateful. These were not normal circumstances. Ty was out there in Florida, and things had taken a downward turn. He needed to get out of Barbados.

Lock looked back at the departures board as the status of his flight flashed a change. The word "delayed" was replaced by "cancelled". It looked like his partner was on his own, and there was nothing he could do about it.

53

R J eased his truck to a stop. He still didn't know if this was the right thing to do. The past few days had felt like a much more intense continuation of his life. To speak or remain silent? To do what he knew in his heart and mind was right, or protect the woman he loved?

The young black woman, the brooding presence of the man escorting her and a spiral of events had left the choice urgent and stark. He had no idea if she was alive or dead. He didn't know either how that would change what he had to do now.

If she was dead most people, if they were being honest, would tell him to leave the whole thing alone. Not get involved. After all, nothing he could do would bring her back, not under that circumstance.

RJ didn't think he agreed. Knowing where a dead person was, or having no idea and living with that doubt, were two very different things for their loved ones.

And if she was still alive? Then his decision was made for him.

He had thought about it on the drive. He might not even have to implicate anyone. He could claim he had happened upon the car. It would be a stroke of good fortune rather than a grave betrayal.

Yes, he thought, as he climbed down from the truck cab. That was how he would play it. As a chance encounter. He was just driving along when he'd noticed something sitting in the swamp that didn't look right. Maybe the sun had caught the windshield and he'd seen the glare. That could be it. That was plausible.

He walked back down the road to where Mimsy and Lyle had tried to conceal where the Honda had taken off and gone into the water.

He had to hand it to Mimsy, she and Lyle had done a pretty good job. Things might be easy to see, as long as you knew what you were looking for, but most people would have driven straight past this thirty-yard stretch of road without so much as a second glance.

He stepped off the road, moving a broken branch out of his way, and walked toward the edge of the swamp. The car was there, exactly as it had been, passenger side down, submerged in the water, the other half sticking out above the waterline. The front had concertinaed in, but besides that it was in fairly decent shape.

Raising his hand over his eyebrows to shield the sun's glare, he peered at the cabin. It was empty. It was only then that he saw her, stretched out across the driver's-side door panels. One arm hung limply over the edge.

She looked like some old painting you'd see in a fancy museum. A deathbed scene. A beautiful maiden laid out to die, maybe after drinking poison. Only instead of her body being arranged over some fancy red-velvet couch she was lying on top of a car in the middle of a swamp, quietly frying in the heat as the insects feasted on her.

No, he thought, he couldn't leave someone like that. It wasn't right. No more than leaving Carole Chabon hanging from that tree, like strange fruit.

It wasn't just that it wasn't right. It wasn't decent. That was the word his momma would have used, God rest her soul.

He stood there for a moment, staring at her, and thinking about how wasteful all of this was. Another young woman who only wanted to do something good was dead.

Then she moved.

54

"Hey, can you open this?" Ty called again, rattling the handle for effect, only to be met by silence.

He took a half-step back and almost lost his footing. She was there. He could hear her moving around, no doubt enjoying every second of his frustration.

"I could just shoot the lock clean off," he shouted, anger starting to rise a little in his voice. "I don't want to do that, but I will if I have to."

She had stopped moving. He couldn't hear any more soft footfalls. But there was a different sound emanating from the other side of the basement door.

He pressed his ear to it. He could hear her talking, but not to him. It sounded like she was on the phone to someone.

It didn't take him long to figure out who she was speaking with.

"Yes, he was going crazy. I managed to lock him in the basement. Yes, he has a gun. Can you get someone here?" she was saying.

Ty rolled his eyes. From childish to pathetic. She was trying to get him arrested. Cast him as the angry black man threatening the little old white lady.

She must have hung up because she stopped talking. Ty stayed silent, listening. She started speaking again, it sounded like another call, but this time the panic was gone from her voice, replaced by a tone that was cool and calculating.

"Mimsy, yes, it's me," she said.

She was speaking more quietly, aware that he might be listening, not wanting him to hear this call.

"Yes, you were right. He's here."

Ty cursed under his breath. "You mother—"

"Yes, yes, they're on their way," Miss Parsons said. "No, it's really no trouble. I'll make sure he doesn't go anywhere."

Hearing her say that did something to Ty. He was beyond rage now with her, with this town and its mealy-mouthed residents, who smiled to your face while they planned your death. It was done. If she or anyone else thought he would go gently, they were about to be proven very wrong.

He felt himself shifting into a different mental state. One he hadn't experienced in a while.

Back in the Marines one of his buddies had had a name for it. He'd called it Berserker Mode. It was a place of focused warfare where everything fell away other than the primary objective.

Right now his objective was to get the hell out of there. Ty pulled his SIG Sauer P226 clear, and made sure he had one in the chamber. He called out a warning to anyone who might be on the other side of the door, and squeezed the trigger.

He watched as the wood around the lock splintered. He took another half-step to the side, adjusting his angle, and squeezed off another round. This one took out the lock dead centre.

He holstered the SIG and shouldered the door open. He walked out, shoulders hunched, head on a swivel.

The librarian was nowhere to be seen. He started toward the long desk.

He kept his steps heavy. It had the desired effect. There was movement.

A black-shod foot protruded from under the desk. Ty walked over and pulled out the chair she'd dragged under the desk to help conceal her position. He tapped her heel with his toe of his boot. Just hard enough to get her attention.

She didn't move.

"Get up before I pick you up," he told her.

"Please," she was saying. "Please don't."

She scooted herself out backwards on her hands and knees. He reached down with a shovel-hand and helped her to her feet.

"It's Mimsy. She . . ."

Ty shook his head, slow and deliberate. She quietened down.

The begging started up again. "Please, I have . . ."

He looked at her with total contempt. "You think I'd shoot you, in cold blood? Murder you right here?"

She was crying, big fat tears rolling down her cheeks.

"You people are right about one thing," said Ty. "I'm not like you, and I pray I never will be."

He turned and strode out of the library, shoulders back, chest out, head high, mind still set firmly to Berserker Mode.

55

Cressida had heard people speak about the will to live—the ability of a human being to summon the mental fortitude to keep themselves alive when their body wanted to give in. Back in New York she had interviewed an army ranger who had been blown up while serving in Iraq. He had tourniqueted the stumps of his own legs to keep from bleeding out, and survived for almost four hours before he could be medevac-ed to safety.

When she had asked him how he had managed to push through the pain and suffering to survive, he had looked her straight in the eye, and said, "I just decided I wasn't going to give those assholes the satisfaction of watching me die."

At the time she remembered asking herself if life was as simple as deciding to keep going.

She had taken him at his word. Now she wasn't so sure. She wasn't willing death, but she was in so much pain and so thirsty that she would have taken almost any relief right now. And death had to be the ultimate relief, an eternal black void of nothingness.

Pain was her present. So was thirst. And right now the present sucked.

Then, from nowhere, she could feel eyes on her. Human eyes.

Not that she could see anyone. Not at first. But she knew someone was there. On the bank, by the road. Looking at her.

She had been lying flat on her back because it took some of the pressure off a searing pain that ran from her lower back all the way up her spine and into her neck. Her leg was still unforgiving, as bad as it had been all night.

She could feel her skin burning, and the dryness in her mouth made calling out impossible. Her throat felt swollen, so did her sinuses, and her face burned hot from the sun.

Part of her hoped to lose consciousness, for the decision to be taken out of her hands. It hadn't happened. She had stayed awake and tortured by the pain.

She tried to get onto her side so that she could face the bank and get a glimpse of whoever she could feel looking at her. Shifting her hips set off another knife-jab of pain that trapped her next breath in her chest.

Trying again, she managed to move an inch or two. She put down her hand and immediately drew it back as the car panel burned her palm.

Reaching over with her other hand, she pulled on the sleeve of her jacket so that it covered the palm of her hand, her dress riding up over her belly. She managed to get her hand down, and move her hips so that she was partly on her side.

Narrowing her eyes, she scanned the bank. No one was there. Not that she could see. Her mind had been playing tricks on her.

She looked from the bank to the trees, then to the water surrounding the car with its pop ash and reeds. The 'gator was still there, unmoving, sunk half into the mud, keeping cool while she baked. Waiting for its moment.

Part of her thought about sliding down from the car into the cool water. Allowing whatever would happen next to happen. But the primal part of her, the lizard part that lay at the base of every human brain, held her back.

There was sound now. A low hum, like an engine, but not a car engine. More like a boat of some kind. It was far off in the distance but she could hear it.

This time she decided not to get her hopes raised. A second ago she was sure someone was watching her from the bank only to look and see no one there. Maybe the sound of the boat was another piece of her imagination that had broken off and floated to the front of her mind.

RJ HAD RETREATED BACK to his truck. He dropped the tailgate, and climbed up to sort through his gear. He had rope, an ax, some camping gear, spare oil, and some offcuts of lumber.

In the cab he also had his shotgun, and a hunting rifle.

It might just be enough to get himself out there, get her off the car, and back to the road. He could use the shotgun on the 'gators if he needed to. There weren't many who would hang around if you put a round near them, never mind in them. They were scavengers, opportunists.

The only ones you had to worry about were the ones you didn't see when the water was too deep. Then no amount of firepower would save you. They could glide on up, and take you at the knee, drag you under and spin you in that death roll. Up close and personal, a man was no match for a big 'gator, even with a shotgun.

He grabbed the rope, the ax, a couple of metal tent stakes and the shotgun. He started back to the bank. He would plant the stakes in the ground, and wade out with the rope, tie it off on the car, and that would give him a line to hang onto as he dragged her back.

Any 'gator made a move and he would clear it out with the shotgun. One good blast would be sufficient to buy him the time required to get her back onto dry land.

He could call the cops. He had thought about that. But he needed to be the first to her.

He didn't know what she had or hadn't seen. What she would or wouldn't say.

If he saved her perhaps he could persuade her that was sufficient. She would owe him, and the price he would charge was her silence.

She could tell people it was a regular car crash, a temporary loss of control on an unfamiliar road. If she said it, they would believe her. She could go back to New York, and they could return to their lives. No one need ever know.

Silence in return for a life. It seemed like a bargain when he thought of it like that.

He stepped back off the road, and started scoping out where to place the tent stakes. He needed somewhere they would hold but also somewhere close to the water's edge so that he could keep a good hold of the rope on the way back.

He heard the deep bass whir of the airboat. It was coming in. He couldn't see it yet, but it was a sound he was familiar with.

He stood stock still, scanned the swamp and watched as a wash of water rose toward the bank. The boat rounded a stand of pop ash trees about fifty yards out from the car.

RJ saw who was onboard, and bile rose from his stomach to bite the back of his throat. Lyle was piloting it in while Mimsy stood behind him. They were headed straight for the half-submerged car.

Profanity spilled from RJ's mouth. He turned tail and hustled back up the bank, seeking cover before they saw him. Halfway up, he threw himself onto the ground. He turned belly down and watched as the boat's engine cut out and it inched in closer to the Honda.

56

R*escue.*

Cressida didn't know of a word that had ever sounded sweeter. There was a boat and it was heading straight for her. It had a huge fan mounted in a cage on the back that whipped up the water behind it as it glided nearer.

A boat rescue made sense, she thought. There would be contact with the water, however shallow. No worry about 'gators, or snakes, or anything else lurking nearby.

The pain in her leg seemed to recede a little. It was the same sensation a person might have when they'd just been given some powerful painkillers. Before they could even hit the stomach, the pain would dull as the mind anticipated what was to come.

Hope had to be the most powerful drug of all. Especially if you feared it was gone for good.

She could already envision being plucked from the car, strapped into a seat, or laid out on a deck. *Water.* There would be water. Then something to dull the hot poker that she felt had been somehow inserted into the marrow of her leg.

A trip in an ambulance, sirens blaring. People with her. More water, probably an IV with fluids to replace all the salts that had washed out in sweat. Oxygen, maybe. Being able to lie down on a gurney, shielded from the baking sun. A cool, dark womb with all manner of modern technology plugged in, restoring her.

Then a hospital room. In Miami. With more water and then, when her stomach had settled, some food. And a television so she could watch her own rescue on the news – heroic reporter almost killed tracking down cold-case murderers.

There would be police. Maybe even FBI agents. Oh, the delight she would take in telling them what she knew.

Maybe someone would bring in her laptop after a few days and she could set to work on the story. Only it was no longer a long article on a website. This was more *New York Times*, *Washington Post*, maybe even a book. No, definitely a book. The story of her aunt and then herself. Justice delayed but not denied.

But first, water. Sweet, cold, fresh water.

With each new part of the fantasy she was building in her imagination, she felt better. She was going to make it. She was going to live.

She tried again to raise herself on her elbow. It looked like there were two people on board. The sun was behind them. She could see them only in silhouette. They both looked large, and doughy, not like park rangers or cops.

But what did that matter? As long as they had a boat and could get her to land, they could be dressed up as Santa Claus or the Easter bunny for all she cared.

As long as they got her off the side of this damn car. Before the bugs that were still swarming around had eaten her straight down to the bones.

The boat's fan cut out and the breeze it had brought died down. The water became still again. She could see a man on the boat. He had stood up, and was making his way to the side. The other person onboard seemed to be steering it in.

It was coming in side on to the underside of the car.

She tried to push off with her hands, and get some leverage to sit up. That way he could help her swing over, and drop down into the boat. If he put his hands under her armpits she could ease down without jacking up her bad leg again.

They were talking to each other. In whispers. That struck Cressida as strange.

She blinked salty sweat from her eyes, and tried to focus.

She saw their faces for the first time.

No, she told herself, it can't be. She was imagining it. It couldn't be them. They had left her out here to die.

Why would they come back like this? Why would they return to the scene of the crime? What sense did that make?

Inch by inch the boat edged closer. Bringing Mimsy Murray with it.

They were close enough that she could see Mimsy smiling at her. It was that same damn faux-concerned smile as before. A smile that she already knew was a harbinger of bad things to come.

Cressida tried to scoot back down the side of the car toward the rear driver's-side door. The pain was too immediate, and she knew that a few more feet and she would run out of room.

The man, Lyle she remembered his name was, was reaching out his arms to her. "Come on, let's get you off this thing." He turned back to Mimsy. "Get it in closer."

The boat inched down, bringing him with it. He lunged for her, and she almost slipped off the car. He grabbed her wrist, and began to pull her with him.

She tried to break his grip. It was no contest. He was way too strong. He dragged her along the side of the car. He reached out his other hand and managed to grab her at the waist. He hooked his arm around her, and hauled her off the car.

He almost lost his balance. He fell back, and she landed on top of him, catching her bad leg. She screamed.

He struggled, getting back on top of her. His knee dug into her stomach. As he scrambled back up, his knee forced all the air from her lungs. She reached down to her bad leg, almost sobbing again with the pain.

"Oh, don't be such a baby," said Mimsy, staring down at her with that same smile.

Lyle moved out of the way. The engine started up, the fan whipping round faster and faster until it was spinning so fast it was a static blur.

Mimsy reached down, and lifted Cressida. She placed her in one of the two rear seats.

"Let's get out of here," Mimsy instructed Lyle.

The boat was moving off, skirting round the car, and sending a shallow wave crashing all the way back to the road. The prow pointed out, away from land. It began to skip over the surface of the water, weaving in and around the pop ash trees.

Mimsy reached down into a cooler, coming up with a bottle of water. She twisted off the cap and handed it to Cressida. "Small sips," she told her.

Cress lifted the bottle to her lips as land disappeared behind them. Now there was only swamp on every side. They kept moving. She snuck a look at Mimsy who caught her in the act.

"You didn't think we'd just leave you there, did you?" she said to Cressida, in a way that chilled her to the very core.

57

The Ford rode up on two wheels, threatening to flip, as Ty threw it into the corner. The sirens were more distant. But they were still coming.

With arrest a near certainty now, he was heading for Mimsy's house. If anyone knew what had happened to Cressida it had to be her. He planned on getting her to talk, one way or the other.

She would cough up where Cressida was, and he would deal with the consequences of how he'd got the information later on. If it meant prison time, then so be it. He had already made his peace with that. He had been lucky enough to dodge that fate after events in Long Beach. Maybe there was only so long you could face up the law before the law faced *you* up.

His cell phone rang. It looked like a local number but it wasn't one he recognized.

If he'd had to guess he would have said it was the cops trying to save themselves the inconvenience of chasing him around southern Florida. If it was, they were likely to be disappointed.

He eased his foot off the gas and answered.

"Ty Johnson."

"Mr. Johnson. It's RJ."

RJ?

"We spoke this morning."

"I remember, but I'm kind of busy right now, RJ. Is it important?"

"I'd say it is. I found your friend, but she's in trouble."

Ty took his phone away from his ear and did a double-take. He checked his rearview mirror for red flashing lights behind him. Now would not be a good time to be apprehended. It was clear. The only thing he could see behind him was the dust from his tires.

"Where is she?"

"You know the dock with the airboats. It's out between Adelson's and my place."

Ty had a vague idea.

"Kind of."

"You think you can find it?"

He looked around. "I'm not sure."

"Okay, where are you now."

He scanned the road for some kind of landmark. A sign that looked like something from the 1950s. A mailbox with a family name on it. Anything.

He kept the Ford rolling. Up ahead was a gas station. He relayed the information to RJ.

"Okay, you're real close. There's a turning on your left about a quarter-mile on down. Take that, and when you come to the fork, go left. It's at the end of that road."

"Left and left at the fork," Ty repeated.

"That's it."

"Is she there?"

"Just meet me there," said RJ. Then he was gone.

58

The Ford skidded to a halt, gravel and stones spinning up into the air. The driver's door exploded open, and Ty got out. He looked around the rickety old dock, scanning the half-dozen boats that were either bobbing gently in the water at their moorings, or loaded onto trailers on the nearby grass.

RJ's pickup truck with the Confederate-flag bumper sticker was there, but no sign of the man. Ty kept one hand on the butt of his SIG, on edge and wary that this could be a trap. If Cressida was here he couldn't see her either, or the Honda for that matter.

"Hey, over here!"

RJ's head popped up from behind one of the huge airboat propellers.

Ty walked down the dock towards him. "So where is she?"

RJ nodded out to the wetlands beyond the dock. "Somewhere out there."

"What the hell are you talking about? What do you mean she's out there?" said Ty.

"Listen, we don't have time to talk about it now. I was just making sure I had enough gas," he said, lifting a five-gallon red metal container. "Get on board. I'll explain what's happened on the way."

Ty held his ground for a minute. "If you're messing me around . .
." he said.

"I know, you'll kill me."

"That's what I'll do if you're lucky."

RJ hauled himself up into the airboat's elevated pilot's seat. "Like I
said, we don't have time."

Sirens whooped somewhere off in the distance as the sheriff's
deputies criss-crossed the roads around Darling, hunting for Ty. It
didn't seem like he had much of a choice.

He couldn't stay there without them catching up with him. And
he had no useful lead or idea where Cressida was, other than the
man in front of him who was telling him he knew, kind of.

It was this or try to get to Mimsy before the cops got to him.

RJ stared at him, frustrated. "I can't do this on my own, man."

"Do what?"

"Get your friend away from Mimsy."

That was enough. Ty clambered into the shallow fiberglass-
hulled craft, RJ sitting above him.

"Stay in the middle," RJ told him. "These things tip real easy."

He flicked three switches on the engine-control panel to his right-
hand side on and then off. He pressed a rubber-domed button, like
he was priming a lawnmower. The engine choked into life. The
propeller started to turn, picking up revolutions rapidly.

RJ tapped gently on the metal pedal and the airboat took off,
skimming over muddy-green water, pushing reeds out of the way as it
moved out and into the Everglades.

The din from the engine was deafening for the first few seconds.
Then it seemed to die down slightly. Ty remembered that the original
airboats, as the name suggested, used aircraft propellers and engines.
He'd seen them once while on duty in Iraq, in the southern part of
the country, an area that had been one of the largest wetland areas in
the world until all-round asshole Saddam Hussein had ordered most
of it drained, destroying the ancient way of life of many Marsh Arabs
in the process.

RJ leaned down as he expertly moved the stick that controlled the vertical rudders at the back, which directed the airflow and thus the direction of travel. Watching him, Ty noticed that when he pushed the stick forward they moved right, and when he moved it back they went left.

"Oh, one more thing, these things don't have any brakes, so if you see anything holler, and holler loud. I'll ease up on the gas and we can cruise back round."

Ty knew there had to be a reason why he'd never had the urge to travel by airboat before. It was pretty much an aircraft propeller hooked up to a big engine, and stuck to the back of a big chunk of fiberglass. If it hit anything solid it would sink like a rock into the swamp.

It was only now that he realized neither he nor RJ was wearing a life jacket. Not that the water looked deep, but he was sure that could change as they got further out.

He twisted round so he could shout up to RJ. "So why do you think she's out here with Mimsy?"

"I don't think, I know. I saw Mimsy and Lyle pick her up and put her on Lyle's boat."

"What?" shouted Ty.

"If I tell you what happened, promise not to take it out on me? I didn't much like the way you were hanging on to that gun when you got here."

"I'm not promising anything," said Ty. "Either tell me or don't."

They had moved out into a carpet of sawgrass. It extended far off into the horizon.

"Last night, I guess your reporter friend was out looking for some answers. Mimsy and Lyle ran her car off the road into the swamp. Then they left her there to die, covered up where she left the road so no one would notice it."

"She was trapped in the car?"

"Not exactly," said RJ. "She was pretty banged up from what I saw, but I think she was more worried about one of the 'gators picking her off on the way back to the road. I was about to get her out of there when Mimsy and Lyle showed up and took her."

"Wait a minute," said Ty. "You knew she was there, but you only went to rescue her just now?"

RJ tugged at the brim of his John Deere cap, pulling it down lower over his eyes. "Guess my conscience got to me."

"And what about Mimsy?" Ty asked.

"I guess once she saw all the sheriff's deputies crawling all over the place she figured it was only a matter of time."

"So her and Lyle . . ."

"They're taking her somewhere she won't be found."

"And you know where that is?"

RJ dug into his breast pocket for some chewing tobacco. He offered some to Ty, who waved it off. "I have an idea, yes."

"So where are they taking her?"

"Devil's Pond," said RJ. "It's way out here about fifteen miles or so. It's an old sinkhole pond. Lots of 'gators too. That's if you don't drown first."

"And how does Mimsy know about this place? Doesn't sound like much of a tourist attraction."

"Oh, it's not, believe me."

"So how does she know that's where to take someone?"

"I told her about it, a long time ago."

"And how did you know?"

RJ plugged a wad of tobacco into the corner of his cheek. He didn't answer. He just stared out over the vast expanse of sawgrass that sprouted from the water, a floating green carpet of nothingness.

"How did you know?" Ty shouted.

"I know because it's where I took Carole Chabon's body after they lynched her."

59

"Over here. Carnes, over here."

Deputy McGraw scrambled frantically back up toward the road, almost tripping over a cypress branch in his haste. He waved his hands, beckoning to Carnes.

"I found it," he shouted to his partner.

They had been driving down that stretch of road on their way to old man Shaw's to see if the big black guy, Johnson, was there. And to warn old Adelson Shaw to keep his doors locked and call if he saw him.

They had no idea what had got the man so heated as to take a shot at Miss Parsons, but it was looking like they had their answer to what might have happened to Cressida King. Who knew what a man who'd take a shot at a little old librarian was capable of?

That was the theory they were working on now, anyway. Who the heck knew what had been going on between those two, the reporter and her so-called bodyguard, before or since they'd arrived in town?

Not only had the big guy been arrested for DUI, there had been a pretty bad incident in California. Firearms had been involved, but some fancy legal work seemed to have gotten him off the hook. Well, their boss had told the deputies when they'd assembled for a quick briefing, that kind of thing might fly in Long Beach, California, but it sure wasn't the way things worked in little ole Darling, Florida, or anywhere in Florida for that matter.

"Blue lives matter," the sheriff had told them. "That means if you see him with a gun, don't hesitate to do what you have to do."

So they had been a few miles short of Adelson Shaw's when McGraw had noticed branches that had been torn down from a couple of cypress and pop ash trees, and scattered at the top of the bank. 'Gators didn't do that kind of thing. Nor did any other animal around here, apart from humans. It was way too green to burn, didn't make for good kindling. It just didn't make any sense.

Carnes had eye-rolled the younger deputy but indulged him. They were in no particular rush. Let someone else find an armed Marine who'd gone crazy was what Carnes figured. He was ten years off his pension and not looking to be a hero. There was a reason he'd taken the job down here, and that was because it was quiet, and you were likely to make it long enough to collect that pension and go fishing every day.

Carnes waddled over to McGraw, a little on edge, ready to draw his weapon, hoping he still remembered how to shoot the damn thing properly and wishing he'd spent more time at the gun range, like the other cops.

"What is it?"

"The car. I found it."

Gingerly, Carnes picked his way over the branches. He stood on the bank and looked to where McGraw was pointing. Yup, that was it. The rental car they'd been driving around town.

"You think they're still in there?" he asked McGraw.

The car was lying on its side, half sunk into the muddy water. McGraw scooted down the bank, trying to get a better angle to look into the cabin.

He looked back up at Carnes. "I don't know. I can't see anyone."

"Okay. Well, let's call it in," Carnes told him.

"Wait!" McGraw shouted suddenly, scrambling further along the bank. "What the hell's this?"

His hand rested on the blade of an ax that had been stuck, stake-like, into the ground. For a second Carnes had visions of that big Marine charging around the swamp with an ax. Or killing the reporter with it before driving the car into the swamp.

He pulled himself back to reality. A missing person, and his imagination had taken over. He needed to get a grip on himself.

McGraw was still looking around for clues, stomping all over an accident scene, maybe a murder scene, with his big old boots.

"Come on," said Carnes, getting exasperated. "We ain't investigators. This right here is way above my pay grade. We need to call it in."

McGraw wasn't for moving. He was like a bloodhound who'd just caught a scent and wasn't for coming back, no matter how hard you whistled. He reached down, rolled up his pants legs, and started for the edge of the water.

"McGraw! What the hell are you doing?"

"What do you think?" said McGraw, grimacing as he waded into the slimy green water. "There could be someone in there." He bobbed his head toward the car.

"Hey!" said Carnes.

McGraw stopped.

Carnes pointed at a clump of cypress where a 'gator was sunning itself, taking in the show. McGraw stood there for a moment, obviously torn between his heroics and his fear of what might happen if the 'gator made a move.

"Don't be a damn fool," Carnes chided.

McGraw finally took the hint. He waded the few steps back to the bank, climbed back onto the grass, and shook the water off his boots as best he could.

He squelched back to Carnes, stopped again, and hunkered down, trying to find an angle where he could see into the cabin. "Looks empty," he said.

Carnes tapped his partner's elbow and indicated they should get back onto the road. "Come on. Looks like we might have a real manhunt on our hands," he said, with a final glance back toward the ax.

"You think?" McGraw said, his excitement spilling over into a broad grin.

60

Mimsy had taken Lyle's place in the pilot's seat. She sat atop the airboat, stick in hand, looking, to Cressida, like some mad English queen of old, ready to order her enemy's execution with the drop of her handkerchief.

Lyle was sitting on the row of seats below Mimsy, a shotgun tucked between his thighs, which strained the seams of his denim jeans. Cressida was next to him, an empty seat between them. He looked like he'd rather be anywhere else in the world. She knew how he felt.

She had already sipped her way through one bottle of water. She held it up and shook it. "Do you have any more?" she asked.

Lyle began to reach for a cooler that was tucked in under one of the seats. "Here, I got you."

"No, Lyle," Mimsy said. "No more water until later."

Cressida was still thirsty. It wasn't that trade-your-life-for-a-sip kind of thirsty but she still wanted more.

She decided not to argue. There was no point. And she wanted to see if she could work on Lyle somehow. Gain his sympathy. Perhaps make him change his mind.

As soon as they had set a course further into the Everglades, Cressida had realized what was up. They weren't saving her. They'd have taken her back to Darling if they had been. By now she would have been living the fevered fantasy she'd had less than an hour ago. Or the first part of it, anyway.

Lyle reached into his breast pocket and pulled out a pack of Marlboro Reds. Cressida eyed them. She hadn't smoked in a long time. Now she could use one.

He tapped two out and offered one to her, palming it over so that Mimsy wouldn't see. It was an offer that had the ring of the condemned woman. He fished out a cheap plastic lighter.

Mimsy's hand reached down and slapped the lighter from his hand. It fell onto the shallow deck of the boat and skittled under the seat. "You can have one on the way back. Not before," she chided him.

He shrank down into the seat again. Cressida had an urge to reach down, grab the lighter, light up and blow smoke rings in Mimsy's face. If Mimsy was going to be the road-trip mom from hell, Cressida could play the rebellious teenager.

Repressing the urge – what would it get her other than maybe tied up? – she shot a sympathetic smile in Lyle's direction. She needed to get him on her side. Maybe not even that much. Just to a point where he wouldn't be willing to go along with whatever Mimsy had planned.

The way back. Cressida had a feeling that she wasn't part of the plan for the return leg. Not that anything had been said. But it didn't take a genius to work out that this wasn't a nature trip. They planned on killing her and leaving her out here.

Just like they had with Carole. Just like, no doubt, they had with Timothy French.

Rehydrating had given her back some of her faculties. Her leg still screamed with pain at every twist and turn the boat took but her mind was functioning.

Think, Cress, think. How are you going to make this work?

The shotgun was the obvious move. But Lyle was big, not in great shape like Ty, but size counted in a fight. Even more if she had to attempt to wrestle the long gun from him.

She closed her eyes for a second, trying to visualize how she could make this work.

She would have to either kill or get one of them off the boat. She'd need the other to get her back to land. If they both went out of the boat, or she shot them, she'd be almost back to square one again. Maybe worse. On top of the car she'd been in sight of land and a road.

Out here no one would find her. Likely not in time anyway.

The landscape had changed in the past minute. From the open plains of water-rooted sawgrass, the vegetation had become thicker. Every few yards it seemed there was a fresh stand of cypress or pop ash trees, branches bowed to the water. Cressida imagined it would make spotting the tiny boat from the air close to impossible. All it would take would be for them to squeeze through a stand of cypress on either side and a spotter would miss them entirely.

Yes, she would need one of them to get her back. Assuming they both knew the route they were taking, and also assuming she had a choice, it was a no-brainer. Queen Mimsy back there could meet her maker out here.

There was a poetic justice to it. The thought made Cressida smile.

Okay, she told herself, so kill one, and keep the gun on the other.

But how?

She would have one shot. She knew that.

She had to wait for the right moment. A second of distraction, a window of time where she could go for the gun, or maybe even tip one of them into the water.

And if that moment never arrived? Then she would have to engineer it. Create some kind of distraction.

She opened her eyes again. Lyle wasn't sitting in the seat. He had moved. Now he was standing at the big scooped prow of the boat. He had the shotgun trained on her chest.

A hand tapped her shoulder from above.

"Not long now," said Mimsy.

Cressida twisted around so she could see her. "Where are we

going?" she asked Mimsy, doing her best to sound casual, like this was a little pleasure ride.

"Oh," said Mimsy. "I think you'll find it fascinating." She let out a little laugh, as if she was amused by her punchline before she had even delivered it. "Let's just say it's a site of great historical interest."

Cressida knew what she was talking about. It had to be the place they'd dumped her great-aunt after they'd lynched her. It was likely where Timothy French had ended up too. "I think you might be surprised by how interested people are in murder," she shot back.

Mimsy grinned. She obviously got a kick out of the jousting— when she had the whip hand, of course. Take away Lyle's shotgun, and Cressida doubted she'd be having as good a time right now.

"Murder involves killing another human being," said Mimsy. "I'm not sure your kind qualifies."

61

U p ahead, the blaze of sawgrass that seemed to Ty to have extended all the way to the end of the earth gave way to a dense jungle of trees and vines. It looked more Louisiana bayou than Florida Everglades. As they closed in on it, he was glad of RJ's expertise.

Not all the trees still stood. Some had fallen into the water, blocking the path of even a craft like this. The airboat was making sense to him now. With no parts below the waterline and a shallow flat bottom it couldn't run aground. A regular craft, anything apart from a rowboat, would have been in trouble within seconds in terrain like this.

RJ eased his foot off the pedal. The boat slowed, the propeller noise fading to something closer to a whisper. Their own momentum kept it moving forward as RJ scanned the water ahead, deftly moving the stick back and forth to adjust the vertical rudders and shift direction.

"How far have we got to go?" said Ty.

RJ took off his John Deere cap and swiped the sweat from his brow, then tucked it back on his head. "Couldn't say exactly. Been a while since I've been out this way."

Ty didn't say anything to that.

"Can't say I've missed it either," RJ added.

"Listen, whatever you tell me out here, it can stay between us," said Ty, unsure if he'd be as good as his word on this particular promise.

"Like Vegas?" smiled RJ.

"Something like that. What happened back then? I mean, what really happened? I know Carole Chabon was lynched and you dumped her out here. I also know that Mimsy was up to her neck in it, and Cress suspected something went down between Carole and Adelson that might have triggered it."

"Long time ago now," said RJ.

"Not that long. If it was, none of this would be happening now. We wouldn't be out here."

RJ seemed to chew that over. Ty studied his face. People might have assumed from looking at him that he was some kind of dumb redneck. They'd be wrong, thought Ty. The lines on his face, and the way he'd spoken, told of a man who was struggling with past events, unable to reconcile who he'd been with who he wanted to be.

From experience Ty knew that was a battle all of its own. Your moral compass might be pointed due north, but the tide could take you a few degrees off course. Over time the end result was that you ended up miles from where you thought you'd been headed.

The good news, thought Ty, was that there was always an opportunity to get back. He guessed that this was what RJ was doing now. Trying to get back on course. Before he checked out and it was too late.

RJ pulled the handle back a little from ninety degrees. The boat shifted left and edged its way between two clusters of cypress. "That was the story," he said. "Mimsy finds that horny old goat in bed with Carole Chabon. Course he was a horny young goat back then. What they called a tough dog to keep on the porch, if you know what I mean."

Ty had an idea. "So Mimsy killed Carole instead of him?"

"Let's put it this way. It wasn't the first time that Mimsy had caught him having a nooner with another woman. But this was a little different."

"Because Carole was African American," said Ty.

"Precisely. You see, to Mimsy it would have been like her finding Adelson having sex with . . . I don't know . . . an animal or something. No offense."

"None taken," said Ty. He realized RJ was explaining Mimsy's mentality rather than his own.

"Boy, she flew into some kind of a hot rage," he went on. "Had everyone in town the same. That poor girl didn't stand a chance."

Both men lapsed into silence. The boat glided on, the canopy thickening, the bright sun fading a little.

"Want to know the real kicker in all of this?" RJ asked.

"Go on." Ty was solemn.

RJ swallowed hard. When he spoke next his voice cracked a little. "She didn't sleep with Adelson Shaw. He forced himself on her."

Ty stared at RJ. "What? How could you know that?"

"Because that's what she was screaming when they put that rope around her neck," said RJ, tears starting to brim in his eyes. "'He raped me.' She kept saying it over and over. Except the more she said it, the more it made Mimsy angry. And Miss Parsons."

"The librarian?"

"Oh, yeah. Bet she told you that she was in college when it happened."

"Not me but, yes, that's what she said to Cress."

"She and Mimsy were right in the middle of it."

Despite himself, Ty felt a lump in his throat. He flashed on old pictures he'd seen of lynchings. The angry white faces of men, women and even children, all gathered around to witness an execution with no trial. Not monsters, but regular people.

"Worst part of it?"

Ty wasn't sure how much worse it could get than what he'd just been told.

"Sue Ann, my wife. She was there too," said RJ. "She helped yank on that rope along with the rest of them."

And you married her? Ty wanted to ask, but didn't. He needed this man to take him to Cressida.

"She regrets it. I know she does. She has the same nightmares as me."

Fresh silence that lasted as they wove through another deep thicket of vines and pop ash trees. Ty wasn't outraged so much as sick to his stomach, and more than a little sad for how people could be. "You can't change what happened," he said. "But you can put it right."

RJ stared at him. "And how do you do that?"

"You do what you're doing now, and when we get back you tell the truth."

"I'm not going to lie. I can't make any promises. I've made enough to myself over the years . . . and broken them."

Ty appreciated the man's honesty. He respected it too. The world was full of people who would tell you what they were going to do. It made a change to find someone who knew themselves well enough not to do that. "So how long do we have to go?" Ty asked.

RJ scraped the bill of his cap against his head. "Like I said, it's been a while since I've been out here but I reckon maybe another fifteen minutes. Give or take."

The follow-up question hung in the air. How long until Mimsy got there with Cressida? How far behind them were they?

And beneath all of those, would they make it in time? Or was she already dead?

From his time in the military, Ty knew how ultimately useless those questions were. Right now, their mission objective was to chase down the other boat. They couldn't legislate for reaching it in time. All they could do was stay focused on the task in hand.

Deal with what was in front of them, which was swampland and lots of it.

As they edged between another two clumps of trees there was a thrashing sound from the propeller at the back of the boat. Ty spun round to see something in the blades, tangled between them and one of the vertical rudders.

RJ cursed loudly. His hand shot down to the engine control, and he flicked a switch, killing the engine.

As the propeller blades slowed Ty saw that a long strand of vine had worked its way into the propeller cage somehow. It was wrapped around the blades, stopping them turning properly.

Looking around, they were in thigh-high water, surrounded by clumps of trees, a thin layer of pollen coating the surface of the water.

RJ moved to the back of the boat. He poked his fingers through, trying to get hold of the vine, or whatever the heck it was, that had got caught in the blades. Ty started to the back of the boat to help him.

It began to tip, one side lurching down close to the surface of the swamp, water threatening to capsize the vessel. Ty quickly adjusted his position, moving sideways to place his considerable weight back in the center, and steady the small craft. "Sorry," he said to RJ.

"It's my fault. I wasn't concentrating."

"Tell you what, let's save the recriminations for when we get ourselves out of this almighty shit show. How's that sound?"

"Deal," said RJ. "Man, I didn't even think to bring my tools with me."

"That's what I'm talking about," said Ty, with a smile. "You were in a hurry. We both were."

Ty had a thought. He always carried a multi-tool with him, either a Gerber, Leatherman, or similar. It was a habit he'd acquired from Lock, who had acquired it when he'd served in the Royal Military Police specialist close-protection unit. Deployment to far-flung locales had meant that calling for a tow truck or roadside rescue were often not a possibility. If you were on your own in the middle of East Africa when your Land Rover broke down, you'd better be able to fix it. Hence the multi-tool.

"Have Gerber, rule the world," was how Lock had put it once.

Ty dug out his Gerber, and took a closer look at the propeller, tracing the route of the vine that had wrapped its way around the blade all the way down to the prop shaft. He made his way down toward the cage that enclosed the prop, taking each step with care.

The boat bobbed in the water, but didn't tip. He squeezed past RJ. He got a better angle as he got closer. He would have to cut it close to the prop or it would just wind back around when they started up again. He opened the Gerber, and pushed the small saw blade through a gap in the cage near the prop shaft. Thankfully he had a strong grip, the result of lots of hours of dead hangs, pull ups and deadlifts.

Keeping his hand tight around the handle, he managed to saw away at the root of the vine, aware that they were busy squandering time they simply didn't have.

As he worked, fraction by fraction, he reminded himself of another military mantra.

Slow is smooth, smooth is fast.

Finally, he sawed through the vine, freeing it from the shaft. Squeezing his fingers through the cage, he got hold of the other end, and pulled it through with a couple of firm wrenching movements.

The vine came away in his hand. It was a lot tougher and more fibrous than it looked. It was lucky RJ had cut the engine or it would have burned out.

Ty flung it as far as he could from the boat. It landed in the branches of a pop ash, safe from doing them any more harm.

"Okay, let's get going," said Ty, a minor victory won.

He clambered back to his position at the front of the boat as RJ reached down to restart the engine.

It coughed, spluttered into life, and died. The propellers didn't move.

He exhaled, gave it a few seconds and tried again.

A third time and Ty's heart began to sink into his boots.

"Someone's gonna have to get out, and hand start it. Only way," said RJ.

Ty looked from RJ, with his hands on the controls and all the knowledge of how to keep the engine moving once it caught, to the murky green waters. It looked like that someone had to be him.

62

"You remember those old movies about World War Two where they'd have to start the fighter plane's propeller by hand?"

Ty was standing knee-deep in the swamp water, doing his best not to fall over, and wondering how he'd be able to yank one of the propeller blades with the force needed to get it started, but without it taking one of his hands clean off at the wrist. So far he wasn't sure he could. But right now it looked like he didn't have much choice. "Haven't really seen that many, RJ, but I have an idea how this goes."

"Okay. Well, when you're ready. Try to get yourself out of the way if it catches."

"That was the plan," said Ty, trying to keep any hint of sarcasm out of his voice and not doing the best job of it. He reached up to the nearest blade, grabbed its upper edge and yanked it as hard as he could. It moved down, then stopped. Ty took a breath. His pants legs were soaked, and he could feel the cool mud of the swamp bottom oozing into his boots.

The toughest part was trying to keep his balance while finding enough downward force. It would have been a hell of a lot easier standing on solid, even ground.

He already had visions of pulling down so hard that the momentum folded him at the hip, carried him forward and moved his head into the propeller blades at the very moment they caught. Of all the ways he had considered he might buy the farm, being decapitated by an airboat had never entered the betting. He'd always figured he'd be shot and bleed out alone in a motel room. Something gritty like that. Not die like he was going for a Darwin award.

He focused back on Cressida, alone with the Everglades' answer to Annie Wilkes, and a guy whose day job was flipping burgers.

"Let's go again," said Ty, straightening, taking a fresh grip, and tensing his core muscles.

"Okay," said RJ.

"Three, two, one," said Ty.

He gave it a fresh yank. The blade clicked round, but nothing more.

"One more time," said Ty. "Man, this really is like being back in the Corps."

"How's that?"

"Doing something dumb up to my knees in mud, with every chance of something biting me in the ass when I least expect it."

He grabbed another blade, reaching up as far as he could to get some good downforce.

"Come on, you son of a—" He yanked, pulled his hands out of the way.

It turned, and took.

The propeller catching and turning. The blades picking up speed in seconds, creating a blast of wind that almost blew him off his feet and sent him tumbling ass over elbow into the swamp.

He took a few steps back as RJ tapped the pedal, revving the engine.

"Okay, Ty, close the cage."

Ty moved round to the other side to secure the cage that had done such a lousy job of shielding the blades from objects inanimate or otherwise.

· · ·

RJ TWISTED round in his seat and watched as Tyrone moved to lock the cage. He'd begun to think that the propeller dying like that was some kind of a sign. A sign that he shouldn't be out there. That he had made a terrible error of judgment.

Likely the young reporter was dead by now. Lyle and Mimsy had been ahead of them before this delay. What chance did they have of intercepting them in time?

And then what?

He had spilled his guts to this man. Even giving up the guilt of his wife.

Now he felt unsure, conflicted.

Confessing had felt good in the moment. But how would he feel when they were both back in Darling, facing down Mimsy and the might of the law.

Sue Ann had warned him. Justice was the preserve of the rich, and they were dirt poor. It was all well and good being noble, but it didn't always work out for people like him and Sue Ann.

If he wanted to change his mind, there would be no better time than now. Ty was out of the boat. He would never get back if RJ left him here.

All he needed to do was tap down on the metal pedal at his foot. He'd be clear and gone before Ty could react.

He looked back at Ty, exhausted, soaked in sweat. A man determined to save someone he barely knew. A man who had served his country and been prepared to die for it. A man RJ would never have spoken with, but also a man he had come to respect in a very short space of time.

Ty began to wade around the side of the boat. RJ could still go. Tap that pedal and be gone. Wash his hands of this whole sorry mess.

The big Marine reached out a huge clenched fist to him. "Teamwork, baby," he said to RJ, offering the bump.

RJ's decision was made in that moment. He closed his hand. They bumped knuckles. RJ opened his hand, and grabbed Ty, helping him to crawl belly first back onto the boat.

63

They were close now. Cressida knew it. Not from anything that had been said—barely anything had been said. That was part of how she knew they were drawing close to their final destination. Her final destination. And, if Mimsy got her way, her grave.

The last ten minutes or so, any chatter had stopped. Mimsy had cut out the wisecracks. There had been no more taunting.

Lyle, already silent for the most part, had sunk inside himself even further. Every time Cressida looked at him he turned away.

There were other ominous signs. Mimsy had relented on the question of water, and Lyle had handed Cressida another bottle, which she had gratefully chugged down.

He had asked Mimsy if he could have a smoke. She had agreed to that too, as long as he held his cigarette over the side of the boat when it wasn't in his mouth, and made sure the smoke didn't blow into her face.

Mimsy, it turned out, was as passionate an anti-smoker as she was a racist. Cressida made a mental note of that for the article she would likely never get to write now. She had thought about asking if she could smoke the Marlboro that Lyle had palmed to her. She had decided against it, even though she was sure it would annoy Mimsy, and confirm the old lady's prejudices about 'her people'.

Smoking, like so many other things, was an activity that Cressida enjoyed the thought of more than the reality. A bit like six a.m. runs in Central Park. It was one of the things that looked cool when other people were doing it.

Beyond the lack of chatter, her two companions' body language had undergone a subtle metamorphosis. Where Lyle had seemed jittery, he now appeared stoic. He had the vibe of a man steeling himself to do something he wasn't looking forward to.

Mimsy sat bolt upright, all her attention directed on piloting the small airboat through trees that seemed to have grown larger than the ones they'd seen up until now.

There were 'gators here, too. Cressida had seen them. More of them as they moved yard by yard through the swamp. There had been a couple of snakes too. Lyle had pointed them out to her. Non-native species, he had explained. They had escaped from people's homes and wound up here where they had bred and pushed out the native species.

There was a metaphor in that, but Lyle seemed oblivious to it. Cressida noted it as another interesting interlude for the big exposé that would never appear with her byline under it.

Which wasn't to say she had resigned herself to her fate. She was just being realistic. With her bum leg, and Lyle having the shotgun, she didn't rate her chances of turning this around. She was down by six in the last minute of the game, and the other team had the ball in her half of the field.

But that didn't mean she wasn't going to try. There was always the interception and Hail Mary pass into the end zone.

And, if nothing else, if she had to go, being shot once or twice, through the head or chest, sounded infinitely less distressing than being left out here to be the next meal of some 'gator and their family.

She fiddled with the cigarette in her hand.

Mimsy had been super squirrely about Lyle smoking in the boat.

As soon as he'd taken his last drag, she had told him to make sure it went into the water.

Cressida could only assume that a cigarette in a gas-fueled boat was the reason for her tetchiness. She didn't know if the fuel they were using was flammable, but Mimsy seemed neurotic about it, and that was all she needed. A small neurosis would do the job.

She tapped the end of the cigarette into her open palm and gave Lyle her most plaintive look. "Do you mind?" she said.

He reached for his lighter. Mimsy coughed, stopping him before he could spark it.

"I promise I'll dispose of it safely," Cressida told her. "And I won't blow the smoke anywhere near you."

Mimsy made a harrumphing noise of assent and Lyle flicked the lighter wheel with his thumb. He held the flame up to the tip of the cigarette.

Cressida took a draw, and blew the smoke carefully away from Mimsy. "Thanks."

She drew the next puff in as deep as she could. She began to cough. Not even having to fake it. She kept coughing, and doubled over. Lyle went to thump her on the back. She could see the shotgun loose between his thighs, not tightly clamped, like it had been.

She half dropped, half flicked the cigarette up and over her shoulder, toward Mimsy, the back of the boat, and presumably the fuel tank.

She held up her hand in apology and kept coughing as Mimsy flipped out.

"Lyle! Lyle! Get that the heck out of the boat. Before we have a fire."

Lyle lumbered into action, first turning side on, so he could try to swing his legs around the edge of the seat, reach down to grab the lit cigarette before it rolled back any further.

Cressida put out her hand towards his side, as if reaching out to him in support. Her hand kept moving. She braced herself for the sharp jolt of the pain that was coming as she pushed off with her good foot, launched off her seat and grabbed for the shotgun.

Torn between reaching for the errant cigarette, and keeping hold of the shotgun, Lyle flailed his arms. His left hand caught Cressida's lip, opening a cut as it smashed into her lower teeth.

Mimsy, meanwhile, leaned down from her chair and threw a mean roundhouse punch. Cressida ducked, and the closed fist whistled over the top of her head.

Cressida had one hand around the barrel of the shotgun. She reached over with the other, trying to get that on it too.

The cigarette abandoned for now, Lyle spun back round and tried to wrestle the gun from her. Meaty paws, used to spending all day doing heavy work over a hot stove, began to prise painfully at her fingers.

It was a losing battle and Cressida knew it. There was no way she was going to beat a man a hundred pounds heavier than her in this fight.

Time for another strategy, she told herself, as Mimsy kicked out, catching her shoulder painfully. It wasn't much of a kick, but in her present state it jarred her more than it should have.

She gritted her teeth and pressed on. She took her hands off the gun without any more struggle. "Okay, okay," she said.

Lyle did what she hoped he would. He began to lift the gun up and into him by the barrel. As he did so, Cressida reached down, and felt for the trigger, falling onto one knee, her other hand up, blocking his view with it and her upper body, in a gesture of surrender.

He kept his hands firmly around the barrel, like a toddler pulling their favorite toy into their chest to save themselves from having to share it.

Cressida's free hand, which Lyle couldn't see, closed around the trigger guard. Her finger slipped inside, closing around the trigger. She squeezed and kept squeezing. Her angle was all off. It took everything she had. Finally, it discharged.

Lyle flew backwards, blood and cartilage spraying over the three of them as his lower jaw exploded into fragments. The round continued on up, taking off the front of his nose, and scraping the overhang of his forehead.

He let out a distended scream, blood pouring from what was left of his mouth. His grip on the barrel loosened. Cressida moved her free hand down, and wrapped it around the stock, prising the gun from him.

She lost what little footing she had, and began to fall back. The barrel of the gun went up and over her head as she tumbled back.

Mimsy launched herself from the pilot's seat before Cressida had the chance to recover. She fell on top of her, making sure to shift some of her weight onto Cressida's broken leg. Cressida let out a yelp of sudden pain as Mimsy dug an elbow into the side of her knee. The boat was rolling hard to one side. The back of Cressida's head was over the edge. She still had her hands around the shotgun, but only just. As the pain surged through her leg, she could feel her grip weakening with every second that passed.

Mimsy kept digging her elbow in, working it right into the joint, making it as painful as she possibly could. At the same time, her other hand kept the shotgun pushed back, stopping Cressida from getting the business end pointing at her.

On the other side of the airboat, maybe less than six feet away, Lyle was staggering around, zombie-like. His hands had come up to his face as he tried to staunch the blood that was pouring out. The sound he made, somewhere between a cry, a groan and a scream, was of pure distress.

Cressida, locked in her death battle for the gun with Mimsy, could hear him trying to form words. She couldn't make them out. The damage to his jaw and mouth was catastrophic.

Mimsy withdrew her elbow. Cressida felt immediate relief.

It proved short-lived as the same elbow crashed into her face. Cressida's head snapped back from the impact, her grip weakening further. Mimsy's hand clawed at her face, nails raking down her cheek, a finger poking into her eye.

Mimsy was strong. A lot stronger than she looked. And she had weight on her side.

Cressida knew she had to try a different approach. Go on the offensive. If she stayed like this, with Mimsy pressing down on her, clawing at her face and poking at her eyes, sooner or later she would be overpowered. It was only a matter of time.

Behind them, Lyle was still staggering about, drenched in blood.

Tilting her head down Cressida watched Mimsy's free hand as it came up to take another finger jab into her eye.

If you want to fight dirty, we can do that.

As Mimsy's finger slid up past her jawline, Cressida snapped at it. Her teeth closed around the end of Mimsy's index finger. She bit down as hard as she could. She could taste blood, salty and strangely satisfying.

Mimsy tried to pull her finger out of Cressida's mouth. Cressida kept her teeth clamped down, her incisors crunching into bone.

Mimsy moaned in pain.

Yeah, see how you like it.

The older woman's other hand let go of the shotgun. She jammed the heel of her palm into Cressida's septum, pushing her nose back up into her skull.

When that didn't make Cressida open her mouth, Mimsy jabbed two fingers into her eye. It was enough for Cressida to loosen her grip on Mimsy's trapped finger. It came away with the tip hanging off.

Cressida could see Lyle lumbering toward them. If he made it over to this side of the boat, they'd capsize. Nothing was surer.

Mimsy must have figured the same. "Stay where you are, Lyle!" she hollered at him.

Even with his entire body in total distress, something about Mimsy's voice seemed to command his attention because he sat down suddenly on the other side of the boat. It tilted back, leveling out on the water.

Backed up against the side, Cressida tried to lower the barrel of the shotgun. If she could only get it angled, she could pull the trigger and this nightmare would be over. This part of it anyway.

Mimsy made a fresh lunge, pushing off with her feet, and diving down low. Her shoulder slammed into Cressida's stomach, knocking the air from her lungs. Mimsy's knee came and slammed into her bad leg.

The one-two shock of it made her lose her grip on the shotgun almost entirely. Mimsy peeled it from her, sat back, and brought it up, her finger on the trigger.

Cressida lay back, completely spent, no more energy left.

Mimsy had the shotgun aimed at the middle of her chest. They were both sucking in air in big gulps. It felt like the two bottles of water Cressida had drunk had sweated back out again in the struggle.

Lyle was rocking back and forth in a sitting position. His hand came up with a jagged fragment of jaw bone. His fingers closed round it. He raised it to his face as if he could just click it back into place.

Pushing off with one hand, Mimsy got slowly to her feet, her eyes never leaving Cressida. She shouldered her way past Lyle, seemingly unconcerned with his suffering, and hoisted herself back up into the pilot's chair.

Cressida could only watch. Even if she'd had another lunge left in her, the distance was too great. Mimsy would pull the trigger before she had even made it halfway.

Back on her throne, Mimsy had the shotgun in one hand, while the other felt for the stick.

"Look what you done," she said to Cressida, nodding at Lyle's bloody face.

64

At the sound of the first shot, an egret took flight over the boat. Ty and RJ looked at each other.

Ty picked it out as probably a shotgun, the sound too low-range and sonorous to be a handgun or a small-caliber rifle.

"It sounded like it came from over there," said Ty.

"It's hard to tell out here," said RJ. "The way sound travels, you can think someone's behind you when they ain't."

"Let's keep moving," said Ty. "If they're headed to where you think they are then we're bound to run across them."

RJ pressed down a little more firmly on the pedal, and pulled the stick back, the back end of the boat sweeping out as they cornered around a fresh stand of cypress. Ty stood at the bow, scanning as far ahead as the terrain allowed, which wasn't very far.

When he saw anything directly ahead in the water, he called it back to RJ, who adjusted course. They kept moving like that for another two minutes, RJ pushing the boat as hard as he could without risking a fresh entanglement with the vegetation.

At one point they came up too fast on a fallen ash, almost fully submerged in the water. Ty saw it late, and RJ cleared it with inches to spare.

Neither man spoke about the shot they had heard. There was little point. They had no way of knowing what it signified until they caught up with the other airboat.

Then, from the swamp silence, a fresh shotgun blast. This one louder. Closer.

Ty glanced back, the two men sharing another moment of quiet dread. "Let's keep going," said Ty, another echo from his days in the Corps.

When all seems lost – keep. After. It.

65

Mimsy stepped delicately down from the pilot's seat, a curl of heat still fresh at the tip of the shotgun. Her brow was furrowed, as if she was still weighing a decision in her mind.

Blood had pooled under the seats, oozing from one side of the craft.

Lyle lay splayed against the side, arms flung out in a gesture of surrender. What remained of his head lolled to one side. Blood oozed from a meaty black cavity near the center of his chest.

The slug had hit him almost square in the heart, tearing through his pectoral muscle, and shredding both atrial and ventricular chambers, killing him almost instantly.

Cressida sat balled up on the other side of the boat, only her bad leg extended. The oozing blood from Lyle's wounds gathered at her heel.

"See?" said Mimsy. "See what you made me do?"

"I made you do that?"

"If you hadn't shot him, I wouldn't have had cause to put him out of his misery," Mimsy said primly.

Cressida stared at her. Maybe the scariest thing of all about this woman was that she actually believed what she was saying. By murdering Lyle she had done what she had to.

As soon as Cressida had realized why she was aiming the gun at Lyle, she had said what he couldn't. She had begged Mimsy to spare him.

"We can turn back. Go and get him help before he bleeds out," she had said.

Mimsy had studied her for a long second. "You should have thought about that before you shot him. But don't worry. At least you'll have yourself some company."

Lyle had been halfway to his knees, his hands clasped in a gesture of supplication when Mimsy had pulled the trigger, blowing him back against the side of the boat.

The woman was stone-cold psycho, thought Cressida. There was no depth to which she wouldn't sink to get her way.

Mimsy snapped the shotgun open, and reloaded. It was an action so smooth that by the time Cressida realized what she was doing the window of opportunity to try again to take her down had gone. She exhaled, all but resigned now to how this was going to end. She knew she had to keep fighting. But knowing and doing were two different things, separated by an ocean of exhaustion, bruises and broken bones.

66

The airboat slowed. RJ stood up on the seat, one hand shielding his eyes against the sun as he scanned the area ahead.

"It's up here somewhere."

Ty bit back a smartass comment. There had been no other gunshot blasts since the second. But that was cold comfort.

One minute RJ had told him they were almost there, the next he seemed to have lost his bearings. It was beyond frustrating. However, expressing that would serve only to make matters worse.

Patience was not Ty's strong suit. But right now it was what he needed. If RJ couldn't reorient himself, and bring them to this place the locals called the Devil's Pond, whatever slim chance they had of finding Cressida would be gone.

67

Cressida watched Mimsy cut the engine, which allowed the boat to glide through the narrow approach that would lead them into the Devil's Pond. Towering bald cypress trees, some more than seventy feet tall, lined a narrow, watery avenue. Grey-green tendrils of Spanish moss dripped from the lower branches to kiss the water.

The narrow channel opened into a huge pond. The sight of it made Cressida shiver, despite the overwhelming heat and humidity. The sinkhole, created by the collapse of an old salt dome cavern, had left an area of water around a hundred feet wide, and easily twice that length.

It was encircled on every side by smaller hat-stand cypresses. The Spanish moss that hung from those trees was thicker and whiter. As the bow of the airboat cleared the green layer of duckweed from the surface, Cressida caught a brief glimpse of the world beneath: crystal clear water that faded into darkness without revealing any bottom.

Skirting close to the trees on one side, a butterfly orchid revealed itself, then a cow-horn orchid, both yellow. They seemed to be scattered randomly. Rare. Precious. Delicate. A first glance wouldn't reveal them. But once you'd spotted one, they were everywhere.

Cressida thought of the botany student who had stumbled over Carole Chabon's remains out here, and another piece of the puzzle clicked into place for her. What else would bring a person to a place so remote and treacherous?

Beauty would be one reason. She peeked at Mimsy, sitting astride the pilot's seat, the shotgun laid over her lap. Cruelty would be another.

Deep, sparkling water shadowed by trees. The wisps of Spanish moss that cascaded over the branches, like tinsel on a Christmas tree. The tiny flashes of perfectly rendered color from the orchids. It was a place that appeared ethereal, other-worldly.

There was something else, though. Another element of nature that was far less benign. Fauna rather than flora. Fauna that took the scene from dream-like and twisted it into nightmare.

Cressida had never before seen so many alligators in one place at the same time. Not in a zoo. Or a 'gator ranch. Or even on the Discovery Channel. She began counting them, and quickly gave up. Like the orchids, once you'd seen one, your eyes were immediately drawn to another, and then another. And the next place your eyes settled you saw two or three, sitting side by side.

Some lay at the edge of the water. Dozens floated in it, or swam lazily at the edges. Others, the majority, stayed near the trees, bellies resting on the huge gnarled stump roots visible just above the surface.

At the far end of the pond there was an island of bright red gumbo-limbo trees that lay in a broad curve extending out beyond the end of the sinkhole. A half-dozen smaller 'gators lay under the trees, ready to scuttle back into the forest behind them.

This was it, the place where Carole Chabon had been dumped, like so much garbage: a grisly Neverland of nature where no lost boy, or girl, could possibly survive.

The snap of the shotgun pulled Cressida from the place's spell. Mimsy climbed down from the chair.

"Well, here we are," she said to Cressida. "Isn't this what you wanted to see? You know, for that story you planned on writing."

Cressida brought her good knee up into her ribs, pulling her arms around it, and bundling into a near-fetal position. Her back was pressed into the side of the airboat. She was shaking uncontrollably. It was a primal panic that seemed to travel from the base of her skull all the way down her spine and into her limbs.

Right now she would have traded this for being back on top of that baking hot car, with only a couple of 'gators to contend with, rather than the hundreds that were here.

Mimsy stayed on the other side of the boat, lunging distance away from Cressida. Not that she had much lunge left in her. Perhaps if her leg hadn't been broken . . .

"Okay, missy," Mimsy began. "I'm going to need you to get Lyle overboard and into the water for me."

Cressida looked at the dead man sprawled opposite her, his eyes as glassy as those of the 'gators. He was big. Quite literally a dead weight.

Even if she had wanted to, she wasn't entirely sure how she would be able to get him over the side and into the water.

She didn't move. She didn't speak.

"Listen, I can't exactly turn my back on you and do it myself. Otherwise I would," Mimsy continued.

"I can't."

"No such thing as can't. What you mean is you won't." Mimsy lifted the gun, tucking the stock into her shoulder. "You ever seen anyone who's been shot in the gut? Not the heart, or the chest, like Lyle here was. The gut."

Cressida shook her head.

"Didn't think so. Well, allow me to educate you. It's pain like no other. It's slow too. Agonizing. You think you've experienced pain. You ain't. Not when you've been shot in the stomach. All those nerve endings. Everything down there all mixing in together."

"Maybe you should have been the writer," said Cressida.

Mimsy's brow furrowed. Her lips thinned. So did her eyes. "Get yourself up, get over here, and get him in the water."

Cressida racked her brain for some way out of this that didn't involve being shot in the stomach. She knew she had to close the distance between her and Mimsy.

She put her hand down to lever herself up, and fell back with a groan. Then she reached out to Mimsy.

"Help me up."

Mimsy lowered the shotgun barrel and began to laugh. "Oh, boy, you must think I fell off the turnip truck. Maybe I could give you my gun to use as a stick. How about that?"

Cressida grimaced, reached back and grabbed the side of the boat. It had been worth a try. She levered herself up, like someone would if they kipped up onto their feet from the ground.

Keeping her weight on her good leg as far as she could, she hobbled over to Lyle. Mimsy stepped off to the end bow, making sure she stayed out of the way.

Cressida reached Lyle. She hunkered down, her broken leg splaying uselessly behind her. The coppery smell of his blood caught at the back of her throat, mixed with his body odor. Her stomach lurched. She pressed on, reaching under his arms, and trying to lift him up.

It was no use. She got him about an inch off the deck before the weight overcame her. She let him go again. "Keep going," Mimsy barked at her.

She tried again, hooking her hands under his armpits and pulling him into her. She failed again. His body slumped back onto the deck.

It was no use. He was too heavy.

She turned back to Mimsy, her clothes soaked in the blood and gore of his wounds.

"Okay, get back there," said Mimsy, gesturing to the stern with the shotgun barrel.

Cressida didn't need asking twice. She hauled herself out of the way. When she had made it to the back of the craft, Mimsy put the shotgun down, but within reach, hooked her arms under Lyle as Cressida had done, then lifted the top half of him up and over the edge.

He stayed there as Mimsy stepped back and picked up the gun

again. He was half in and half out of the boat. Slightly more in than out, his pelvic bone just above the lip.

"Okay," said Mimsy. "You think you can manage it now that I've done the hard part for you?"

Cressida wasn't sure what she was trying to prove. Was there a point to all this, other than making her last few moments as unpleasant as possible?

She sighed, and half stumbled, half limped back to Lyle. If she reached down, grabbed his legs and lifted them, gravity would take care of the rest.

Mimsy had the shotgun trained on her back as Cressida squatted and grasped Lyle's thick calves, then moved her hand down to his ankles when she couldn't get a grip. She heaved upwards. He started to move.

She said a prayer as he began to tumble, head first, over the side and into the pond.

The 'gators are in for one hell of a treat, she thought, as she felt a shove in her own back, lost her balance and began to follow the dead man over the side and into the water.

68

RJ was steering carefully through the narrow channel, the propeller turning just fast enough to keep the boat moving forward, when they heard the splash. It was followed, fractions of a second later, by another, and then a woman screaming, long and loud.

Then silence.

Ty, who was standing at the very apex of the bow, turned back to RJ. "Get this thing moving."

Reluctantly, RJ pressed down on the gas pedal. The airboat lurched forward. At this speed, he risked losing control, and capsizing. He looked to Ty, and eased up on the pedal. Ty glared at him.

"I can't go any faster," said RJ.

"Try it," Ty shot back, as the pond beckoned a hundred yards ahead of them and the distant sound of thrashing water reached them.

69

Cressida scrambled back toward the boat, the water taking the pressure from her bum leg, and allowing her to use the strength in her upper body, and good leg to kick out toward the side. Out of the corner of her eye she was aware of a long black shape slipping into the water on the other side of the pond.

She crawled forward, and tried to reach up to grab the fiberglass hull of the boat. In the deep water, with nothing to push off, it was hard to get up high enough to grab the lip.

Finally, after a couple of efforts and with splashes behind her, as more 'gators headed to investigate the commotion, she managed to get the fingertips of one hand onto the edge of the airboat. Like a mountaineer who'd lost his harness, she did her best to hang on, her forearms burning.

Reaching up with her other hand, she managed to get a better grip. Half an inch by half an inch she improved her position until her hands clamped over the lip. It would take another huge effort, but one more surge and she might be able to pull herself up and out of the water. Then she saw Mimsy's face, looming over her, all teeth and gums. The same smug smile Cressida had come to despise. The butt of the shotgun came up over the edge and crashed down hard, slam-

ming into the knuckles of her left hand with sufficient force that she
heard the crunch of bone. Pain ripped its way down her hand and
into her arm.

Cressida tried to keep hold with her right hand, and use it to haul
herself up.

The hard wooden butt came down again. It smashed into her
other hand. She lost her grip entirely this time, and slid down, back
into the water.

Her head went under. Panicked, she inhaled a lungful of water,
arms flailing wildly.

There were shapes at the edge of her vision in every direction
now. It looked almost like a shoal of large fish filling the pond. Only
they weren't fish. They were 'gators.

Looking across, she saw Lyle's body about twelve feet to her left,
barely on the surface. A huge 'gator moved in, took one of his legs in
its jaws, and pulled his body down into the pond.

Some of the other 'gators flicked their powerful tails, making
their way towards the body, as the 'gator that had him went deeper
and deeper, rolling over and over, its belly flashing white every
second or so. The death roll continued. Another gator 'darted in to
grab at one of Lyle's arms, setting off a fresh rush from some of the
others who had been warily circling.

Cressida struck out, back towards the boat. A black shape closed
in on her. She could see its teeth. At the very last second it changed
direction, and dove down to join the frantic fight over the newly
arrived spoils. Its tail slammed into her as it moved past, winding her.

She surfaced for a split second. The boat was moving away, the
propeller turning slowly. If it left without her, she was dessert. That
much she did know. Except "dessert" didn't fully capture the horror
of how she'd live her last moments.

Reaching her hand over her head, she began to front crawl as fast
as she could for the back of the boat. She kept going, knowing that at
any moment jaws could clamp around one of her legs and take her
down to the limestone bottom to join Lyle.

She settled into something approaching a rhythm, closing in on the boat. There was no propeller below the water to slice her up. If she could reach the back of it, maybe she could find something to hold onto. She could tow behind it and hope that the noise of the airboat's propeller would be enough to keep the 'gators at a safe distance.

As her head once again cleared the surface, she saw the stern of the boat pulling away as it headed back towards the channel. It was pulling away faster than she could swim.

70

A s the scooped bow of their boat cleared the channel, Ty saw Mimsy, atop another airboat heading towards them. She steered with one hand. In her other, she held a shotgun.

Her eyes went wide with surprise as she saw them. She took her hand from the stick, took the shotgun in both hands, and swung the barrel toward them.

"Threat!" screamed Ty, as she pulled the trigger and the echo of the shotgun boomed around the pond.

RJ ducked down as her shot whistled overhead.

Ty's SIG cleared his holster. He clambered toward the bow, duck-walking low, and scanning the other airboat for any sign of Cressida. He couldn't see her, but he didn't have the best angle. She could be lying down. If he returned fire, he couldn't afford to aim wildly. He'd have to pick his shots with care, and allow for the wash from the other boat as it headed for the channel.

Thankfully for him, Mimsy was up top, sitting on the pilot's seat.

Ty topped his head above the bow, took a two-handed grip on his gun, and squeezed the trigger. The shot slammed into the bottom of the chair where Mimsy was sitting, sending shards of metal sparking across the deck.

Ty ducked down, and scooted across on his butt. He doubted a fiberglass hull had many ballistic resistant qualities. At the end of the day they were floating in a huge plastic bathtub with a propeller strapped to the back, not an Amphibious Assault Vehicle, like the ones Ty had used in the Corps.

Ty twisted round. RJ had climbed down from his seat, and taken cover with one hand so he could steer. "Bring us alongside her," Ty shouted to him.

"Are you crazy?" RJ screamed back at him.

Ty treated the question as rhetorical.

"Ty!" shouted RJ, jabbing a finger at the pond.

"What is it?"

"Look!"

Ty popped his head back up, and tried to see where RJ was frantically pointing. All he saw at first were 'gators. Everywhere. At the sides, and swarming to a part of the pond where the green duckweed had been replaced by a bloody slick of deep scarlet.

"No," RJ hollered. "There! There!"

Ty looked ten feet to his left. Someone was in the water. He could see their head, bobbing on the surface. Their arm came up above their head for a second. Then both arm and head disappeared under the surface as more 'gators slid into the pond.

Mimsy's boat was almost parallel to them, separated by no more than thirty feet of open water. Ty whipped round to see Mimsy, back on the seat, taking one more shot.

It slammed into the lip of their boat on the port side, taking out a chunk. She threw down the shotgun, and kept moving, accelerating towards the channel opening.

Ty stood up, and took off his boots. He held up his SIG, holding it by the short metal barrel and tossed it to RJ. RJ caught it one-handed.

Ty scooted his legs over the side of the boat.

"You see any 'gator heading for me, turn the asshole into a handbag and a pair of boots," he said, diving into the cold water.

71

Ty pushed off the boat with his feet, and struck out for where he had seen her go under. He took a couple of strokes, and surfaced. He couldn't see anyone. He looked back to the boat. RJ had taken up his position at the bow, the SIG in his hand, scanning for approaching 'gators.

He dove underneath. The water was clear. He could make out what seemed to be a human shape over to his left, legs paddling frantically. Beyond her was a mass of 'gators, swimming past each other, and diving back and forth between the bottom and the surface. A cone of blood blossomed in the water at the center of them.

Ty swam for her, using his broad powerful shoulders to power through the water. A bullet fizzed through the water beyond him. He saw a 'gator that must have been heading straight for him zigzag off in a change of direction.

Too many more of those, too long in the water, and RJ would be out of ammunition and Ty would be out of luck.

He came up and gulped a deep breath. He dove back under, figuring that staying beneath the surface was the safer option.

He kept moving, finding his stride, parting the water with his big hands, and putting his back and shoulders into it.

Getting closer, he could make out Cressida, eyes closed, leaking blood into the water, her hair fanning out in every direction. He looked for air bubbles coming from her mouth or nose but couldn't see any.

Another shot fizzed, this time off to his right where a much larger beast was floating on the surface. This one didn't move.

Ty came up, took two gulps of air, and went back down. Dolphin-kicking with his legs together, he coasted for a few feet, then spread his arms out to quicken his pace.

Up ahead he could see that she was slowly sinking.

His lungs were bursting, but there was no time to surface. Doubling down, he pushed on, moving into a breaststroke to power himself faster through the water, diving down a few more feet so that he could come up under her.

A shadow fell over him and his heart jolted with a fresh shot of adrenalin. He twisted his torso, looking up to see the outline of the airboat passing overhead.

Two more strokes, and he reached her close enough to touch. He kicked out, grabbing hold of one of her legs. She made a sound, and kicked out with her other leg, catching him hard in the head.

He moved up her body, wrapped one arm around her slender waist, and kicked for the surface as she continued to struggle free.

They made the surface together, both gasping for air. He looked around for the boat. Just as he was starting to panic, he saw it.

RJ hung over the side, the gun still in his hand. Ty lifted Cressida as best he could. She was spluttering water, panting for air. RJ reached over, and managed to grab one of her arms. With Ty pushing, he managed to haul her up, clear of the water, over the side, and onto the boat.

Ty trod water, scanning the immediate area as RJ got Cressida settled. The 'gators were still swarming, the blood pooling ever outwards, diluting from scarlet to pink.

This was the first chance he'd had to take in where he was. If you wanted to get rid of someone, this would be the place to pick. Unfortunately Mimsy would be halfway down the channel by now and, if she had any sense, booking it back to Darling as fast as she could.

Ty had plans for the mayor. But they all relied on him not having his legs bitten off by a frenzied 'gator in the next few minutes. His mind floated to the speech in *Jaws*, where the gnarled old fisherman tells the story about the USS *Indianapolis* sinking and the crew being eaten by sharks, and how the worst part was just before you were rescued.

Roger that, mother—

"Ty!"

His name had never sounded sweeter. He turned back. RJ reached down, grabbed his hand and gave him the boost he needed to clear the smooth surface, and get back on board.

"I thought black folks weren't much at swimming," said RJ.

Ty smiled, swinging his legs up and over the side. "We are when a 'gator's about to chew us a new asshole. Anyway, I've been taking lessons in case I wanted to re-enlist. SEALs get all the glory, these days."

Cressida was lying on her side in the recovery position. Ty crouched next to her. "How's she doing?" he asked RJ.

"Well, she's breathing. That's a start."

As he said it, Cressida made a gagging noise akin to a cat expelling a hairball, and vomited noisily over the deck.

"I'll sit with her. Can you please get us the hell out of here?"

72

A welcoming committee of a dozen sheriff's deputies was waiting for them as RJ's airboat limped toward the dock on its last thimble of fuel. As soon as they had been able to get a signal, Ty had called in a request for medical personnel to meet them when they docked. He had handed over to RJ, who gave them an update on what had happened, including the fact that Darling's best pancake-maker, or what was left of him, was at the bottom of Devil's Pond. Ty sensed that the story was better coming from a local than from himself.

There had been no sign of Mimsy or her boat on the return journey. Ty had spent most of it tending Cressida. He'd made sure she got some more water, and did what he could with her broken leg. It looked to be a straightforward fracture of the tibia, but no less painful for that.

Given everything she had been through, the fact that she was still alive bore testament to her spirit. With her capacity to endure sheer misery, she'd have made a damn fine Marine. When he'd told her so, she'd given him a wan smile and asked if he had any morphine. Okay, so maybe not, he'd figured.

Ty had stashed his gun on the boat, hoping they might miss it in all the excitement. He could easily purchase another, but he had a sentimental attachment to that one. As they eased toward land, he made sure to stand at the bow with his hands clearly visible.

He disembarked first, and was immediately placed in cuffs. Not that he had expected any different. To their credit, the deputies were polite to the point of apology. However, there was still the outstanding matter of him discharging his gun in the library.

It was what it was.

He asked to hang back while Cressida was taken carefully off the boat and loaded into the back of an ambulance for the trip to hospital. She managed a weak wave in his direction before she disappeared inside. Hands cuffed behind his back, he had to settle for a stoic nod. She'd be fine.

More than anything it was a relief not to have lost his principal. He sat in the back of the patrol car, and looked out over the swamp. A shudder ran the length of his body as he thought of Devil's Pond. He could add that one to his running list of nightmares.

RJ was busy talking to the sheriff. It looked like he was going to avoid being detained, for the time being anyway.

Ty wished him well. If there was anyone in Darling who had redeemed themselves, it was the 'gator farmer. He had come through at the most important time of all—when it truly mattered.

In a world where saccharine hand-wringing apologies on social media were the primary currency of absolution, Ty found it refreshing to have met someone whose apology came in the form of naked honesty. Not to mention a more than meager dose of real bravery.

If RJ had been a conspirator way back in '74, Ty truly believed he had been a reluctant one. It might not count for much to a judge, but Ty thought it should. When contrition was genuine it was hard to entirely condemn a man.

73

Soaked through, and covered with all kinds of swamp filth, Mimsy watched the two sheriff's deputies parked in plain sight outside her house, awaiting her arrival. She had hoped to grab a shower and fresh clothes before she did what she had to do. So much for that.

She thought about calling Claire Parsons but decided against it. RJ's betrayal had shaken her. But she still held out hope of turning him around. He needed to be reminded of where his loyalty should lie. If not with his race, or the Klan, or people like her, who had kept the town white, he should think of his wife.

If Mimsy could sway him, this might all still work out.

She watched the deputies for a few more seconds as they dusted the powdered sugar from the doughnuts they were wolfing down off the front of their uniforms. Then she turned and melted back into the stand of trees.

74

R J's hand shook as he took the mug of coffee from Sue Ann. He had told her as much as he could, but had spared her the more grisly details, especially about Lyle.

He didn't know where this would take their marriage. The sheriff had already told him they wanted to speak with him, just as soon as they had located Mary Elizabeth Murray. This time he planned on telling the truth, so help him God, with one minor exception.

As far as he could, he planned on airbrushing Sue Ann from what had happened on the day Carole Chabon was lynched. He would offer himself up to the law instead.

"Poor Lyle," said Sue Ann, staring out of the kitchen window at the rear pond.

"Yup."

He guessed in some way Lyle was also a victim. He knew the hardest part to explain in all of this was how Mimsy had exerted the influence she had. How she had been able to make people do the most loathsome acts, and commit the most venal crimes. In truth, he wasn't entirely sure he knew the answer. It was as if she had been able to cast some kind of spell over the town. She was a master manipulator, always able to pick out a person's weakness.

Then she had met Cressida King and Ty Johnson, and her magic hadn't worked so well.

He smiled at the thought.

"Oh," said Sue Ann. "Big Bertha's eggs hatched. There's a bundle of little hatchlings out there," she went on, with a nod to the back pond. "See."

He looked out. He could see Big Bertha by the side of the water. He couldn't pick out the hatchlings. They were far too tiny to see from this distance with the naked eye.

They looked more like lizards when they first hatched. It was the cutest thing.

The momma 'gator would scoop them up into her mouth, and take them down to the water so they could begin learning to swim. She would open her mouth and drop them out. They would scoot about and then she would scoop them back up again, holding them carefully between jaws that could bite through sheet metal.

He would go out and take a look later. Once he'd gotten some rest.

"I'm going to the store. You want anything?" his wife asked.

He shook his head. The last forty or so years of my life, he thought. "No, I'm good."

She put her hand on the small of his back. "Yes, you are. You're a hero for rescuing that girl like you did."

Some people might see him like that. But it wasn't who he'd see every morning in the shaving mirror. He'd see a man who'd been asleep and finally woken up.

Sue Ann walked out of the kitchen, leaving him alone with his thoughts.

75

H e tried to sleep. It was no use. He was still way too pumped up.

When he had tried to lie down, he saw Devil's Pond on the back of his eyelids. It rolled across, like a movie. The start was fine —he could pick out the orchids. So fragile, so beautiful. But those words took him to the faces of dead and nearly dead women.

He stopped fighting, and got up, took a shower, then changed into shorts and a shirt. He would do some work outside, and hope that would bring him relief.

There was always work to do around the place. It was both a blessing and a curse. At times like this, he took it as a blessing. Keeping occupied was no bad thing.

As he walked outside he saw Mimsy's car. It was parked over by the barns, out of sight of the road but where he or Sue Ann would clearly be able to see it. It hadn't been there when Sue Ann left. He knew that because he'd rushed out to remind her to pick up some smokes and a six-pack of Coors. He'd had a feeling he was going to be doing some real drinking to help him get over all the upset.

Her car was there but he could see no sign of Mimsy. RJ walked back inside, pushed open the bedroom door, and retrieved the gun

Ty had given him for safe-keeping. He hit the magazine release, checked he had rounds, and slapped the mag back in. He tucked it away, out of sight, in the back of his pants, pulling his shirt tail out to conceal it, and went outside again.

He didn't have far to go, or long to wait. Mimsy heard him slam the front door and appeared from the side of the house with that dumb old shotgun she loved so much.

She saw him, without a care, clue, or firearm, and didn't even bother to raise the gun.

A dumb move on her part.

He kept his left hand nice and loose by his side, and hooked the thumb of his right hand, nice and casual, into his front pocket, ready to move round and reach for the gun if he had to.

"Mimsy," he said.

"RJ."

This was Mimsy all over. Good manners, even as she planned on putting a bullet into him right here on his own property.

"We need to talk," she said.

"Yeah, we sure do," he said. "I'm kind of busy, though, so you're going to have to walk with me."

He started toward the pond. Curious George was up near the fence that separated the big pond from the one where Bertha was tending her hatchlings. Curious George, always where the action was, always wanting to be in on everything.

Mimsy raised the shotgun. RJ ignored her. If she'd come here to kill him she could have hidden her car better, snuck up on him, shot him through the window. It wouldn't have been too hard, and he would never have known about it until his brains were shooting out of his skull and splashing all over the wall.

"Go on, shoot me in the back," he said, still walking. "They'll probably bring back the chair for you."

He could hear her, stomping behind him.

"Hold up, RJ."

"I can walk and listen," he said, all casual. "Been married long enough to have those two down."

"How much did you tell the sheriff about what happened out there?"

He kept walking up to the ponds. He stooped down and grabbed an empty plastic bucket that was lying next to the fence.

He turned as she jabbed the shotgun between his shoulder blades.

"She shot Lyle. Blew his jaw clean off. I'll take a polygraph to prove I'm not lying."

"Good. You do that," he told her. "Then you won't need me."

"You could tell them that Ty fellow made you go out there. Forced you. At gunpoint."

That was it. He started to snicker. Had she somehow convinced herself that she could talk her way out of this? If she had, she was more delusional than he'd thought. "Yeah, that's what I'll tell them. It was all the big black dude's fault. Usually works, right?"

He turned back around and, swinging his bucket, set off again for the pond. He wanted to get a better look at the new arrivals. New life among all this bad history. It had to be a good thing. We're born and we live and then we die. Humans, 'gators, everything on earth.

"How do you think Sue Ann will get on in Lowell, RJ? You know what her nerves are like. She wouldn't last a month among all those animals."

Lowell was one of the largest women's detention centers in Florida. It had a fearsome reputation as a rat-and-bug-infested hell on earth, with countless unexplained deaths among inmates.

RJ stopped dead. Mimsy had been looking for a reaction and now she was going to get one.

"Yeah, that's got you thinking, hasn't it, RJ?"

He turned back to face her. His right hand moved from his pocket, to his back. He was watching Bertha, up close near the fence, standing guard as her hatchlings scurried after each other in the grass at the edge of the water.

"It surely has," he said, bringing the SIG up before she could get the shotgun to her shoulder or her finger on the trigger.

"Put it down, Mimsy, or so help me I'll kill you right where you stand."

She hesitated. "You wouldn't dare."

He didn't say anything. He started to squeeze the trigger.

"Double-action trigger on this baby," he said to her. "But did I already have it good to go? That's what you have about one second to guess."

She knew enough about guns to follow what he meant. Either this squeeze would simply ready the gun to fire, or he'd shoot her.

"Take it easy, RJ. I was just saying."

She lowered the shotgun.

"Put it on the ground and step back," he instructed her.

She did as he'd said. He reached down, and picked it up, covering his free hand with his shirt sleeve to keep his prints off it.

"Let's take a walk," he said, moving behind her, and jabbing her with the shotgun barrel. She hesitated.

He poked her again, harder this time. "Move it."

"What are you doing, RJ? Going to feed me to one of your 'gators?" she sing-songed.

"Nope," said RJ. "That wouldn't be sporting, now, would it?"

"So where are we going?" she asked.

"You and me are going to have a wager, Mimsy."

He pushed and prodded her up to the second pond. As they walked toward it, he noticed Bertha, gathering up her newborns in her mouth and hurrying into the longer grass on the far side of the pond. True to his name as well as his nature, Curious George positioned himself at the fence so he could take in whatever the show was.

RJ and Mimsy got to the second, smaller, pond that held Bertha, who was now well hidden on the far side.

Mimsy stopped at the gate that led into the enclosure. "Well?"

Even at gunpoint she didn't appear to take him seriously. She viewed him as a joke. He'd always known that. Someone to push around, and do her dirty work, just like Lyle. Just like everyone in

Darling. And as soon as they'd outlived their usefulness, she disposed of them.

"Take off your clothes," he said. "You're going swimming."

"Don't be ridiculous."

"If it was good enough for that reporter, it's good enough for you. Odds are better too. There's only one 'gator in that pond, and she's as old and slow as you are."

"Go to hell, RJ."

He pointed the SIG at the ground in front of her and pulled the trigger. The shot buried its way into the ground a few inches short of her left foot.

"Next one goes into your foot, and then I work my way on up until you get in that water."

Her mouth fell open.

"One length over and back. You make it back, you can have your clothes and be on your way. Or you can keep your clothes on for all I care. But they'll slow you down."

She looked from RJ to the perfectly calm pond and then back. "You want to humiliate me."

No, thought RJ. "Yes," he said. "I want you to feel a little of the shame I've felt all these years, with you bossing me and Sue Ann and Lyle around like we're peasants."

"Very well then," she said. "You think I haven't been in swimming holes with 'gators around before?"

Not with 'gators that have young to protect you haven't, thought RJ.

He took a set of keys out, and unlocked the gate. She stepped through, smirking at him. He closed the gate behind her and watched as she took off her clothes until she was down to her underwear. "This how you get your kicks?" she sneered.

The irony of the question seemed to be lost on her. She was the one who had taken Cressida King to Devil's Pond and thrown her in. She could have shot her, but she hadn't. She had wanted to watch her die there for her own sick amusement.

"Over to the side, and back."

"And you'll let me go?"

"I'll even give you a towel to dry off," he said.

She looked at the pond. It was maybe eighty feet to the other side and the same eighty back.

She didn't move. She appeared to be weighing something in her mind. She turned back to face him. He kept his eyes up: there were some things he didn't want to see, not at his age, and Mimsy Murray in her underwear was one of them.

"I make it over and back, I want you to tell the sheriff that girl shot Lyle. Which she did."

"But I wasn't there," said RJ. "I only heard the shot."

"Then lie."

RJ was through with lying, but Mimsy wasn't to know that. "Okay," he said. "Deal."

She seemed pleased, like she'd got one over on him.

She walked the last few steps to the edge of the pond, and dipped her foot in. She shivered a little, then eased herself down and into the water. Anyone round here who swam in the wild knew better than to dive in when there could be 'gators around. Splashing got their attention.

She was neck deep in the water now. She pushed off the bottom, and began to swim in steady, ladylike strokes, keeping her head above the water.

"This is the easiest bet I'll ever win," she announced.

"There and back," said RJ, watching the reeds and grass on the far side.

Bertha was still hunkered down out of sight. But she would be watching this strange interloper, RJ was sure of that.

Mimsy seemed to tire a little. She found a second wind, and moved from a breaststroke to a crawl. Her arms pummeled the water. Her legs kicked up and down, creating lots of disturbance.

The grass began to move on the far side. Bertha was crawling forward, placing herself between her hatchlings and the strange creature coming straight towards them.

Oblivious, Mimsy kept coming. She was twenty feet from the

other side. Then ten. She was coming faster, making more noise, the splashes getting louder.

She reached the bank, and climbed out. She held her arms up, triumphant.

"You're going to lose, RJ. Get that towel ready for me."

As she crouched down, ready to dive back into the water, Bertha lunged from behind her, taking down Mimsy at the back of her knees, and pushing her off balance and into the water. The 'gator followed, snapping her massive jaws, and clamping around Mimsy's ankle.

Mimsy let out a shriek, and twisted round to see what had hold of her. Bertha kept moving, tightening her grip around her ankle, and pushing forward, moving Mimsy out into deeper water.

With the woman's ankle firm in her jaws, Bertha pointed her snout down, and dove, taking Mimsy with her, under the surface. The water churned, legs, arms flailing.

Bertha's tail flicked fast as she took Mimsy out further. Then she let go of her. Mimsy re-surfaced for a second, screaming for help. Then Bertha was back, taking her around the waist this time, and pulling her back down.

RJ looked over at Curious George. He was at the hatch that separated the two enclosures. He butted his snout against it, increasingly agitated by the sounds and smells of the carnage as the water frothed red.

Finally, after a few more seconds, the water began to still. Bertha resurfaced. Mimsy's body floated lifelessly in the water. One of her legs had been sheared at the knee, and a huge chunk of her torso was missing. Her arms extended straight out.

RJ walked along the narrow concrete gangway to the hatch, and lifted it up. It was time for George to satisfy that curiosity of his.

RJ SAT ALONE in the cab of his pickup truck and smoked a Marlboro, savoring the taste of the smoke. He reached down to his cell phone and opened up a music app. You could get pretty much any song by any artist for a monthly fee. He usually listened to seventies and eighties rock.

Lynyrd Skynyrd, Van Halen, Creedence Clearwater Revival.

This didn't seem like a time for any of that music. He tapped a name into the search box. Billie Holiday. Then he scrolled down to the song he'd had playing in his head for a while now. He smoked his cigarette, closed his eyes and listened to the saddest song ever written about a strange and bitter crop.

76

F*our days later*

WEARING a sober grey suit that his girlfriend, defense attorney Carmen Lazaro, had picked out for him, Lock walked out of the courtroom and into the corridor. Ty sprang off the wall, and the two men shook hands. Carmen followed a few steps behind, with the Miami counsel Ty had retained to expedite matters as quickly and painlessly as possible.

"You're going to have to stop making a habit of this," Lock said to his partner.

Ty shrugged. "Wasn't part of the plan."

"Come here," said Lock, throwing his arms around him and pulling him in for a hug. "I'm sorry I didn't get to you in time."

"I'm sorry I messed up your vacation."

They stepped back. "Call it even?" Lock asked.

"Sounds fair."

Carmen linked her arm with Lock's, happy to see the two of them reunited and Ty a free man. "Why don't we go get something to eat? Ty, you're always hungry."

"True dat."

"There's a little place nearby where you can get deep-fried alligator, if you can believe that," said Carmen, poking a finger into Ty's ribs.

"How about steak?" said Ty. "You don't have to worry about what a cow's been eating before it's slapped on your plate."

"Or vegetables," said Carmen, who had already started to steer Lock to eating more greens, which Ty found disturbing.

"Yeah, let's not get carried away, sister."

A HALF-HOUR later the three were settled into a booth at Red, The Steakhouse. Carmen watched in wonder as Ty ripped through a prime ribeye that even a 'gator might have struggled with, and a side of Florida creamed corn alongside another of Parmesan Tater Tots.

Lock had ordered a bottle of red wine to celebrate Ty's freedom, and was tucking into a NY Strip with Béarnaise sauce, while Carmen had gone for the mouthwatering house salad of candied walnuts and goat's cheese on a bed of baby greens.

Lock raised his glass in a toast. "Tyrone Johnson, one-man army."

They clinked glasses.

"Damn, this tastes so good," said Ty, slugging down some of the hundred-dollars-a-bottle Cabernet Sauvignon.

"So what was the good word from these overpriced Miami attorneys?" Lock asked Carmen.

"They're not overpriced if you walk free."

"I'll drink to that," said Ty, looking up briefly from his food.

"Firing the gun is going to be tricky, but not insurmountable. They think, after everything that happened in Darling, putting a black ex-Marine in the dock is going to be a bad look."

"In other words, political correctness rules the day," said Lock.

Ty hoisted his glass. "I'll drink to that too."

Lock topped him up and signaled for the waiter to bring them another bottle.

"There'll be a bunch of hand-waving and it'll get buried and go away would be my guess," said Carmen.

"Okay, Tyrone, so no more guns in libraries or walking out of hospitals butt naked," said Lock.

"I make no promises," said Ty.

77

After a short period at the University of Miami Hospital on 12th Street to get patched up, and have an MRI to assess the damage, Cressida had been transferred to the Baptist Hospital of Miami to recuperate until she was well enough to make the trip back to New York.

While Lock and Carmen headed to the airport to fly back to Los Angeles, Ty checked in at the Baptist Hospital reception. With Mary Elizabeth Murray dead, any immediate threat to Cressida had receded.

He took the elevator up to the floor she was on, carrying flowers, a takeout bag he'd procured from the restaurant, and a couple of books he'd picked up for her at Barnes & Noble. He checked in at the nurses' station and they took him down to her room.

She was sitting up in bed, her leg in a cast, a laptop propped on a table. Other than a few scrapes across her face, she looked pretty good, all things considered. She smiled when she saw him. "My savior," she said.

"Savior's part of the job description. You writing your article?" he asked her.

"Book proposal," she said, lifting her cell phone and angling the screen so he could see her flooded inbox. "Haven't even been able to go through all the offers yet."

"I can imagine," he said

The news story of how a young black reporter had gone looking for the killers of her great-aunt was gold, and it had taken no time for it to go national. Ty had done everything he possibly could to minimize any mention of his involvement.

"So what did you bring me?" Cressida asked.

"You assuming this is all for you?"

"Wait, don't tell me, you wander hospital corridors with flowers."

He laid out what he'd brought on the bedside locker and the bed. "Flowers are for you. I was going to get orchids but I didn't want you having flashbacks."

She didn't laugh.

"Sorry, grunt humor. I forget."

"It's okay."

He put down the bag with the food. "Lunch, from one of the best places in Miami."

"Thank you."

"And two books. I wasn't sure if you'd read them so the receipt's inside the first if you want to switch them when you get out."

She took the books from him, and looked over them. The first was a history of the civil rights movement called *Parting the Waters* by Taylor Branch. The second was *Invisibles* by Jesse Holland, a history of black slaves who had worked in the White House.

"Thanks. These are great. I've been meaning to read the Branch book for years. Never got round to it."

"Well, when you do . . ."

She laid the books next to her on the bed. "Thank you. For everything. I really mean it. And I'm sorry if I wasn't completely upfront with you at the start."

"Apology accepted. I'm glad it all worked out."

That part was true for Cressida and Ty. For people in Darling, the next months were looking strained. The FBI office in Miami had opened an investigation into the recent and historical deaths. Divers had found the remains of Timothy French at the bottom of Devil's Pond after the National Guard had secured the scene so they could get down there safely.

Skeletons, both literal and figurative, were being dug up.

Ty had been in contact with RJ's attorney and offered to be a character witness, should it be required. At heart, RJ was a good man. Ty recognized that. He also knew that circumstance could dictate someone's actions ... actions they might come to regret.

That was why justice was often depicted as a woman holding a scale. With the bad, there was good. With the dark, there was light.

"Hey," Cressida said. "You want to see something?"

"Sure."

She put the books to one side and patted the bed. Ty managed to park himself next to her. She clicked on a file on her laptop and an image appeared, a color picture of a young African-American woman. She was in her early twenties, with long, straightened feather-cut hair and cat's-eye-framed tortoiseshell glasses. She was smiling, full of hope.

"This was Carole."

"Your great-aunt?"

"It was taken a few months before ..."

It was only in that moment that Ty realized he had never before seen a picture of Carole Chabon. He studied it, taking his time. He thought of Adelson Shaw, and a feeling built inside him that he had to tamp down.

Some things were best left to the law, and he knew the FBI had spoken with RJ about what he believed Adelson Shaw had done when he'd met the young Carole Chabon, and set the whole thing spinning wildly out of control.

Ty looked from the picture to Cressida. He could see the resemblance in her features. "You done good," he said to her.

She gave a somber nod.

"No, I mean it," he said. "She deserved justice, and you've helped deliver it."

She reached out and took his hand, folding her fingers around his. He left it there for a moment. Then he got up. "I'll be around for a few more days before I fly back to LA. If you need anything just holler."

"Thanks, Tyrone."

"Sure thing," he said, walking to the door.

When he looked back to her, she was hunched over her laptop, getting ready to write her and Carole's story. He stepped out into the corridor and headed for the elevator.

ABOUT THE AUTHOR

To research his books, Sean Black has trained as a bodyguard in the UK and Eastern Europe, spent time inside America's most dangerous Supermax prison, Pelican Bay in California, undergone desert survival training in Arizona, and ventured into the tunnels under Las Vegas.

A graduate of Oxford University, England and Columbia University in New York, Sean lives in Dublin, Ireland.

His Ryan Lock and Byron Tibor thrillers have been translated into Dutch, French, German, Italian, Portugese, Russian, Spanish, and Turkish.

ALSO BY SEAN BLACK

Sign up to Sean Black's VIP mailing list for a free e-book and updates about new releases

Your email will be kept confidential. You will not be spammed. You can unsubscribe at any time.

Click the link below to sign up:

http://seanblackauthor.com/subscribe/